A Hell of a War

www.barbarianspy.com

This book is copyright © habu 2017
habu asserts his right to be known as the author of this work.
Published by BarbarianSpy in 2017
Cover design © S Bush 2017
Cover images: manipulated: © bereta | Depositphotos.com
ISBN: E-Book: 978-1-925568-20-2
Paperback: 978-1-925568-21-9
All rights reserved

BarbarianSpy
Toronto, Australia

A Hell of a War

Habu

Table of Contents

Introduction

In *A Hell of a War*, habu brings together nine previously published, but expanded, and one new gay male stories set in, leading up to, or closing out on World War Two. Six of the mostly bittersweet stories are set in the European Theater of the war and four are set in the Pacific Theater.

None glorify war; all deal with sexual relationships between men that are fostered by the tensions and uncertainties of war and the conditions of being thrown together with other men, with no one but men to share sexual tensions with on a daily basis. The stories in this anthology emphasize the intensity of sexual need and the expansion of opportunities for satisfying this need in young, fit men exposed to life-threatening danger and the need seek out what they need when they still can have it. This is not a military warfare book; it is a book of stories about gay male relationships in crisis that have been formed by necessity and opportunity.

In "Chameleon Love," the first of the European Theater stories, a French village male prostitute is challenged to balance the demands of the occupying Germans, the needs of the French Resistance, and the survival of his family and himself. In "War Letters," wartime letters between an Army officer and an enlisted man slogging up Italy in the Anzio beachhead campaign en route to Germany reveal a bittersweet, increasingly intense, and doomed gay male military romance. A family photo hinders a military hospital developing romance in "Photo Barrier." Two stories, "The Aviators" and "Long John Silverman," provide a nostalgic look at the short life expectations of military aviators in World War Two and of the "grasp life while you can" attitude fostered by this grim reality.

In "Mountain Memory," a painting captures both the tragedy and tenacity of surviving the aftermath of war and of adapting to the sexual limitations set by wartime conditions.

The final four stories move us to the Pacific Theater of the war and start, in "Naval Dilemma," with life on the ground for a young Hawaiian rent-boy immediately prior to and on the day of the Japanese attack on Pearl Harbor. In "Trapped" a downed American pilot is imprisoned and put to service in a Japanese World War Two male brothel. The short story, "Tea with the Prince," spans the entire war in the Pacific from the late 1920s and the Japanese invasion of China through to the end of the war and American occupation of Japan as told through the eyes of a young American involved in a long-term relationship with a Japanese prince and German military officers. The section, and the anthology, concludes, in "Relocate?" with a never-before-published story of a naval enlisted man's dilemma of whether or not to resume his military service and a homosexual relationship with a married naval officer in California at the end of the war.

European

Theater

Chameleon Love

June, 1940, Blaye-et-Sainte-Luce, France

Henri noticed how quiet the square was as he left the bakery shop with the piles of baguettes under his arm to be delivered around the village. Was this the day, he wondered. The Germans would enter the town to occupy it any day now. Their month-long movement was just about to reach the Bordeaux region, arriving in his own village on the southwest coast at the Gironde Estuary before the push into Bordeaux. The only saving grace was that they wouldn't billet many troops here, saving the bulk of them to occupy the far larger and better strategically placed Bordeaux.

Many of the villagers had already left, so he had just two deliveries to make—to the large, but deteriorating villa directly across the square and then to the house of the teacher, Samuel Levin, in the smaller building at the edge of the square. He would dither at the teacher's house until it was time to scrum with the village's rugby team out in the field to the west of the village. The first delivery was to his own house, where he lived with his grandfather, Ansel, a former, greatly revered town mayor, now almost immobilized by gout, and his maiden aunts, Suzanne and Marie. The Ballard family, once the richest and most prominent in the village, had fallen on bad times financially, with the deaths of Henri's parents in one of the plague-like influenza outbreaks that had passed through the village a decade earlier. The bread he was bringing to them from the baker was part of Henri's wages from working in the bakery in the morning.

What else Henri did to earn money for his family's keep was what he had to do—and what he did basically because he enjoyed doing it.

After the delivery to his relatives, Henri crossed the still-ominously and atypically silent square to the house of the teacher to deliver his daily bread as recompense for the tuition for the baker's four children. As usual, the door to the small house was ajar, the first floor of the building being two schoolrooms. Henri mounted the stairs to the dwelling of the teacher above, and knocked on the door.

"Is that you, Henri? You alone?"

"Yes, teacher. As always."

"Enter."

Henri did so, leaving the bread on the counter in the kitchen, living, dining and nearly everything else room and then moved to the doorway to the back room—Samuel's bedroom.

Samuel, a Jewish rabbi as well as the village teacher, dark, hirsute, forties, and bearded, was Orthodox in appearance, other than the fact that he was naked and sitting on the side of his bed in full erection. He motioned Henri to come forward and kneel before him, which the young, perfectly formed and handsome man in his early twenties did, without hesitation. Henri knelt between Samuel's spread thighs, took the teacher's erect staff in his mouth, and gave it suck.

Later Henri became as naked as Samuel. Samuel was still sitting on the side of his bed. Henri's body was reclined toward the floor, supported by Samuel's legs, with Henri's legs wrapped around Samuel's gaunt torso, ankles crossed behind his back, while, gripping Henri's wrists, the strong Jew pulled Henri off and on his cock.

When ejaculation was achieved by them both, Henri was belly down on the arm of Samuel's reading chair in the corner of the bedroom, with Henri looking down on the side table where Samuel's wire-frame glasses rested on student papers he was correcting, and Samuel crouched over Henri's back and fucked him from behind and above.

When both were dressed, Samuel, as usual, walked Henri down to the front door of the house after Henri picked up the coins, representing his payment, from the kitchen counter where he had laid the baguettes. After surveying the supposedly empty square—but not too well—the teacher and village male prostitute kissed inside the shadows of the hallway—although not far enough inside. After drawing away from the kiss, Henri looked down, laughed, and pointed out that Samuel's trousers were not buttoned. Henri did the service for him.

What neither had noticed was that there was an open-roofed German military command car sitting at idle across the square, where the Wehrmacht Hauptmann—captain—sat in the back, waiting for the column of foot soldiers to arrive for the formal occupation of the village. Hauptmann Gerhard Rein watched the farewell of Samuel and Henri in Samuel's doorway, the buttoning of Henri's fly by Samuel not the least, with great interest and with pleasure that it would not require much effort to set up his routine while in this village.

It was known to only a small segment of the population of Blaye-et-Sainte-Luce—mostly those connected with the activity—that Henri, the greatly attractive young heir to the declining Ballard fortunes, was also the village male-on-male prostitute. All villages had them, of course. In many villages they were barely tolerated—but tolerated nonetheless because they were a necessity of life. Henri was from a tragic, prominent family and was so likable—and of such a handsome countenance and sweet disposition—that even those who knew of his nefarious function in the village and who were not connected with it tolerated it and accepted him. Those who would publicly disapprove were simply kept in the dark to ensure village stability.

For his part, Henri enjoyed doing what men wanted him to do, and he needed the extra money and services to keep his family fed. His grandfather could do nothing any more but dispense wisdom and affection. His aunts took in sewing, but that was hardly enough to keep the roof of the large villa from caving in on them. So Henri had his arrangements—the morning work at the bakery and bread for the family for an occasional side fuck by the variety-loving baker. The coins from the teacher. Select meats from the village butcher. And so forth.

From the teacher's house Henri walked west of the village to the field where the town team practiced its rugby.

Henri was a popular player there because, though smaller than most of the rest, he was strong, fast, and clever on his feet. And he was good with his hands in finding and holding the ball. Even a few of the rugby players could attest to how good he was with his hands—and with holding balls. The village butcher, Giles, a huge, muscular man, was both the team goalkeeper and its captain/coach. He was the power player on the team, defending the goal fiercely and well.

Following the practice, while the other teammates, muddied but highly pleased with the practice and each other, headed east toward the village, Giles placed an arm around Henri's shoulder, with the excuse of pulling him aside to give him some strategy pointers. The others looking in the direction they were headed, Giles marched Henri into a grove of trees next to the field. Neither noticed the military staff car that had been parked near the field, with Hauptmann Reins watching the practice—both the play and the obvious after play.

In the grove of trees, Henri lay on his back between the roots of a tree with his soccer shorts off and his legs raised and spread, as Giles, shirt off and soccer shorts pinned down under his balls, knelt between Henri's thighs. Henri arched his back, panted, and cried out at the initial penetration as Giles's oversized cock entered his ass channel. As the bigger man began to pump Henri's ass, the younger, blond beauty slitted his eyes, licked his lips, and ran his hands over the bulges of the butcher's chest and biceps. There would be a fine cut of meat on the Ballard dining table tonight in exchange for the fine cut of meat the butcher was now receiving from Henri. And Henri wasn't the least bit embarrassed at how he was providing for his family. He enjoyed the attentions of men, and it was a precarious life for all in the village, especially with the uncertainty of the now-arrived German occupation.

Henri loved the fucking. He didn't have to love all of the men who provided it. But if he had to be a chameleon about showing his love for what they did to him, a chameleon he would be.

After Giles left him, Henri lay there for several more minutes, his legs spread, calming his breathing. Giles had the biggest, cruelest cock by far of all the men Henri took in the village. It took Henri a few minutes to recover.

In those few minutes, however, Hauptmann Reins appeared at the edge of the trees, and the eyes of the two met. Henri defensively reached for his soccer shorts to cover his privates, but neither of them was fooled about what had transpired there.

Henri's first response was feeling a chill of fear run up his spine. The Germans were reputed to be highly puritanical—to persecute any variant activity. Would Henri be sent to the camps he'd heard about on the first day of the German occupation?

But then Hauptmann Reins smiled broadly at Henri, and Henri understood that that was not to be his fate. He smiled back, tossed the soccer shorts off to the side again, spread his bent legs farther apart, rolled his hips up, fisted his cock with a hand, and gave the German captain a provocative look. If a chameleon he had to be, a chameleon he would be.

The German army officer unbuttoned his trousers, pulled out a long, thin, erect cock, and approached and sank between Henri's thighs. As the cock made a long, cruel thrust up into Henri's channel and Reins closed his hands around Henri's throat and began to pump his ass, Henri, the chameleon, arched his back; gagged, gasped, and groaned, as he knew the German would want to hear; and began to move his hips in the rhythm of the fuck. There must be some way he could gain advantage from this for himself and his family in the German occupation, he mused.

When Reins had ejaculated and was holding Henri close and breathing hard, his cock still buried deep inside Henri's channel, Henri whispered in the almost adequate German he'd learned thanks to his liaison with Samuel Levin, words to try to bind the German to him—words of loving the fuck, of wanting it again. Of how handsome and masterful the German officer was. Of how he melted to the attentions of a man in uniform.

Beaming not only because of how sweet and willing Henri's body had been, or even that the young man knew some German, but mostly because the sweet piece wanted to be fucked again immediately, seeming eager to have Reins plowing him again, Reins took as little time as he needed to comply.

He'd been of two minds—whether to use the public humiliation of this young man and the resulting punishment as an example to cow the people of this village into subjugation, or to use him and hold the vilification for later. The Frenchmen's succulence and willingness had determined that he would live his life of service to men a little longer.

* * * *

Henri's premonition of what was to come and an understanding of the high-stakes risks that now existed propelled him into motion as soon as he returned to the villa. Luckily, he got no argument from Suzanne and Marie and stalwart support from Grandfather Ansell. Of course he didn't tell them the real reason this had to be—but they weren't stupid. They'd heard about other French villages the German had occupied. They could discern what some of the safer options were.

On his way back into the village, Henri had stopped at the stablery and hired a buggy, horses, and driver to appear at the back gate of the villa grounds. He had no trouble doing so, as the stable master, Pierre, was one of his men. He only had to promise two free lays, which he thought cheap, considering the short notice and how far up the coast the farm of the Ballard cousins was. The deal was struck on the spot, with Henri giving the stable master a quick blow job, which he made clear was in addition to the lays he had promised.

While Marie packed trunks for herself and Suzanne, Henri and Suzanne scoured the house for valuables the absence of which wouldn't be noticed by first-time visitors and hid them away in the recess in the chimney in Suzanne's room that had been used for similar emergencies in the two hundred years the villa had stood here. There were more secrets in the house than just this hiding place.

The women had been gone only a short time when the knock on the door that Henri had anticipated came. Standing on the landing in front of the door, backed by two soldiers— one older and grizzled and one almost as young as Henri and wide-eyed and full of unspoken questions—was Hauptmann Gerhard Reins, eyes aglow from the servicing he'd received earlier in the day. Henri didn't regret having given into the man. He was maybe in his late thirties; ramrod straight, not just in his spine; and tall, on the thin side, but muscular, hair even blonder than Henri's—nearly pure white—and piercing, cruel pale-blue eyes. The mouth was set in a superior-attitude near-sneer, which contrasted with the older soldier behind him, whose sneer was knowing and demanding. When he was honest, Henri had to admit to himself that he preferred a demanding—and, yes, even a bit cruel—man. This soldier, at least, had been told of Reins's earlier tryst with Henri, Henri was certain. And it was just as likely that he wanted to claim a share.

"We require billets," Reins declared. "Your house has been identified as the most appropriate one in the village. And I expect it to provide full amenities." The captain gave Henri a meaningful look.

Henri knew there were houses in better shape, but he had to admit that this villa was the most imposing one, sat on the village's main square, and had the most furnished bedrooms. This had been his premonition—that the German captain would come straight here for housing—and other benefits. The "other benefits" fit in with Henri's desperate plans, though.

Henri merely inclined his head in assent and acquiescence.

"This is Obersoldat Johan Mueller," Reins said, gesturing to the older solder, "and this is Soldat Hans Kant," he said, pointing to the younger and obviously junior—and certainly only nervous one—of the trio.

And then Reins said what Henri had been hoping for. "We do not pay for the use of the house, but we pay for the food, enough for everyone under the roof—and who will that be?"

"Just my grandfather and me," Henri answered. "He is old and hard of hearing and won't be in your way."

"Ah, good. And for the bad hearing when it comes for us to need that." He gave Henry a meaningful look, which Henri fully understood, "and do you have servants?" he continued.

"Just the cook and a day maid," Henri responded.

"They will be included in the food ration. And because of the special circumstances, I will pay extra for your exclusive services—for me and these two soldiers who will billet with me. Am I right that you receive payment for your services? That this is a function you serve in this village? For men? I have seen you with the rabbi and the butcher."

The look was piercing. The younger soldier didn't seem to understand what was being said, but the older one certainly did. And now Henri was certain he knew the real reason his house had been chosen by the captain for billeting.

"Yes," he answered demurely, eyes downcast. "These are the services I provide. For men." He didn't add, which you well know, but he could have. Of course the captain hadn't known that Henri got paid for his services in the village. Henri didn't expect the captain to pay for them, if he didn't want to.

"And to my two adjuncts too?"

"Yes, of course."

Then Henri looked up—his smile went behind the captain to the Obersoldat, Mueller, conveying his particular interest in the rougher of the three. "If you'll come upstairs with me, I'll show you to bedrooms. All are prepared"—and, indeed, part of the work of Suzanne and Marie's departure was to remake their rooms, both quite comfortable rooms dominated by four-poster beds with heavy, durable canopies and strong corner pillars. They would withstand the moving weight of two men—or more—in them. There also were thick draperies on the windows and thick, sound-proof walls. To be sure they understood, Henri noted, as they mounted the sturdy staircase from the front foyer, "There are four bedrooms on the second level. The bedrooms on the third floor are not in use. Both the cook and my grandfather have rooms on the first floor in a wing beyond the kitchen, well away from the main house. The rooms on the second floor are for you, your two soldiers, and me. My room connects to yours, Captain. I hope this meets your needs."

The German captain quite explicitly said that it did. Perversely, Henri had assigned Reins to Suzanne's room, the one with the fireplace that hid the family's most precious possessions.

That night Reins showed his fetish streak. He had his two soldiers tie Henri's wrists to a corner of the frame of the canopy bed in his room, with him, naked, stretched below. The grizzly and wiry older solder, Mueller, held Henri on one side by pulling Henri's leg up toward the headboard, his heels on top of the headboard, while the younger, magnificently built private, Kant, did the same on the other. Kant wasn't just the one in the best muscular shape; he also was the lowest hung of the three. Reins knelt below Henri's buttocks, ramrod straight other than the forward jut of his pelvis, with his long, hard cock thrust upward, while, his two soldiers maneuvered Henri's rolled up hips in position and then, screwing his ass channel on Reins' cock, moved Henri back and forth on the shaft.

Knowing what he had to do and sensing even then that he needed to enlist the sympathy of at least one of the three, and the choice being obvious to him, as he could tell there would be no sympathy of any kind to expect from Mueller, Henri turned his face to that of the youngest soldier, and the two kissed deeply.

Later, as Mueller cruelly pistoned Henri from behind, bent over the side of the bed, Kant knelt in front of the reclining Reins—by his own choice—and sucked Reins to an ejaculation.

Before dismissing his attendants, Reins had them tie Henri, wrist and ankle, to the four strong posts of the bed. They tied him high off the bed, so that the droop in his buttocks surpassed six inches off the surface of the bed. Bursting one of the feather pillows open, the captain poured the feathers over Henri's body and blew and delicately pushed them along the surface of Henri's delicate skin to take pleasure in Henri's moans and begging for relief and in watching him struggle against his bonds and writhe in midair. When Henri was whimpering from exhaustion, Reins moved onto the bed, knelt between Henri's suspended thighs, grasped and spread Henri's buttocks with his hands, and pulled Henri's puckered entrance onto the bulb of his cock. With a vicious pull and an accompanying gasp from Henri, Reins pulled Henri's channel on the shaft and then deeper and deeper on the cock, as Henri writhed, arched his head back and marveled in words he knew the German wanted to hear of how deep the cock was reaching. Reins pulled Henri on and off his buried cock to a mutual ejaculation, and Henri's murmurs of maximum pleasure.

Guarding the tone of his voice and pulling a wan smile across his face, Henri told the sadist German captain that this masterful sex made him love Reins and wish for all of the inventive ways his body could be used to stimulate and serve the German's needs. He hoped that Reins's inventiveness would last him for some days to come.

That seemed to be enough for Reins's wants for the night, although in days and nights to come he was to devise many more unusual and decadent fetishes in the taking of Henri, much of which entailed the bondage of Henri and the use of the strength of the bed pillars and overhead canopy. All four men retired to their respective bedrooms.

To further Henri's own plans, he crept into Hans Kant's bedroom in the middle of the night; climbed under the covers with the young, hung, magnificently built German soldier; assured him his captain need never know that Henri came to him; coaxed him to the hardest of woods with mouth play; straddled the young soldier's pelvis; and rode him for an hour, leaving the young soldier glassy-eyed and murmuring of awe, love, and devotion. It also left the young soldier with a secret from the captain that he and Henri shared—including that Henri enjoyed Kant's cock far more than he enjoyed the captain's.

Hans's hands on Henri's waist were strong and calloused. He was a young stud, new enough to sex with men to be surprised and jerk and tremble when Henri, thoroughly experienced in the pleasures of men, surprised him with intimate touches—eating out Hans's ass as he writhed and luxuriated in the first such intimate service, taking the young man's balls in his mouth and humming, taking Hans almost to ejaculation by deep-throating the whimpering warrior's throbbing staff before mounting him, kissing and pinching Hans's nipples while rising and falling on the cock, nipping his nipples and his neck for the feel of his flinching and driving his cock deeper, begging constantly in broken German for the cock to dig deeper, reaching back and entering the young stud with a finger at the conclusion and rubbing Hans's prostate to make him explode deep in Henri's ass.

Other than one of the village priests, who was delicate and almost effeminate in sex even though he was on top, Henri was mostly fucked by older men. It was a thrill to have a younger, perfectly cut, vigorous, and virile man between his thighs—and he told Kant so. And even after an hour, it wasn't just the one fuck, with Henri riding Hans's thick cock. The young German soldier lost his shyness and, after a short recovery, took control and rode Henri—and then rode Henri again—and again.

The German was fast and furious with fire-off power; Henri more controlled. Hans was kneeling over Henri's prone body, his knees separating Henri's bent legs as he released a bucket of cum across Henri's heaving chest. Learning fast, the blond god rubbed the bulb of his bubbling cock over and over again on one of Henri's cum-slicked nipples while taking Henri's cock in his other hand and pumping him. Seeing through the slit in the draperies that it nearly was dawn, Henri gave the German his seed, arcing it up to mingle his cum with the young soldier's on his chest.

Hans's breathy whispers of devotion, in which Henri discerned the word *Liebchen*—lover—assured Henri that he had won one ally in the cruel triumvirate—and that he had driven a wedge between Kant and his superior officer.

* * * *

The days stretched into weeks, and it wasn't hard for Henri to make clear to the men he normally serviced and received favors from that he now was exclusively taken—and by the enemy. This had ominous results, though, even though it was out of his control and the men he had gone with in the village should have understood that. It wasn't just the attitude of the village men that became ominous, though. The first thing he noticed was that the house of the Jewish teacher, Samuel Levin, was closed up, the windows boarded up, but with scorch marks on the bricks around them to indicate that there had been a fire.

It was Ansel who told Henri of the village gossip that Samuel had been taken away in the night and torches thrown through his windows that caused fires that the neighbors put out after Samuel had been dragged away. Henri had known nothing of it even though it had occurred just across the square from his family villa, because he was being strung up facing a pillar of Suzanne's bed at the time, in her room with the thick walls and noise-dampening draperies and having his legs held up and stretched out at either side by Mueller and Kant, while Reins fucked him from behind.

He did recall afterward that Reins kept going to the window on the front of the villa and peeking through the curtain, so it was highly possible that the captain had prior knowledge of what would happen with Samuel that night.

The next day, Henri found there was no need to make excuses about not going to the bakery, as the bakery was closed up tight. So was the butchery. And so were the stables, the stable manager, Pierre, having melted away without calling in the two fuck sessions Henri had promised him. The baker, butcher, and stable manager, as well as more than half of Henri's rugby team had taken to the countryside to form a resistance group, Henri's grandfather was told in a whisper by the day maid, and Henri's father had passed the information on to his grandson.

As tough a choice as it was, Henri's giving in so readily and easily to the wants of Hauptmann Reins had worked in the Ballard men's favor. If the soldiers had not billeted in the Ballard villa, the family's source of bread and meat would have evaporated. Instead, Reins had forced both businesses to remain open with new proprietors and more than sufficient food was being supplied to the Ballard villa kitchen.

The secret of the totality of Henri's collaboration with the enemy came out full blown in the village gossip stream not too long afterward when the captain decided he wanted to treat his unit of men to an evening of debauchery.

He commandeered the local *maison close*—brothel—on the edge of the village, complete with the two women prostitutes who worked the two rooms above the barroom, and put on a lavish party. Henri didn't have a head for liquor and probably didn't know fully what he was doing when he was coaxed to stand on top of a table with the two women prostitutes, all naked, and danced a sensuous dance until each was pulled down by the eager hands of soldiers, laid out on separate tables, and gang fucked by a succession of randy and drunk German soldiers, all the time with their captain looking on, laughing and egging them on.

The brothel's staff—other than the two unfortunate prostitutes—fled the bedlam early in the evening. But they looked on from safe positions and all later attested to the willing wantonness and fraternization of Henri with the Germans when, long after the two prostitutes had curled up into bruised, whimpering balls of withdrawal, Henri was sitting on Hauptmann Reins's lap, riding his cock, and waving his arms like he was an American rodeo star.

After that, all doors in the village were closed to Henri—with the exception of the village church. The next afternoon, when Father Christophe entered the main sanctuary, it was to find Henri lying, belly down, arms outstretched in front of the altar and murmuring prayers of confession. In the day's light he fully understood what his drunken behavior the previous night had revealed to the village. His ability to be a chameleon was abruptly being compromised.

At the soft voice of the priest, Henri looked up. He groaned. He had hoped it would be old Father Marc who would be there to hear his confession, but it wasn't. It was the younger Father Christophe.

"Come. Rise. Come through with me and we will discuss this," Father Christophe said. In the father's spare cell behind the church kitchens, Father Christophe gently pressed on Henri's shoulders to make the young man sit down on the side of his bed, raised his cassock to reveal he was naked underneath and in erection, and, cupping Henri's chin, guided Henri's mouth to his cock.

Of all the men in the village, it was the young priest who was willing to continue sinning with the village male prostitute.

An hour later, when Father Christophe, one of Henri's regular hookups in the village, had fucked Henri in a side split from behind in a spoon position on the cot to ejaculations by both, Father Christophe said, "I can hear your confession now."

Henri dutifully confessed his sins in trying to be the chameleon and do the best he could for his family under the conditions of the German occupation. Christophe took the confession, named the penance, which was mild, but added the word of advice, "The resistance here will become violent, I'm afraid, son. It would be in your best interests to withdraw to somewhere else considering what the village is saying about you."

It hadn't been a full confession, as Henri had heard that he wasn't the only one cooperating with the Germans—that Christophe was falling into their line too and was fraternizing with the enemy as much as Henri was. Indeed, as the priest led Henri back to his sleeping cell, Henri caught a glimpse of a young German soldier withdrawing down a corridor.

Henri didn't think really that he needed to be told that he should leave the village—and he wondered who heard Father Christophe's confession and suspected that much of the melancholy in the priest's voice in giving him this advice came from the regret the advice would end these occasional trysts in the priest's bed. He was trapped, though. He knew the priest was right, but there was Grand-Père Ansel to think of. What would befall him if Henri just left? It was Henri's responsibility to put the well-being of his family first.

Oh what a pickle his attempt to play chameleon to solve problems that were unsolvable had placed him in.

* * * *

By listening to the Hauptmann and his two attendants converse, Henri was able to discern that the occupation of the village was in trouble, both because the resistance here was threatening to swamp the resources the Hauptmann had been given and because the resistance in nearby Bordeaux was necessitating the retrenchment of forces there. Bordeaux was, by far, a higher priority for occupation than this small village was.

Increasingly, Reins was showing his worry and concern—and his fear. The soldiers he had under his command were drawn closer to the Ballard villa, strengthening the defenses here, but acknowledging their weakness against the activities of the resistance elsewhere in the village and surrounding countryside. His worry was shown also in the frenzied way he and his attendants were using Henri's services throughout the day—like each fuck might be their last.

As active as Henri had been before, although he'd never been involved in threesomes before now nor been put in the positions of bondage and cruelty before, as now, he had never been double penetrated. Now that was happening routinely, with the third usually using his mouth at the same time. Henri had no idea how much crueler Gerhard and Johan could get, with regularly now riding him on all fours on the floor while digging the heels of their boots into his calves and beating every exposed surface with a riding crop. Only the young soldier, Hans, held back from this—satisfied, no doubt by Henri's nightly visits to his bed for more intimate and loving fucking.

Having the Germans comfortable with his presence, though, helped Henri in the timing of what he knew needed be done. This was brought to a head by Hauptmann Reins himself one night over dinner.

"I'm afraid we pull out tomorrow," he informed Henri. "We have been called to pull back to Bordeaux to strengthen the defenses there."

"I . . . I will miss you," Henri answered, halfway believing it himself. He had not done much self-analysis of his response to the captain's form of lovemaking—halfway in fear of what he had to admit his response was—arousal, and to a high degree, pleasure at the cruel use of his body, especially now by the gaunt and grizzly Obersoldat Mueller, who made no bones about testing Henri to the limit. Catholic that he was, despite the light penance Father Christophe had given him, Henri knew that he deserved what Mueller was doing to him. And, to his embarrassment, he longed to have more of what Mueller did to him.

"You don't have to miss me. You are coming with me," Reins said. "I am comfortable with your services. I don't see the need to find a new young man who will serve my needs as well as you do. I'm sure you realize—and appreciate—that I could have you thrown into a camp at any moment for deviant behavior and have not done so."

This was the way Henri realized it could go with Reins and it was the direction in which Henri had tried to develop the relationship. It wasn't a final answer, he knew. He no longer believed there was a final answer that would save him. But this could save his family and help his country.

He crept away to Grand-Père Ansel to tell him in as limited a way as he could what he must do and why—although he was sure that the old man had known all along and hadn't seen any better choices for Henri and the family than the one Henri had made.

"You must go now, Grand-Père, by the secret door in the fence to the neighboring lot." The villa was guarded front and back by German soldiers and the two adjacent house had been commandeered and vacated. But there was access across the lots through hidden doors in fences that had long been devised and maintained by the residents.

"You must find the resisters. I know that the butcher, Giles, is leading them. You must call me out as a German collaborator and say that you and the aunties have managed to escape me. And then, after the Germans have pulled out—I am going with them—you must live as quietly as possible. You and aunties must learn to be chameleons. The Germans may return, and, when they do, it may be for all time."

Understanding, Ansel hugged his grandson, and, with tears in his eyes, shuffled away to the secret door into the neighboring lot.

Before returning to Reins and his attendants for a last frenzied night of demanding sex in the Ballard villa, Henri told the cook to put out a breakfast on the buffet in the dining room early in the morning and then, herself, to use the secret door to escape—and to assure Giles, in the function she had been serving of slipping messages to the resistance from Henri, that he would continue to do all he could to get whatever information on German plans and movements back to the resistance as he had done all the time he was with the captain.

"Ahh, you should not be taking all of this on yourself, Monsieur Henri," she objected. "You have been the best of patriots yourself, sacrificing yourself like this—letting the villagers, and now, even your own grandfather, believe you are a collaborator. When you are not."

"I am whatever I have to be, Lisle," Henri responded, knowing that the safest way to continue life as a chameleon was to maintain pretenses as much as possible. "Grandfather is too infirm to be expected to keep the secret. So he must not know yet. And you must denounce me in public after I'm gone, as well. If justice prevails, Giles and the others will vindicate me someday when the Germans have been expunged from France. For now my collaboration must be believable."

The next day Henri rode out of the village of Blaye-et-Sainte-Luce in Hauptmann Gerhard Reins's open staff car, not knowing what the future held, but continually looking for the opportunity to use chameleon love to survive.

Reins sat close to him on his right and Mueller on his left, and they were barely on the road when both began to fondle his body and put upon him—with Mueller even managing to reach into the folds of his clothes, grasp his balls, and squeeze to the point of making Henri gasp and want to faint. It would have been so much better to be able to sit next to the young golden god, Hans Kant, now in the front seat of the vehicle, who was so besotted with Henri now that he would do anything—including passing on plans of German troop movements and intentions.

Still, the chameleon in Henri made him work up all options. The last thing he wanted to have happen to him was to be exposed as a male-on-male prostitute and sent to a camp. He'd rather die than that. When the car was stopped on the road for Reins to confer with a group of soldiers, Henri turned his face to Mueller and whispered, "It is my hope that someday you and I can be alone and I can enjoy the full attentions of your specialties."

Mueller glowered at him, his mouth twisting into a cruel leer. "Trust me, if I get you alone, I'll break you for all time."

It was an ultimate option for Henri. Something to keep in reserve in case his attempt at patriotism came to a dead end.

~

War Letters

Now that he'd gotten this far with it—contacting the man and driving all the way up to Gettysburg from Washington, D.C.—Hal Collins was having second thoughts. He arrived at the house fifteen minutes early, but he drove right by it and pulled over to the curb two blocks farther on. Several minutes later the pain in his hands registered in his brain, and he realized he'd had a death grip on the steering wheel. He took his hands away and popped his knuckles.

The old wooden cigar box was sitting on the passenger seat beside him. He remembered seeing it in the bottom drawer of the general's desk in his study when he was a boy and the family was visiting the general, his grandfather. While the older folks sat out on the porch and talked, Hal would sneak into his grandfather's study, which was stuffed with memorabilia from three wars his grandfather had fought in: World War II, the Korean Conflict—as it was called until recent decades when it was finally given the respect of having been a war—and Vietnam, which his grandfather had fought from the Pentagon, having been called back into duty from retirement. Generals were always subject to being recalled, and Hal's father was a symbol of extraordinary bravery, honor, and service.

But the general never would talk to his family about his war service. Hal's father—and later Hal—had to find out about the general's war service and the stories behind all of his medals and citations through magazine articles from the time, or, like Hal did, while his parents and the general chatted on the porch, by surreptitiously going through his grandfather's study.

For some reason, although Hal always checked that the wooden cigar box, closed by two rubber bands, was always in the bottom drawer of the desk, he never, while his grandfather was alive, had had the courage to open it.

After his grandfather's death—ironically from lung cancer contracted by chain smoking the same cigar brand of what Hal thought of as the general's secret box—Hal's father had quickly packed up all of the memorabilia and sent it off to the general's regimental museum.

For years Hal had kept thinking about the box and wishing he'd had the courage to open it to see what was inside when he was a child. When his own father died, Hal was surprised to find the box—the same one; he'd memorized every torn scrap on its sides and top—tucked away in his dad's attic along with other things Hal knew were very private to his father.

The rubber bands no longer were on the box. Now it was closed with thick string. His father must have opened the box and seen what was inside. He must have read the few notes that were inside, crudely penciled on yellowed paper and secured with a black ribbon.

And when Hal read those notes, he was glad he hadn't read them until now and he knew why both his grandfather and his father had kept them secret—and, most of all, why his father hadn't sent them off to the regimental museum with everything else he'd sent there. Underneath these ribbon-wrapped notes was a short letter from his own father, addressed to Hal. His father not only had kept the notes, but he had known that Hal would find them.

Hal: As it is evident that you have now found and read of your grandfather's secret, I turn over to you the request that he made of me but that I was not equipped—either emotionally or by nature—to fulfill, as you are. You can understand all of this better than I can, I'm sure, and are much better able to decide what to do about this. The enclosed notes were written to your grandfather when he was a young army officer during the Allies' Anzio invasion in World War II, when his unit marched from the boot of Italy to Germany. At the last, the general begged me to find what had happened to the young private who wrote these notes, Benjamin Montgomery, and to pass on the general's highest regards and appreciation and his apologies to Montgomery or his surviving descendents, if any.

I had no idea what he meant before I found and read the notes. When I did find them, I regretted having promised to try. And I put off trying until it was too late for me. But by then I knew you would be the one to fulfill this request, if anyone could or would. Both because of who you are and because you have the means of searching the records from the Pentagon. So, I leave it entirely up to you on what you can or wish to do about this.
Dad

Hal sighed, picked up the box, opened the car door, and started walking back to the house wherein lived Benjamin Montgomery's grandson. It had taken some time to trace him through the Pentagon files, but Hal had done so. He now wished he hadn't been persistent in doing so. He had assumed he would find nothing, and then when he did find what he found, he assumed that Montgomery's grandson wouldn't have any interest in a few notes his grandfather had written in World War II.

He had called ahead and he had said the minimum he thought necessary to be able to claim—to himself—that he'd done what he could to fulfill his grandfather's death wish. But the young man on the other end of the line, Bud Montgomery, had surprised him. There had been a pause before he had spoken.

"General Henry Collins? Yes, I know of him. You say you have some notes from my grandfather, sent to him in World War Two?"

"Yes, and I promised my grandfather when he was dying to try to track down what had happened to your grandfather in life and to pass on his regards, appreciation, and—he said—his apologies. It might be enough to have done this over the telephone . . ." Hal certainly hoped it would be enough, and he had now passed on the three things the general had asked for, so this would be enough for Hal. "There are just a few notes, probably in your grandfather's hand. But you may not want those, and perhaps just this connection over the telephone is enough." Hal hoped the young man wouldn't want the notes. It was bad enough that Hal knew about them and had read them.

"Where are you?" the young man answered. "I think we should meet."

"I'm in D.C., but I can come to you, if you wish," Hal said, hoping that the young man didn't wish. "But perhaps a meeting isn't . . ."

Hal had done what his grandfather had wanted. He didn't really want to get any further into this.

"I think we should meet. I think I have the notes your grandfather sent mine in this exchange."

Oh shit, Hal thought. "Maybe we should just leave this . . . I don't think it would do either of our families any good to . . ."

"It's fine, Colonel Collins," he answered. "This need go no further than the two of us, but I loved and respected my grandfather, just as I'm sure you must have yours to be doing this. I think we owe it to them to put these notes together, if they do go together, just to give them both some peace and closure."

And thus Hal found himself knocking on the door of a neat little bungalow on the edge of Gettysburg, Pennsylvania.

A trim, handsome young man met him at the door. "Colonel Collins? I'm Bud. Please come in. The living room's over there. Would you like to have a beer?"

While the young man was getting the beer, Hal entered the living room, which was minimally but neatly furnished. He sat on the sofa and looked around. There were photographs across the room on a table. A wedding photograph, obviously of Bud Montgomery and a pretty, young blond woman. And a few others, of a couple of older couples—their respective parents? And a more recent one of Bud and his wife and two small children. And one of an older, but handsome man. The Benjamin Collins of the notes?

Despite the table full of photos, Hal got the distinct impression that he was alone in the house with Bud Montgomery.

After bringing in the beers, Bud left for a few minutes and then came back with a small wooden box—not a cigar box, but obviously an old one. He took a small stack of folded, yellowing paper out of it, and sat on the sofa next to where Hal was sitting, the general's cigar box in his hand.

"Well, if these are the two parts of a story, we'd best see what the story was," Bud said.

"Are you sure?" Hal asked. "The notes I have are very . . ."

"From what I have here, I have no illusions about what these represent," Bud answered.

And so, they began.

* * * *

"It would be suicidal, Major. And it would be cruel to the soldiers who we know won't last the night or beyond tomorrow. We need to let them die in peace. Then in a couple of days we could—"

"It's what regimental headquarters wants, Captain. We must move with the regiment and they are moving on from the Monte Cassino area."

Captain Collins knew that Major Dunlap was lying about that. Collins was the "Sparks"—the commo operator—for the unit of fifteen soldiers of the 157th who had been assigned to maintain the wounded until the ambulance corps unit could catch up with them. And since they'd been assigned those duties and managed to pull the wounded up to this warren of caves around the base of the mountain that the Monte Cassino monastery supported, all hell had broken out on the battlefield below. They hadn't heard from regimental headquarters for two days. A German artillery unit had advanced to support the Italians, and Captain Collins strongly suspected there wasn't a 157th regiment anymore.

The unit had landed in Oran, Africa, in June of 1943 to stage for the invasion of Italy at Anzio at the end of January 1944. The landing had gone well, but by early February, as the regiment worked its way up the peninsula, the Germans began throwing everything they had left at the invasion force and the 157th had stalled at Monte Cassino, seventy miles short of Rome.

So, Dunlap and Collins were the officers of a fifteen-man unit guarding thirty-two wounded soldiers in a series of caves opening up onto a broad ledge. The wounded, a good third of whom would inevitably die soon, were stashed in the

31

caves. The fifteen combat-capable soldiers were pulling eight-hour shifts of five men each at positions near the edge of the ledge, watching for Germans or Italians, while five soldiers maintained a mess and other support needs and the other five were sleeping in a cave dedicated to their needs. Dunlap and Collins each had a shallow cave for their own billet.

The ambulance unit consisting of seven medics had reached them less than an hour previous to the disagreement conversation between the major and the captain near the entrance to the cave holding the terminally ill. To the major's great disappointment they arrived with no news of the rest of the regiment's disposition or condition.

Major Dunlap was about to reiterate the order to prepare the men to move out, when the head medic, a corporal, came out of the cave.

"We have assessed the wounded, Major," he reported. "Three of the soldiers will die within the next couple of hours, and I doubt that five others will last the night."

"That's unfortunate, Corporal, but we must be on the move to meet up with the regiment."

"How far will that be?" the corporal asked.

Captain Collins, who had been turned away from this discussion, turned back and said, "We have no idea how far it is. We have no idea where the regiment is now. Or do you know, Major?"

The major looked irritated—but also fairly calm. "No, it will be up to us to find them."

"Many of the wounded can't move on their own, Major," the corporal said. "We've just done our assessment. Now we have to dress the wounds. Some of the soldiers still have bullets in them. It will be hours before we can stabilize the wounded."

"And by then it will be dark," Captain Collins said. "We will stand less of a chance finding the regiment through enemy territory in the dark than in the light. And, as I said, it would be cruel to force march men who will be dead, one way or the other, in the morning—and the able-bodied soldiers can't fight, as needed, with two wounded men each on their back."

The major's face was beet red. He didn't like to be second-guessed, even by clear logic. But the logic, in fact, was clear.

"Very well. We will reassess the situation at dawn tomorrow. But I then want us on the move by noon."

Collins and the corporal watched the major stalk off. They turned and looked at each other. Both were fine-looking men, the captain in his late twenties and the corporal, by the look of him, barely twenty-two. They each shook their heads, giving the other a sympathetic look, and walked off to perform their respective duties.

It was late afternoon on February 12, 1944.

That evening, Captain Collins found a note that had been placed under his pillow that gave him some comfort that his near insubordination with the major earlier that day had not gone by without some form of support from the men of the unit.

Shouldn't be doing this, I know, but just wanted you to know that most of us guys are with you on this, Cap. Some of the man we have here are too shot up and played out to be on the move just yet—some of them forever, and it would just be cruelty to bring those men even more pain in something that isn't going to save them. Just want you to know you aren't alone in this, even tho none of the rest of us have a say in anything.

The next day dawned with no further contact from the regiment, two soldiers that had to be buried in the soft soil at one edge of the ledge, and a heavy fog enveloping the mountain. The fog helped them in the respect of making it less certain that any of the remnants of the German and Italian forces roaming around—the enemy having suffered as much in the battle as the Americans had—would find them under those conditions. They still could hear the occasional sound of rifle shots. But the German artillery was silent, and perhaps on the move up the peninsula. The 157th was a vanguard regiment in the march up from Anzio. Soon wave after wave of American forces would be in the area. This was why Captain Collins favored staying put. They could always catch up to the 157th later, he reasoned with the major.

The fog hurt them in the respect that it brought the disagreement between Major Dunlap and Captain Collins even more in the open. There really was no place they could go and not be overheard if the major insisted on blustering his position. And the major did insist on blustering his position.

The fog stayed with them all day, though, and by late afternoon the major had to admit that they were going nowhere that day. Two of the critically wounded had died in the night and two beyond that during the day.

"But what about those with only minor wounds?" the major asked the medic corporal.

The corporal called out a young private, who looked barely old enough to be at war, out of the cave where the less-critical soldiers were being treated. The private was shy, although he managed a smile at Captain Collins when he emerged from the cave. "The major has asked about the progress of the health of the minimally wounded, Private Montgomery. Please report. How many of them would be ready to march tomorrow—and to fight, if need be?"

The private flared up a bit at the question, glaring at the major probably a bit more than the major would tolerate if the soldier were directly under his command, but he calmed down as quickly as he had shown irritation. "Most of the men not in the critical care area could probably march tomorrow, sir. But I doubt if more than a dozen of them could point rifles steadily. Perhaps a few more days and—"

"Thank you, Private," Major Dunlap said with an icy voice. "You may go back to your patients now."

Once again the private gave Captain Collins a smile as he turned and fled back into the cave.

That night Collins received yet another handwritten note under the pillow of his pallet, which gave him encouragement to hold off on the withdrawal from the caves.

Stand up to the major, Cap. There are enough of us who will stand behind you on this. The caves are the best place to be in until the fighting gets beyond us. We got more sick and wounded here than we got men who could fight. We didn't march all the way up from Anzio to Monte Cassino just to get out in the open for Krauts and Spics to pick us off. There's nothing cowardly about it. I, for one, would pick up a gun and join it out there if you tell me to but none of us medics can be doing that and caring for the wounded soldiers and carrying them out of these caves on our backs at the same time. You are told the major right about that.

One who cares and stands behind you.

Late that night, not being able to sleep, Captain Collins had left his cave and was standing by the entrance into the critical care cave, chancing smoking a cigarette to calm his nerves. He normally wouldn't have considered doing this at night, but the fog had settled in again, and he doubted that a lighted tip of a cigarette could be seen at the edge of the ledge from here, let alone down the mountainside.

He thought he heard a strange noise from inside the critical cave—like perhaps one of the patients choking—and instinct drew him into the entrance way. He stopped there, though, instantly understanding what was happening at a pallet over in a corner.

The young soldier on the pallet was one who had been thought not to be alive this morning, but he was still alive. One of the medics was kneeling beside him. The medic had unbuttoned his fly and had his cock out, and the dying soldier was sucking on it, while the medic had his hand inside the fly of the soldier and was stroking his cock.

Collins wasn't surprised. There had been indications about this solider earlier, the one who was dying, but nothing definitive had been established. It was clear from what Collins could see and hear that what the medic was doing for the dying soldier was an act of solace. Regulations, of course, demanded immediate charges and punishment for both of the soldiers. But, muttering "fuck it" under his breath, Collins just turned and left the cave.

Exhausted, he was able to fall into a deep sleep on his pallet for the few hours left in the night. When he awoke, he found another note—in the same hand and on the same lined notebook paper as the two earlier notes—laying on top of his mess kit. The note thanked him for turning his eyes away from what he had spied in the night, and for not reporting the incident.

Just want to thank you for understanding, Cap. There's lots of ways to take care of the wounded and dying. It's not being less of a man to be human and carrying with all this shit going on. Private Craig is on his way out. He knows that. Jimbo knows that. If Jimbo allows him to get what comfort and pleasure is left in life that ain't up to no one but the two of them and God, I say. It's war, and it's still bad out there. Krauts everywhere and the Spics are just shooting at anything that moves. We're probably all gonna die. Probably none of us are going back to a regular life as the Bible tells us to do.

Thanks—for the private Jimbo's caring for in the best way he can see and for the remaining time the private has—for just overlooking it and not telling the major. Everything about where we are and can't get out alive is unnatural. And we're stuck with everything. So, nothing's unnatural here.
With the greatest respect,
Private Benjamin

When Collins checked the next morning, he found that Private Craig had died an hour earlier. Collins also now knew who had been sending him the notes. This one was signed by the private who had been called out to report the combat readiness of the less critical wounded, Private Montgomery. He had signed the note "Private Benjamin," but the only Benjamin in the caves was Private Montgomery.

Other news he received that morning was that Major Dunlap had taken two soldiers and set off on his own to reconnoiter the area, still being hot to lead the unit off the mountain and to meet up with the 157th. This was fine with Collins except for the part of not having been informed that the major was doing this. It was a clear sign that the major didn't trust or want to work with Collins, which couldn't possibly be good, especially when the unit was in the peril that it found itself in.

Still, there was an upside to this. Until the major returned, Collins was in charge. The major had said nothing to the men about the situation. Collins called them together, including the less-critically wounded, after they had breakfasted and told them that, unless the major returned with contrary orders, they would stay here for at least two more days. He didn't say the timing was established with the consideration that by then there wouldn't be critical wounded still alive who could not travel—but everyone listening to him knew the score.

He continued by saying, though, that the unit *would* have to be on the move soon. Little evidence of fighting had been heard or seen from the valley in more than twenty-four hours, he was sure that the main vanguard of the U.S. forces would be appearing in the next day or so, and, most telling of all, they would be running out of supplies and couldn't stay here much longer in any event.

The men listened to him intently and none questioned the wisdom or necessity of what he was saying, his spirits were lifted that night to find yet another note in his cave providing affirmation and a pledge of support from his not-so-secret supporter. It normally wouldn't mean a great deal to receive support from a private—and one from a medical rather than a combat unit and looking barely old enough to shave—but his eyes had met on several occasions with those of Private Montgomery over the past two days, and an affinity had been established between them. For some reason, Captain Collins found himself very much wanting to know that he had the young, good-looking private's approval.

He was not yet able, however, to consider what might underlay this affinity.

You're the man. I'd follow you anywhere. You were right. It's just about past us now. Soon as we're down to those never going anywhere from here, I'm with you a hundred percent on giving it a go. So's all the other guys. The major doesn't come back, we'll do what you say, no question. Even then we'll follow your lead. Me, especially, whatever you want, whatever you tell me to do. You got it. I'll carry a man and a gun. Just say the word.
Your man,
Private Ben

The next morning, Captain Collins's world changed forever. And it happened in the most unexpected way, blindsiding him, deeply disturbing him, and causing him to brood for some time on his life until now to consider whether there had been any foreshadowing for this life-shattering revelation.

The unit had devised a shower behind some rocks at one edge of the ledge, where a small cascade of water dropped down the side of the mountain. Part of the "on mess duty" units duties was to keep buckets filled with water, and when the men were able to break away to douse themselves with the ice-cold water, they merely tipped a bucket over their heads, soaped up, rinsed, and used as little water as they could in the process.

When Collins rounded the corner of the rock-enclosed area, naked, to take a quick dousing, he almost ran into Private Montgomery, who already was there, naked and soaped up. Surprised at the appearance of the captain, the private lost his balance. Collins caught him, preventing the smaller man from falling to the ground. But the positioning of the captain's arms and hands when he caught the naked private was intimate. He was embracing the private's chest from behind him with one arm, the captain's hand palming the private's pecs. And his other hand was cupping the private's genitals.

All would have been fine, if the captain had let loose of the private as soon as Montgomery had regained his footing. But he didn't. They remained, transfixed, in that position for nearly half a minute—time enough for both of them to start hardening up and for each to know the other was doing so. Collins was trembling. Montgomery let out a low moan, which snapped Collins out of his daze. He turned and fled the shower.

For the rest of the day, he dreaded the knowledge that there would be a note accusing him of what he'd had no knowledge of having any interest in—at least until now. He agonized at the realization that the encounter had meant something to him. That it had started to make some feelings of the past click into place, feelings he didn't know he'd had and didn't want to have.

He avoided Private Montgomery for the rest of the day and wouldn't have known what to say to him if they did encounter each other in private. There certainly was nothing he could say to the young man with others present.

He made it to the night without incident, but, just as he surmised, there was a note under his pillow on his pallet when he retreated to his cave. It wasn't an accusatory note, though. Collins realized that it might have been better if it were. It was a "not to worry" note that left him more disturbed and full of guilty feelings than before.

It's OK, Cap. It's more than OK. It was accidental like. But anything you want. Anything you need. Just ask. And not because you're an officer. Because you're you. You don't even need to ask, know what I mean? We all have needs. I have needs too.
Ben

Benjamin Montgomery's note of conciliation—and hinting of more—could not go unanswered. To talk to him would put it all on some sort of official level. Captain Collins decided he had to write a note of his own, the first one he'd ever written to the private. He agonized over the note, not being able to write what his emotions were telling him he wanted to write—to admit to—which wasn't only that feelings he had for other men were beginning to emerge from him but also that he had specific feelings for, attraction to, Private Montgomery. Feelings he should not have, but increasingly couldn't deny.

This had to be nipped in the bud and he had to accept responsibility for what he'd done. Providing it in writing would absolve the private of any guilt and would leave the matter in the private's hands concerning what he wanted done about it. Montgomery couldn't know how he really was feeling. His note to Ben, delivered by slight of hand in passing the next morning, was meant to apologize for the encounter and assure the private both that it wasn't his fault and that it was an anomaly brought on by the tensions of the war—and not an indication of anything real.

Oh, god, B, I'm so sorry. I didn't mean to do that. Just forget I ever touched you like that. I don't know why. I'll be careful not to be showering at the same time again. It's the war, man. I'm not like that. You don't have to tell me it's OK. It isn't.

The note didn't work. Private Montgomery clearly was interested in more contact—and inviting more intimate contact. His answering note clearly opened the door to Collins and caused the captain to retreat to his pallet, pull the cover over himself, and masturbate to gain relief and release the heat of the thoughts that now were racing through his mind. A simple, accidental encounter in the shower had opened a Pandora's box. It had let a genie out of a bottle that Collins didn't seem to be able to bottle up again. And it wasn't being helped by Private Benjamin, who was now giving Collins intimate looks as they crossed paths and was positioning his body provocatively.

The note Collins found after the noon mess clearly signaled that the private wanted more from him. And increasingly, Collins wanted to give the small, cute medic more.

I wanted more. There, I said it. But you're so hung, I was scared. And an officer. You haven't done it, ever before? Don't know how you managed Africa and then up from the boot of Italy without it. Or maybe officers can get at the women. Privates like me sure can't. We have to make do with who is there. And then we find we like it well enough—even more than like it. And it gives us release and helps us go on. I'm not ashamed of what happened. I don't want you to be ashamed either. It's what happens in war times like this. I sure won't say anything to the major or anyone else, and if you're interested, see you at the shower again. If you're not, please just forget that I mentioned it. But don't be sorry for it. I sure as hell am not sorry. In fact, I want to think that . . . well, if you really don't want me to hope about it, do something or say something before tonight.
B

For the rest of the day, there were several times the two came face to face. It was a confined space and there was no avoiding each other. Each time Collins was determined to say something, but he didn't. What he wanted to say wasn't what he knew he should say. So he said nothing and gave no signal to dash the hope the private had put into his note.

That night the private stole into Collins's cave and was naked and creeping under the blanket covering Collins's pallet so silently that Collins thought he was having a dream—a wet

40

dream that he couldn't help but having—before he was awake enough to know that he was hard, that Private Montgomery was straddling his hips, and that the private was fisting Collins's cock and sliding his channel down the pole.

Collins lay there, wide eyed and panting heavily as the small, young, incredibly sexy private fucked himself on the cock.

Collins had done nothing to force the encounter, but when, after twenty minutes of groaning sex, they both had come, Collins had done nothing to cut off the encounter either.

His note to the private the next morning was meant to put an end to it, to take all of the blame, but to say that it would be impossible to go on, to follow his acknowledged attraction farther. And in accepting the blame for someone egging the young man on, he as much as told Private Montgomery to turn him in for rape. He was the officer. The responsibility was fully his.

I'm such an animal. How can I ever let you know how sorry I am I lost control like that—that I didn't say or do anything to keep it from happening. Just a fuckin animal. It's all this stuff about whether and when to make a break for it. I just about had all I can of it. I promise I will never again . . . If you want to report me to the major, I wouldn't fault or fight it. Maybe it's just time for me to be put down. This war is hell. It's making a fucking wild animal out of me.

I couldn't say this to your face. You can show this note to the major, if you like. It's all my fault.
Captain Collins

Private Montgomery's answering note, brushed all of Collins' arguments and noble intentions to take full blame and all responsibility aside and pressed on for more attention from Collins, for the captain, the older of the two and the top, to continue and deepen the relationship. When Collins didn't answer that note, Montgomery sent yet another one, begging Collins to step up to the attraction each undeniably had for the other. The second note was passed by hand, and for the first time the issue was spoken.

"Sorry for the language, but I'm aching here. You have fucked me already, Captain. We have fucked. That cat don't go

41

back in the bag. You want me, I know—as much as I want you. It's the war. We both need this. I'm aching for it."

"You used me to fuck yourself," Collins answered in a strangled voice. "This isn't right, Ben." But he took the note and the private knew he was winning—or the captain wouldn't have accepted the note.

No, don't feel like that, Cap. Don't say anything like that to me. I wanted it. I asked for it. It ain't like you popped my man cherry or anything. That happened a couple of guys ago. I ain't confused about what I want and need. My first officer, tho, and I never had it so big. Not your fault. Once I saw you in the shower. . . . Just the way it is out here on the road to Berlin. The tension and the needs. It's not the real world. We all have needs and urges. Me too. Don't take this on yourself. You need it too. I could tell by the way you just went with it. Well, you need it . . . anytime . . . you got it with me. God, you've got a big one.
Anytime, anywhere,
B

Collins didn't answer, but that didn't stop another note coming.

Like I said already, anytime you want it, Cap. 'Cause I sure want it. I can't stop think of doing it with you—aching for you to do it to me without me controlling it. You giving me that big one. I have needs too. Couldn't you tell by my moaning as you pushed it up into me and how I clung to you and then begged for it again? You're not taking advantage. You didn't hurt me—in none of the ways. I've done it before. Lots of times. And I can get it. That's not a real problem. But you and me. We're real good together. Real good. I gotta say that if you're really thinking of me, as you say is what's holding you back, you'll fuck me again. We both need it. We both need to feel. You're driving me wild here. I'm aching for it.

Collins came to Ben in the shower. The shower wasn't set up in the last niche in the rocks along the far edge of the ledge—there was room on the ledge beyond that and the cliffside was riddled with small caves. Collins pushed the private beyond the shower, into another niche, and fucked him from behind, standing up, with the smaller man bent over in

42

front of him and grabbing his ankles until Collins pulled Ben's shoulder blades up, into his chest. He cupped the young man's chin, and brought his face around for a deep kiss while Collins pumped his ass and released his cum deep inside the young private.

Ben said that wasn't enough for him. Collins admitted that it wasn't enough for him either. They fucked half the night away in Collins's cave, on his pallet, in several different positions, all ones Ben nudged Collins into. It was clear that Ben was the expert here, no novice in any sense of the word. But Collins was a quick learner. The dam had burst. He suddenly knew who he was and what he wanted.

And what he wanted was to fuck Ben silly. It's what Ben wanted too.

The note Ben handed Collins the next morning exuded the glee that he had that, at last, they were fucking with no reservations, no restraints other than keeping it private between the two of them.

Roll me over, Roll me over
Roll me over in the clover
And do it again, do it again!
Fuck me again and again!
Ain't much for poetry, and I never thought of that way of it, but that's all I could think of, you fucking me. Us guys are always singing that song—most in a different way. But that's just how I feel with you now. You put me on one high, you did. First time we done it all the way flat out without any guilt or shame—at least for me, and you sure as hell didn't seem to be holding anything back. And then again. I want you to do me again and again and again, Fuck me. Fuck me. Slide that big one up inside me again. There, I said it. War is hell. But it's not that much hell now.
Roll me over . . . BIG SMILE.
Yours

They had one more night together in the caves. They fucked with abandon, with Collins taking complete control, with Ben muttering over and over again, "Fuck me, spike me, screw me, plow me," in joyful celebration that Collins was mining the depths of his channel, both of them spewing cum multiple times.

The last note that Collins received from Ben in the caves celebrated their exuberant coupling with a crude poem that was to become Ben's mantra as they marched and fucked across northern Italy and into France.

> *Fuck, spike, screw, plow,*
> *Do me anyway you like,*
> *Just do me now, now, NOW!*

There. Hasn't being royally screwed like that last night made me a much better poet? I know that we can't speak about this in the open. But don't deny me these notes. You don't have to answer if you don't want. You let me know in the night what you're feeling. You came to me for it last night. You showed me you had to have it as much I have to have it from you. I am just busting with the want of having your dick inside me. Your big, throbbing dick. Fucking me, fucking me, fucking me. This war is hell, but you have given me a slice of heaven, a reason to live, to be there on the other side. I live for the nights, of you covering me, and kissing me, and holding me tight. And thrusting inside me. And fucking, fucking, fucking me. God, you are hung and hard for me.

I know you don't want to talk of love. But if one man could talk of love to another . . .
Yours. Anywhere, anytime.

That morning, Captain Collins marched what remained of the unit, down in strength fourteen soldiers, including Major Dunlap and the two soldiers he'd taken with him on the reconnaissance mission, out of the caves and down the mountainside. Twice they brushed close to German remnant units, but two days later, without firing a shot, Collins delivered all of the men who had come off the mountain with him safely into the hands of U.S. Forces.

The remnants of the 157th, now, with the addition of Captain Collins's men, were gathering north of Rome to prepare for a march through France, toward Berlin. The Germans were on the run back to the homeland. Of the 705 men in the 157th at the first firing of a gun in the battle for Monte Cassino to the day the Captain Collins appeared with his unit, Major Dunlap never being heard from again, there remained 163 men.

On February 24, 1944, Captain Collins was promoted to major and notified that he was being put in for the Silver Star for bringing his unit out substantially intact and saving as many wounded men as he had.

At the end of the ceremony, Private Benjamin, thinking that his ambulance unit might now be split off from the 157th, slipped a note of congratulations to Collins, and set up an assignation with the new major in the room assigned to Collins in a small hotel that had been commandeered as an officers' billet.

Congratulations, Major. If anyone deserves it, you do. Bringing all of us out of the Monte Cassino caves hell hole alive. I'm so proud of you. But being an even higher muckity muck officer now, does that mean we have to use a rubber? Sorry, that was a joke. But I don't want to use a rubber. The skin of a hard, throbbing cock rubbing me inside drives me wild. Not just any cock—yours. That's what I want to feel. The heat of it. I guess there would be the pulse of it that I love to try to match even with the rubber. But not the heat and the slide of the skin covering the rod of steel and then the filling of me. Your hot jism exploding even deeper inside me—deeper than your big, hard cock can reach. I feel it in my belly. It warms me through the long, wet trod through France. Have I told you that no one has ever cocked me as good as you do? No one has been as thick and long inside me as you have been? Can you feel how hot I am for you even at this moment? Tried to come with you last night. Almost got there. Maybe tonight?

Tell me that majors still fuck privates. If I've worked it right, you are reading this as you turn in. And are getting hard. For me. If so, I am just back in the shadows. Just put out the light and lay down on your back. I'll give you a blow job worthy of a major and then I'll do the riding. Love (Yes, there, I've put it out there in the open)
You know who

The fucking, intense and celebratory not only because of Collins's promotion but also from relief that they had made it to U.S. lines and because this was their first lovemaking in a proper bed, went on for hours. Collins was in full control now, taking Ben first doggie style, bent over the side of the bed.

After drinking half a bottle of Champagne that Ben had managed to commandeer, Ben lay on his back on the bed, his legs hooked on Collins's hips as, pushing his knees under Ben's buttocks, Collins grabbed Ben by the waist and pulled him on and off the cock. They celebrated their first encounter and Collins's first fully controlling fuck, up there by the shower on the Monte Cassino ledge, by fucking in the shower of the adjoining bathroom, Collins standing with his back to the slick tiles of the wall, and Ben plastered to his pelvis, with wrists hooked behind Collins's neck, and Ben placing his feet on the wall on either side of Collins's torso and fucking himself on the cock by leveraging off the wall on the balls of his feet.

One last drunken fuck found them on the floor, Ben on his belly, and Collins riding his buttocks and waving his arms in the air like a rodeo cowboy.

Ben asked for a written note cataloging their evening together, thinking that this might be their last fuck, that they would find themselves in separate units the next morning.

Collins's letter not only celebrated the night, but also expressed the depth of his appreciation for what Ben had given him. It also contained the surprise that they would not be parted—that a major was accorded an orderly and that Collins's request that Ben be assigned to him as his orderly had been granted.

They would march into France together. As a high-ranking officer, Collins would receive billeting in a hotel or private home, wherever possible. That the two would now march by day and fuck in a private bedroom by night, Ben being the most attentive orderly to his officer's needs and desires that he possibly could be.

War or no war, life was good for the two lovers.

Jesus Christ, that was incredible. We've come a long way, haven't we, B? There is so much I want to do with you, to you. You are the reason I can go on. And it will go better for us, now, I promise. A major scores an orderly. And better billeting along the road. Maybe a private bedroom in a heated house. And an orderly to serve him. Guess who services—oops, I mean serves . . . grin . . . me so well. So, guess who've I've asked to be my orderly.

We mustn't sink too far into this, though. This has got to remain the temporary result of the circumstances of war and men thrown together in worry and danger and not the usual outlets. This is still unusual, unheard of in my family, as I'm sure it is in yours. I have a wife and a child. I love them no less than before this happened.

This must, for both of us, just be to see us through this hell of a war. We can't put too much meaning into this—either one of us. But it's important to me. Now, thanks quite a lot to you, I can see a glimmer of sanity on the other side. Not a life completely like it was before Africa and Anzio and Monte Cassino, and now France. I would never regret this: you, being inside you, the release, the pleasure, the forgetting just for those moments, you lying under me, you giving it to me . . . everything. But this isn't the real world, and aren't we fighting to put the world back on its axis—and on the pedestals that civilized societies create for us to honor? I love my wife. I love my baby son—even though I've never seen him in the flesh. And, yes, I have L for you too, B. But it's a different feeling. It's for here, now. That will have to be enough.

But, fuck, B, that was incredible. Yes, fuck, fuck, FUCK.

The only shadow hovering over the concept of their life being ideal—or as ideal as it could be considering that they were still in a war and marching across countries on their feet—was the continued hedging Collins voiced and wrote about concerning the future and the probability that they both would return to normal—more socially acceptable—lives after the war.

Ben continually worked to deflect this, though, and answered Collins with a letter making every effort to hang on to what they now were to each other. Whereas Collins fought to acknowledge reality, Ben grasped at the fantasy that had been woven around them.

I don't know why you lift me up and then push me down. Not when I'm on your cock, of course. You can lift me up and slam me down all you want then. You could have stopped at "score." You sure scored last night. You could write these letters on two sheets and just slip me the first page and burn the other one. But I'll take what I can get. I'm aching for you to slip me something right now, and we've just finished the evening mess. I have hours more to pant for your cock.

I'll take an L that comes with an F and an S or two and a P (Fuck, screw, spike, plow—but do it now. Isn't that the way it went? You'd think I chanted it enough while you were screwing me that I'd remember exactly how it goes). Your body doesn't lie to me, Henry. You are in paradise—far from this fucking slog to Berlin—when you are fucking, screwing, spiking, plowing me. And so am I.

You are right about having privacy and a bed most nights along the march through France. I didn't know you could come up with that many ways to fuck a man. Good thing we don't use rubbers. We'd be out of what few the Red Cross slips under the table to a soldier before we'd gotten out of the caves. Screw thinking about the other world. This is my whole world now. You are my whole world. Even if you can't say it, I can. Love, love, love.

And right now, I would love you to fuck me. And what I'd really love is for you to fill out what that "L" means to you—to both of us. This isn't just because we're in a wartime bubble to me. This is a forever for me.

* * * *

By late July of 1944, the 157th, in separated small units spread across the line of advance, was approaching the Largue River in the Franche-Comté region, preparing to move into the Alsace region. When they cleared Alsace, they would be in Germany itself. They were hot on the tail of the retreating German army. There were few skirmishes between the U.S. and German forces, but the local populace was war weary and panicked and communication were such that they had little knowledge of what army was moving through their region. All they knew was that they had been used as pawns to exploit and ravish.

They were skittish and responding to any danger they saw to their villages and farms.

Major Collins's unit was approaching the small hamlet of Bonfol, which had been brutalized by German soldiers not more than two days previously. Walking in a tree-lined dirt-surfaced avenue between fields that had been churned up by German Panzer units, Collins heard a rustling in a tree overhead. Looking up, he saw a young boy of no more than nine or ten, pointing an old rifle at him. The rifle wavered in the boy's hands and Collins had time to see the fear,

48

determination, and hatred in the boy's face before he turned to take cover. He also had time to shoot the boy out of the tree with his own at-the-ready rifle.

He didn't shoot, though, and because he didn't shoot, as he turned and dove for cover, the rifle in the tree discharged and a single bullets somehow struck Collins in the muscle of a calf, traveled through that calf, and then through the other one as well. As he fell, he remembered having looked back up to the face of the boy in the tree, whose eyes looked sad and weary. The boy was raising the rifle again.

But a shot rang out, from among the soldiers who were catching up to the major, and the boy fell out of the tree and lay, dead, on the ground just beside where Collins had fallen. Before Collins was lifted up by his orderly, he was face to face with the boy on the ground for long enough for it to register than the boy's eyes retained their look of sadness.

Collins was transported to the nearest U.S. Army field hospital near Basel. His orderly, Private Montgomery, stayed with him, having been very useful in tending to Collins on the spot and keeping him as comfortable and stabilized as possible en route to the field hospital because Montgomery himself had been a medic in an ambulance unit.

At the field hospital, the orderly stuck by the bedside of the major, providing additional nursing care twenty-four hours a day in addition to what the busy hospital could afford to devote. The wound was painful and it would prevent Major Collins from preceding with his unit or meeting up with the 157th until they were approaching Heidelberg, in Germany, some ten weeks later. But his wounds were minor compared to others the hospital had to deal with under short-staffed conditions, so the presence of the orderly meant everything in the initial care of the patient.

When the major came out of the near coma, induced by painkilling drugs, though, he turned away from the orderly and refused to respond to him. At length, he asked to be transferred to another hospital and for his orderly to be sent on to catch up with the 157th, which is what transpired.

In the final known, and fullest and most revealing, exchange of letters between the two men who had become war-conditions lovers, Private Montgomery, who was the soldier who had shot the boy from the tree outside Bonfol, pleaded to the major not to turn away from him and the major sadly answered that it was time for both of them to start returning to reality—that their war would be over soon, they both would want to return to a life that didn't include men making love to men, and that this disruptive incident in France was, both of them needed to admit, the best possible circumstance to end their relationship.

August 5, 1944

Tell me that wasn't our last time. Tell me it wasn't because your wounds hampered you and I had to do the work. Tell me that it wasn't because I shot that boy. He was going to kill you. You didn't mind it with the promotion celebration. You seemed so distant tonight. But it wasn't because you couldn't come. I brought you off twice. But it was like you were holding back—and I know you when you aren't holding back in a fuck. Oh, god, do I know how wildly you can fuck when you're loosened up. I thought we were beyond the notes, that we could talk to each other in the daylight. I can control myself in front of the others. You should know that by now. I'm your orderly and also a medic. No one's questioned that I spend the night with you in this hospital room. There's no fucking suspicion about me taking care of you. If you won't speak to me, at least read this note. Don't turn away from me.

Is it because he was just a boy and I shot him? Or is it because you hesitated in shooting him yourself, and are embarrassed that I saw that? I don't judge you for that. Your ability to still be a human after all of this time in the war is part of why I love you. And no one else saw what happened. No one saw you freeze.

It was him or you. And he'd already shot you once—and even though he looked scared as hell, he was going to shoot you again . . . and again until you were dead. And he was dead one way or the other. Someone else would have shot him, if I hadn't. So, of course I dropped him. You have to understand. When it's you and anyone else, if I can do anything, I will. I know what you've said and written, where you've drawn the line. I understand your problem, how you are torn, how you feel you have to hold on to that other world if you can. But that's your line. I draw no such line. I have no other world to lose. I'm yours, all yours. I will do anything to keep you alive.

OK, you don't have to talk to me, but those wounds, even though they are flesh wounds, could easily be infected. Don't turn me away. I'm a medic, not just the young soldier you're fucking and can't fully accept that you are.

>*Don't turn me away.*
>*Benjamin Montgomery*
>*The private you are fucking and who loves you*

August 7, 1944
Ben:

If you are reading this and we aren't both in a stockade, the colonel gave you this letter without reading it—as I requested that he do. You also will know that I have been moved to another hospital—at my request—and that you have received orders to catch up with the unit marching into Germany. Although I've learned we are going to Heidelberg to protect artwork the Jerries stored in the castle there rather than to Berlin. I don't know if you even care about that. But Heidelberg would have been a far better place for us to spend our last days together than what's left of Berlin.

And you must realize that we would have ended it there, in Heidelberg, which isn't that far away considering that we have tramped on foot from the boot of Italy to here in Alsace already.

I'll say it now. I have come to love you, and it isn't all about the sex, even though, you are right, it has been paradise to be able to balance the hell of war with the heaven of fucking you. And, yes, that scares me. I shouldn't have let it go there.

This isn't the real world. We both must return to the real world. I can't believe that you have nothing waiting for you back in Tennessee. You must return to normalcy, as I must. This war has stripped away everything civilized and acceptable in the soldiers who have been forced to clean up the failure of politicians and megalomaniacs like Hitler and Mussolini. To a certain degree, we've been reduced to being primitive animals too—just to fight them on their own level and to survive. It was natural, in a way, there being few women and many frightened men along the road that I let myself be reduced to a primitive animal in this way too. Men thrown in together in fear and uncertainty, need and tension. Testosterone like a bright flame. And being told over and over again that we weren't like the fascists—we didn't loot and rape. And if we did, we'd be summarily executed—in a climate where it was believable that this would be our fate.

It was natural to turn to each other for comfort and release. And you were so desirable—from the first time I laid eyes on you. And then, yes, you have to admit it, so willing and leading me. You accepted responsibility for that from the beginning. It's not that I'm saying you are a schemer. It just seemed so much more acceptable for you in the circumstance we were in. You were the one with the open mind and I was the prude.

That's not an excuse for me, of course. I was an officer and you were a private—not even a foot soldier. You were a medic working to save the wounded men assigned to my unit in the caves of Monte Cassino. I didn't even ask you how old you were. You looked so young that I should have. Thank god your being too young didn't get added to my sins. I should have shown restraint. But it was such a struggle on what to do there, and you were so comforting and supportive—and available and willing. And so damn sexy. I was an animal, a primitive animal. And you took it and did everything you could to have me and to hold me inside you.

I don't think I've ever told you. I never could bury it all with my wife or any of the other women I've had. But you took it all and made love to it. And I was such an animal. I was lost to you—days before I first fucked you. It was driving me crazy. It was what I wanted at the time. When you gave yourself to me, it got me through the lunacy of the war.

But enough of that. I promised myself to keep this formal—for the sake of both of us. No, this is not your fault. None of it is your fault, really. You were young—you still are in years, but certainly not in experience. I'm an officer. It was basically my weakness—my weakness in this so that I could be strong in other ways. You'll chastise me, I think, for mentioning "fault." All along you've taken what we've been doing as natural and right, under the circumstances, and I've been the one who was reserved and expressed the guilt. That said, I have loved your notes; the heat of them spurred me on to something I'll never regret (I hope), and they gave me release when, barring a release such as that, I might have killed Major Dunlap back in the caves of Monte Cassino, and then where would we have been?

A parting is inevitable. I ask you to come to accept that. But that it is now isn't because of anything you've done. You saved my life. I don't discount that in the least, and I forever will be in your debt for that. I was in your debt before that. You gave me everything. You gave me pleasure and release and a will to put one foot in the front of the other during our trek. And you did it all without asking for or demanding anything but the cock in private—which was the easiest thing I could give to you, because it brought so much pleasure to me. (Cock in private. I laughed when I reread that. I'm sure you did when you first read it. You always said I was too serious. I sure had my cock in a private, didn't I?)

I think it was the eyes—the sad eyes—that woke me up. Of course the bullet through the legs was a wake-up call in itself. That young boy in the tree. His eyes looked so sad. He didn't want to be there any more than we did. But he had a duty, just as we did, no matter how futile and irrelevant it was at that point. The Jerries were on the run—all the way back to Germany. His war was over. But the boy didn't realize it, and he did what duty told him he had to do to protect his world, his family—shoot the invaders. He was trembling so bad that I have no idea how he managed to hit me—even through the legs.

I can't help wondering what I would have done—what you would have done—if he'd missed with that first shot. But it was the eyes. I'd seen those sad eyes before. I saw them on your face when you first struggled up to the caves in Monte Cassino with your medical unit and saw the work that faced you—knowing that a good third of those boys would never be coming out of the caves alive no matter what we faced if we had to go back into the battle.

I think when I first saw those sad eyes of yours, I knew that I wanted to possess you. (The rest of the body was great too, I must say.) I had had those thoughts about other men before that. But there was something about you that told me that I needed to have you under me, pinned to the ground by my cock, fully mine. But when I saw the eyes of that young boy who died, needlessly, because I was invading his village and his village had suffered the savagery of all of the invaders who came before us, I knew I couldn't go on like that with you.

And I knew, despite what I've written, that it was all my fault, all responsibility for your life and well-being that I shouldn't have taken advantage of.

Don't write me again—please, Ben. It all has to stop at some time. Now is the time. You won't find me. The colonel has assured me that you will be safe where he assigns you—back in an ambulance unit, but now with the enemy pointed the other way and running. Remember me with fondness, if you can, and as your partner in surviving the hell of war. I know that I will remember you with . . . yes, Love.
HC

* * * *

"That's the last letter I have from your grandfather to mine," Bud Montgomery said. The light was growing dim in the small living room. The men had been sitting side by side, closely, piecing the letters together for a couple of hours.

"I see," Hal Collins answered. "That's sad, so sad."

"Yes, but what I story. I can understand how both of them felt. The sadness was that it had to end."

"As I read the letters, I can see the conflict in my grandfather's view of it—having to consider the social mores of the time—or thinking he had too. Your grandfather's position seemed the purer."

"But it also seems clear that my grandfather seduced yours into the relationship—a private seduced an officer."

"I don't think that would have been possible if the officer didn't basically want it to happen. They just lived at the wrong time."

"You think it would have been better in the present?"

"Well, homosexuality is more readily accepted now, I think. I certainly don't feel the stigma that my grandfather obviously did—probably for very good reason. I'm an Army officer and I've been able to declare, if only recently."

"You? You're gay?"

"Yes, I think that's why this responsibility for putting the letters together devolved on me. My father couldn't bring himself to do it. But in his letter to me, passing on the responsibility, he said that I should understand the need for it better than he did, because I was gay. In that, I think he was right."

"I see." Bud was looking away from Hal, his face turned toward the family photographs on the table across the room.

"I'm sorry if I have offended you." Hal was truly concerned. Since he had arrived here and while they had been piecing together the letters, he increasingly had become attracted to Bud Montgomery. He, of course, could never act on it, but he found the young man's understanding and acceptance of the contents of the letters and the sensuality he exuded arousing.

"How could you have offended me?" the young man, asked turning back to Hal. He placed a hand on Hal's forearm that Hal felt as a burning brand, so much did it arouse him.

"You have been so good about all of this—the revelations in these notes and letters. I'm gay, so it isn't difficult for me. But for you it should be—"

"I'm gay too."

"Excuse me? Those photographs on that table over there. Isn't that your wife? Aren't those your children?"

"Yes, but that doesn't mean that I'm not gay. It just means I didn't come to grips with that fact until after I married and had children. My family is resigned to the fact and we get along fine. They just don't live here. I live here alone, and when I'm feeling brave and am attracted to a man, I bring him back here, and I lie under him. It's not primitive as the officer in his letters kept worrying about. It's natural, and it meets natural needs and can be loving."

"You bring men back here, and you lie under them—when you are attracted to them?"

Bud had not removed his hand from Hal's arm.

"You lie under men?" Hal repeated.

"Yes, I'm sorry if I offend you now, but I'm openly gay, and I want to make the most of the rest of my life. That's what I find sad in the story of our grandfathers—that they so obviously loved each other and yet had to give each other up. I don't even need the love. If I'm am attracted to a man and aroused by him I am happy to let him fuck me."

"Men fuck you casually?"

"Yes, when I want them."

"And that's all it takes? You might, then be attracted to—"

"I have been attracted to you since I heard your voice on the telephone. I have been aroused by you since you walked through my front door. Haven't you felt the vibes too?"

"Yes, I've felt them. But I believed . . . I didn't know . . . I fought them."

"Like your grandfather fought them? To what good purpose? Was he happier for it? I can tell you my grandfather wasn't happier for it. He mourned the loss for the rest of his life. He's the one who forced me to acknowledge that I like men rather than women—and that I liked men to fuck me. He's the one who told me not to resist my impulses, to grab as much pleasure, of my own choosing. He gave me the notes and letters he'd saved from your grandfather. That your grandfather saved the notes and letters he received as well screams of his own regret for what he lost. We don't need to relive our grandfathers' mistakes, though . . . Damned right I want you to fuck me."

Hal stopped further declarations by the younger Bud by pulling him closer, embracing him, and possessing his mouth with his. Bud pulled Hal down on top of him as they turned to stretch out on the sofa, and they rolled around, frantically pulling at each other's clothes until there was nothing else to pull off. Instinctively, Bud scooted down the length of the sofa as Hal worked his way in the opposite direction, raising up in a pushup position on his toes, with the heels of his hands dug into the sofa arm. His face now positioned under Hal's pelvis, he took Hal's half-engorged cock in his mouth, and Hal face fucked him, doing pushups above the younger man.

When Hal was as hard as hard can be, Bud scooted up the length of the sofa again, to where he could guide Hal's cock to his asshole, wrapped his legs around the small of Hal's back, and pulled the cock inside him.

"Shit, you're good at this," Hal muttered as he continued his pushups, this time stroking his cock in Bud's channel rather than his mouth.

"So, according to those letters, was my grandfather," Bud answered. "There's so much I can show you, so much we can do, so much fucking we can make up for for our grandfathers."

Hardened armyman that Hal was, he was able to do hundreds of pushups without breaking a sweat. Bud was glad he could, although they finally both broke a sweat.

When they had both ejaculated and fell into an entwining embrace—and Bud had managed to regularized his breathing—he whispered, "Can you come again?"

"Gettysburg isn't that far from D.C. I think I can manage to make the trip again soon."

"No, I mean can you come again now? Can you make me come again now? This house is small, but it has a bedroom."

"Yes, I think I can manage that," Hal answered, with a grin. "But our grandfathers did it wherever. I don't need to go as far as the bedroom."

Bud gave a gasp and arched his back, as Hal thrust his cock up inside him again and began to pump, showing how fit he was—that he could get hard again quickly.

~

Photo Barrier

Captain Delwin Jackson—Diggs to almost everyone who knew him—opened the only eye he was able to open, seeing first the photo of Tawna and the kids, Jamia and Jeron, that should be in his wallet but, inexplicably, was in a frame too big for it and standing on top of a white laminated nightstand next to the bed. Because he heard the heavy breathing, the second thing he saw when he swept his glance down the side of the bed was the concerned look of a young man decked out in a lime-green tunic. The heavy breathing seemed to be associated with the surgical mask he was wearing.

Diggs felt like throwing up. Was it the lime-green tunic? Then he did toss it up, but strong hands were turning him to the side of the bed, placing a pan under his chin, and wiping his mouth with a wet cloth after he'd retched.

"It's OK, it's OK," he heard the man in the line-green tunic say, spoken with a slightly muffled voice and heard through the shot of pain running mostly down his right side. There wasn't anything fuckin' OK about it, he thought, but he was hurting too much and was too exhausted to care. He lay back in the bed and panted a shallow pant.

"You're back in the land of the living, that's all that matters now. It's the medicine, but you need that. Just get plenty of . . ."

But Diggs had already closed his eye and was somewhere else altogether. Somewhere not nice. Somewhere with loud explosions, permeated with sweat and fear, screams and the sounds of . . . battle.

* * * *

"Back with us again, I see. And not feeling as nauseous, I hope."

The same lime-green tunic. The same face with a mix of smile and concern. Or at least a similar face in the same lime-green tunic. No surgical mask. But then how could he think the face was familiar? How many times had he wakened to this face? A young face, red hair and freckles, but strong, good features. And caring eyes.

"Bucket, bucket," Diggs muttered, and it was there, and he was being helped to turn aside by strong hands, and a pan appeared under his chin. He stayed twisted over for some moments, making sure it was all out. All of the pains of before were still there, but this time he felt the hand patting him on the back and somehow the pain wasn't as intense as before.

"There, that's better. You're doing fine. You'll be just fine."

"Trucker, Jack . . . Steve?" The names burst forth in a drunken drawl through cracked lips. How long had it been since he'd spoken a word? Why those names? Why was that important enough to be his first question in he knew not how long? And then he remembered. The sweat and the fear. Off track, lost in the jeep. Where were they? I shouldn't be here. The explosions, the screams . . . the long silence. "Jack? Jack. Oh, no, Jack." His head hit the pillow and he groaned. The pain was shooting through his right side again.

"You're good. You're safe," the soothing voice said. "You're at the 24th Field Evacuation Hospital, currently in a field in Belgium, but soon headed for Germany, I've heard. That's good news—that we can relocate to Germany now. You're safe, well away from it now. You'll be fine, Captain."

Diggs shut the one eye not already shut—his left eye—tight. He wasn't there, he wasn't here. He wasn't anywhere. Just like . . .

"Major Lord—Doctor Lord—will be by soon to talk to you. I'll let him know you're back with us again. He'll give you the technical talk, but I know it's weighing on your mind, so I'll give you the bottom line from what I heard him say."

Weighing on my mind, Diggs thought. Haven't even given it a thought. But then he realized that he hadn't been as out of it as he thought he had—for some days. It had, in fact,

59

been going over and over in his mind in his semiconscious state. That and Trucker and Jack and Steve. His men. Jack, oh Jack. He was responsible for them, for him . . . for Jack.

"Your eye will be fine," the orderly, Corporal Prentice, continued. "They'll take the stitches out of it and you'll see fine again. Maybe a bit of scarring for a while at least. The arm's almost healed already. They got shrapnel out of your right side, but that's all sewn up and healing. The leg will take awhile, and there probably will be a permanent limp. I'm sorry, I shouldn't be telling you this, but I know you'll want to know. Don't tell Doctor Lord I told you, OK?"

Diggs became aware of the hand laying on the hollow of his shoulder. And that it was skin on skin. He was naked under the sheet. Just now realized that. And he had a cast on his arm and leg. Bandages on his right side, dressing wrapped around his belly. A compress on his eye. A fuckin' walkin' mummy. Except not walking. For the first time he was becoming aware of himself, his body. And of that hand gently laying where his shoulder met the rise in the bulge of his left pectoral muscle. Strangely comforting. Reassuring.

"But . . . but your wars are over, Captain," spoken softly, hesitatingly, unsure of the reception this news would get, but evidently a message the orderly thought Diggs needed to hear. "Time . . . soon . . . to go home to them, the family. I don't know how you feel about that, but I'll bet your family will be glad you made it home."

Diggs looked up into the young, innocent-looking, handsome face, to see that the orderly was looking toward the nightstand—to where the photo of Tawna, Jamia, and Jeron had been placed in an oversized frame.

Diggs turned his head, shut his eye tight, and screamed a scream that only reverberated in his brain. He had to go back. His war wasn't over until Trucker and Jack and Steve were accounted for . . . were safe.

"It's really good news, Captain. You'll be fine; you'll be going home."

Corporal Prentice was leaning over Diggs's chest, wiping the tears away from his closed eyelid with a wet cloth.

Diggs willed himself back into unconsciousness. Hearing he would be fine, would be going home, sliced through him in a more painful way than the wounds on his right side did. He knew then that Tracker, Jack, and Steve wouldn't be fine. They wouldn't be going home. He remembered now how they looked when the explosion upended the jeep—right before he blacked out. Holding Jack in his arms. They had been his responsibility. They were the ones who should be fine, should be going home. Not him.

* * * *

"A handsome family," Corporal Prentice said, smiling at Diggs. He gestured toward the photo on the night stand.

"Yes," Diggs responded in a monotone, but not a belligerent one. He saved his belligerence for himself. The orderly had shown him nothing but kindness and patience over the last two weeks.

If Prentice noticed or was disturbed that he wasn't— still—getting more than one-syllable responses—and no proffered discussion—from the captain, he wasn't showing the knowledge. He knew it would change some day. Maybe today.

Diggs's torso was propped up a bit in the bed, and Prentice was giving him a sponge bath. The cast was off his arm and the dressing gone from his eye. There was progress in everything but his attitude, although it was only Diggs who didn't feel there was a change in the world of his attitude. Those caring for him in the six-man ward—which, primarily, was Corporal Prentice—were gratified at signs that the captain was prepared to reconcile himself to life. He hadn't referred to the men in his unit he'd lost for days.

But he hadn't referred to his family in the photo yet, either. That's what the medical staff was waiting for—for his thoughts to turn to going home . . . home to his family. Prentice was thinking of the captain going home too, but not as enthusiastically as the rest of the medical team was.

"You've healed quickly," Prentice remarked.

"A miracle," Diggs muttered.

Two words. Progress.

"That's not the miracle," Prentice responded.

"Oh?"

61

"Um, sorry, I shouldn't have said. But it surprises me . . . that your muscle tone remains so firm. Really a good body, in musculature. A great body. You must have spent half your life in a gym. I would think that—"

"You think it might be a black thing?"

A whole sentence.

Prentice blushed. And on a redhead that was a noticeable thing. Diggs smiled, both amused and seeing the attraction of the corporal's finely sculpted features when highlighted with a blush. A curl of hair came down over his forehead in an "oh my gosh" touch on a face that had shown so much patience and concern for him over the weeks.

"I'm sorry. I didn't mean to imply."

"It's OK. I've heard that blacks can muscle up easier and keep it easier. Just didn't know that might be valid."

Three sentences. Real progress.

"If you want to keep the muscle tone, of course, you probably should start to receive massages. The doctor has that on your chart. We could start wheeling you down to therapy in a while for that, but if you want to get a start on that . . . you have such a mass of muscle . . . it would be a shame . . ."

"If someone could start me with massages here, that would be fine with me," Diggs said.

The corporal had moved the sponge bath down to the captain's thighs. If he noticed that Diggs was half hard—which would have been very difficult not to notice as the officer was horse hung—he didn't give any indication, other than maybe a certain tremble in the handling of the sponge.

* * * *

"I could take care of that for you, Sir . . . if you needed relief. It's nothing to be embarrassed about. I know it's been a long time." It was spoken in a whisper, as if, perhaps if Diggs chose not to have heard it, it would never have been said. Or maybe in fear that the other patients in the ward would overhear it.

Corporal Prentice had been giving him a massage, and after spending considerable time on Diggs's broad chest, with bulging pecs and biceps, and particular attention to his right arm that was slowly coming back into tone, the young man was working on Diggs's thighs.

There was no ignoring the captain's cock this time. It was fully hard and fully hard to ignore, and Prentice had clearly seen that Diggs had touched it several times with his own hand. It was evident that if Prentice weren't there and there were a way for Diggs to hide the evidence in the sheets, he'd be taking care of himself.

"If it will take away the ache in my balls . . . ," Diggs growled, close to the edge of exploding, increasingly, over the series of massages Prentice had given—themselves increasingly sensual—having become keyed up and aroused.

Prentice was a handsome young man, and the lime-green tunic didn't hide that he was in great physical shape too—nor, in the last few days of massages did it hide that the massages were giving him a hard on as well.

Increasingly over the weeks, Diggs had grown to see the similarities between Prentice and Jack. Jack had been a redhead too, although auburn rather than strawberry-blond. And he'd been handsome and young and well built, like Prentice. And he'd been deferential and respectful—and yielding. And he had given Diggs relief—the sort of relief that Diggs could use now.

"I understand," Prentice said, and then the corporal was pulling the draperies around the bed but was back beside the bed quickly, taking Diggs's cock in hand.

He gave Diggs a nervous half smile but tried to take the tension out of the situation, speaking in a matter-of-fact way and trying a bit of joking. But all the time he was talking as if nothing was going on, he also was slow-stroking Diggs's cock with his hand. Diggs was laying back in the bed, but tense and moaning. The longer Prentice stroked, though, the more Diggs relaxed.

"There's no reason to feel guilty about this, of course. It's a medical need and a medical answer," he said, but, although he had one hand wrapped around Diggs's throbbing cock, he reached over to the nightstand and turned the photograph down on its face. "Not something the family need see, of course."

Diggs didn't join in Prentice's little joke. He wasn't showing disapproval, though, his eyes were locked on Prentice's strong hand fisting his cock, and he was groaning his need.

Prentice worked the cock for nearly ten minutes, sensing the building toward release. "Shall we see if we can hit the ceiling, Sir?"

Virile and in top shape—other than the wounds to body and soul—and not having any for two months, Diggs almost did.

* * * *

"They've moved me to this bed, by the window," Diggs said.

"You're senior in the ward now, Captain," Corporal Prentice answered. "So you get the privacy of the end bed—and you get a window." He was already pulling the drapes around the bed.

"And as far away from the other men in the ward as possible," Diggs added with an amused smile on his face.

"That too, Sir. A massage special today . . . or perhaps the massage deluxe?" His words were bantering, joking, but Diggs could see something else in his face, a certain longing and need.

"I supposed a 'massage special' includes a hand job. But there's a deluxe model massage?"

"I shouldn't have . . . I'm sorry . . . but would you really be interested?"

"Yes, Prentice, if it's what I think it is, I'm interested. But are you sure? Are you really offering to—?"

"Yes, Sir. I'd like to do it. I've wanted to do it for some time."

"Well, then, I'll admit I've been interested too," Diggs answered. "But it's so intimate . . . do you have a first name?"

"It's Paul, Sir," he answered in a small voice.

"Yes . . . Paul . . . I would be very interested in the massage deluxe." Diggs reached over and turned the photograph on its face.

Paul Prentice was leaning over Diggs's midsection, a hand wrapped around the base of the thick, long cock, alternating from sucking on the bulb and trying to deep-throat the monster when the captain reached down the side of the bed and had his hand running up under the hem of the lime-green tunic, through the fly of Prentice's briefs, and encasing a hard cock.

"Sir, you don't have to—?" Paul said, briefly taking his mouth off Digg's cock.

"I want to," the captain answered. "For what you're giving me, I want to give as well as take." He stroked the corporal's cock as it engorged under his attention. The corporal's breathing as he sucked the captain's cock became ragged, but he didn't back away from the bed.

After a few minutes, Diggs nudged him up on the bed brushed the hem of his tunic up to the young corporal's waist—awkwardly, as he had to do it with his right hand and his arm was still in a light cast; pulled off the redhead's briefs; drew in a heady breath of Paul's groin; licked down the strawberry-blond circles of his pubes and inhaled his balls to hear the corporal moan; and opened his mouth over a hard cock.

Lying, spent, the two in a sixty-nine embrace on the bed, Diggs whispered, "Del. The men know me as Diggs. But those closest to me call me Del."

Jack, near the end, had started calling him Del.

"Tell, me, Paul." he continued after Paul had tried out the sound of that name, "how far do you want to go? What is it you'll do? What's your limit? Is there anything beyond the deluxe massage where you're willing to do?"

"I'll take your dick—gladly—if that's what you're asking, Captain."

"Yes, that's what I'm asking, Corporal."

* * * *

That night, amid snores rolling over the ward, the drapes pulled around the bed, moonlight streaming in the window, the family photograph on its face on the floor below the nightstand, Paul rode Del's cock. Del was on his back, his legs bent to give the heels of his feet leverage in the mattress, holding Paul by his slim waist. The heels of Paul's hands were pressed into Del's taut nipples on his massive pectorals, and, leveraging off knees planted on either side of Del's hips, Paul rode the cock in increasing intensity until, with a muffled cry from him and a groan from Del, he collapsed on Del's chest, knowing that Del had released inside him, having a minute earlier felt his own cream flow up Del's sternum.

They sighed and kissed, feeling the pulse of the other calm down.

Eventually, Paul whispered in a trembly voice, "Sorry, Captain, I just couldn't hold it any longer. . . I thought about you—about what we did—all day, and I just couldn't—"

"Shush, Paul. I'm going to turn you now and fuck you again."

He proceeded to do so, turning Paul on the buried, reengoring cock, to where Paul's back was pressed into Del's torso, embraced closely in Del's arms. Del laced his legs in Paul's, spreading and raising the young orderly's thighs, and began pumping up into him again.

Holding him close, a hand muffling his mouth and nose, keeping the young redhead from crying out over the top of the drapes, knowing that he was digging so deep, pistoning so fast, that Paul couldn't stifle his reaction. Fucking Paul just as Jack had liked to be fucked. Fucking Paul but also fucking Jack. Thinking of Paul but also thinking of Jack. And pounding, pounding, pounding. Pounding it all better again—or trying like hell to.

If he noticed that Paul was crying, he didn't remark on it. Del was crying too.

When Paul left, the photo was back on the nightstand, but still laying on its face.

* * * *

"Good morning, Captain. And how are we doing this fine morning. I understand you'll be leaving us in a few days. The hospital will pack up soon too and move into Germany."

66

"We are doing fine, corporal. I haven't seen you in the ward before, I don't think. Haven't seen Corporal Prentice today either."

"Corporal Prentice has been transferred to another ward, Sir. I'm Corporal Shelton. I've come to take you down to therapy. According to your chart, you should have started massages down there, in addition to the leg therapy you've been doing, some time ago. Don't know how we overlooked that, Sir. But you certainly don't seem to be behind in the maintaining the muscle tone department."

"Maybe it's because I'm . . . oh, forget it. Prentice was transferred, you say?"

"Asked to be yes, Sir. Says he likes variety and there was an opening in the burn unit. Oh, is that photo of your family, Sir? Mighty fine looking crew."

"Yes . . . and yes," Diggs answered. But when the orderly returned him from therapy, the captain turned the photo over on its face and turned his head toward the window.

* * * *

"I've come to drive you to . . . oh, it's you, Captain Jackson."

"Yes, it's me, Del, Paul."

"I . . . I didn't know who . . ."

"I asked for you specifically to drive me to the party, and I asked that they not tell you who you were picking up."

They were at the bachelor officer's quarters near the field hospital, which was busy packing out. Del, healed except for the cane he had to use and that still grounded him from driving himself, was staying at the BOQ, waiting for transfer to his next billet. The party in question was a farewell one the hospital was holding for the local support staff being left behind and for those, like Del, who were recovering and sticking around waiting for orders to their next assignment.

"OK, I see." Paul sounded confused, though, like he didn't see at all. "But you're not dressed for the party."

"I'm not dressed at all," Del said, pulling the sash of his robe open and parting it. Paul sucked in his breath at the magnificence of the captain's muscular body. Del was approaching full erection.

"Why did you walk away from me, Paul? Just that one night. You came to me. I didn't demand it. Wasn't I good enough for you? Is it because I'm black?"

"Not good enough for me? Shit." It came out as a gasp. "I couldn't. I just couldn't. It wasn't enough to turn the photograph over. It was your family. You have a family. Even turning the photo over . . . I just couldn't."

"It wasn't because you didn't want to?"

"Shit, no. How could you think that? I came for it . . . even with the barrier of that photo."

"That photo is of my sister and her kids, Paul. That's not my wife; not my kids. I don't have a wife and kids, Paul. I'm gay. I fuck men. You know that; I've fucked you. Usually I fuck one man at a time while it's working out, though. I joined the army to be with men, to fuck willing hard-bodied, young enlisted men. I'm partial to redheads, if you must know."

"Sir. Captain Jackson . . . Del."

"I'm not going back to the States. I've arranged a billet in Frankfurt, just an hour's drive away from where your hospital is locating. So, if you're interested, I think I'm overdue for one of your deluxe massages."

He reached over and slammed the door to the corridor shut as Paul sank to his knees, cupped Del's balls and the base of his cock with a hand, and guided the cock into his mouth.

Jackson didn't require a long massage however. He soon had Paul bent over the bed on his belly and was massaging the young man's ass channel doggie style with a big, black cock.

~

The Aviators

Chapter One: Mission Ritual

The only sound in the dimming summer evening light inside the airplane hangar was his grunting and her moans and sighing. She was perched on her ass on the worn wooden desk off to the side of the two P-47 Thunderbolt fighter-bombers taking up most of the room in the hangar. A lightbulb hanging on a chain above the desk swayed back and forth in the breeze coming from the open hangar doors, the arc of the sway seemingly matching the rhythm of his thrusts inside her, as if he was gauging the coordination of the rhythm. And perhaps he unconsciously was, as his mind was only half there. She was the one who had wanted this. She had come to the hangar while he was waiting for something else entirely and had initiated the fuck.

Her full skirt and petticoats billowed around her waist. Her knees rested on his hips. Her hands clutched his bare buttocks, pulling him inside her with each jarring thrust. Her white cotton panties lay on the concrete floor of the hangar, resting on top of his trousers and briefs, which were puddled around his ankles. Her calves were covered with rough, white cotton knee socks. He'd bought her sheerer stockings but she hadn't dared wear them anyplace yet. Her husband took her nowhere but the local pub and she hadn't come up with an excuse for owning them. They certainly weren't something that her husband could have given her. She put them on occasionally now and again while her husband was in his fields and she wanted to feel rich and decadent.

He held her in place on the edge of the desk with a hand on the small of her back. His other hand cupped a pendulous breast and thumbed the brown nipple couched in a nickel-sized aureole. He'd already pinched and prodded the other nipple as she was giving out little yipping sounds and while he was moving his bulb into position. He'd rubbed his cock head through her folds and over her clit until, through her heavy breathing, she'd reached down, put him in position, and pleaded, "Now. Now. Take me now," through clenched teeth.

He'd almost laughed at her adoption of the accent of some American actress or the other she had seen at the local cinema. This was all a movie drama for her, giving herself to the handsome, ill-fated American aviator on the eve of flying his last mission out over the English channel.

She'd arched her back, given a little cry, opened her eyes wide when he entered her—thick and hard. She doubled her panting and murmured, "Alex, Alex, Alex," as he held barely inches inside her, for her to take his measure and blossom open for him. He knew this was when he should utter her name too, but he suddenly couldn't remember what it was. Eleanor? Emily? Ellen?

Instead, he muttered, "Beautiful. You're so fine." This must have satisfied her, as he could sense the tension draining out of her and feel her go soft inside, spreading open for the shaft throbbing inside her. He reared back, thrust forward, giving her all of it. She screamed; dug her nails into his buttocks; flung her body about within the confines of his strong embrace; cried out, "Mercy, give me mercy," until, riding her hard and fast, she settled down to the rhythm, murmuring, "Yes, yes, yes. Oh, Alex, yes."

Five, maybe six minutes, and he had released his seed, pulled from her, smoothed the front of her skirt down, and rolled to the side to perch on the desk on his rump next to her. His nice-sized cock was still half hard, jutting out. He was young, healthy, and virile. He'd be able to go again within twenty minutes. Perhaps she knew that, as she reached over and wrapped a hand around the shaft. Before, this was when she would go down on her knees before him and take it into her mouth until he'd given her an after ejaculation and it had started to go flaccid.

But not this evening. After he'd offered her a Lucky Strike cigarette, she said, with a bit of regret, "I can't stay.

There's a to do at the pub and Harvey will expect me to meet up with him there." She took the cigarette and lowered her head to the flame he produced from a lighter he retrieved from the desktop—another gesture she'd learned in an American movie, he knew. Lucky Strike cigarettes were American military ration and the designated cigarette of the fighter-bomber squadron that had named itself the Luckies.

Harvey was her somewhat dim husband, who worked a bit with the plane mechanics at the aerodrome and on his ancestors' small farm on the outskirts of Duxford the rest of the time. He was a good fifteen years older than she was, dull as a rock, and nothing close to being able to handle or satisfy her. She worked in the scheduling office at the aerodrome. Once she'd gotten off the farm, the future was sealed for her. If Alex hadn't succumbed to her needs and advances, it would be some other American flyer fucking her. After he was gone, it would be some other American aviator fucking her. It was like they had made it a club. They dyed their hair blonde and went to see American patriotic movies on Saturday night with their girlfriends and they suddenly were in a pool of women who opened their legs for the American aviators.

At least that's how he reasoned the situation. Not that he hadn't fucked another man's wife before—or, for that matter, some wife's husband. Alex was a modern man, and he was an American fighter-bomber pilot in the later stages of the Second World War. The first world war, originally termed the Great World War, had been fought to end all wars. They all knew better now—and they knew this war they now were in wouldn't be the last one either. He was painfully aware of the mortality rate in his chosen field. He wasn't one to pass up a fuck no matter what the origin—female or male. He just took on different roles, depending on who his sex partner was.

"That's a pity," he said, blowing a stream of smoke out. It was the best he could think of doing. He was still trying to work out her name. And she had just appeared this evening. He'd had other things to do, not the least being checking over *Lucky Linda* for tomorrow's bombing raid over Belgium. *Lucky Linda* was the name of his P-47, which he loved dearly—the fighter-bomber, not the namesake Linda, who had sent him a Dear John letter more than a year before. He'd been good up to that time—fighting for home and hearth and the honey left behind. She too had dyed her hair blonde as soon as war had been declared. Since his world had fallen apart, he'd been sewing his oats like there was no tomorrow—because maybe there wasn't. And that's when the young woman revealed the reason for her visit.

"You go up again tomorrow, don't you?"

"Yes," he answered.

"I hate this," she said. "We never know if they are going to come back. I can usually tell by the sound of you boys taking off when you'll be back—and I find myself outside, looking to the sky, counting the planes. There always are more going out than there are coming back."

"Yes," he said and took a puff on his Lucky Strike. This wasn't what he wanted to hear the night before a mission. Mentally, he was retreating from this. This wasn't what he wanted to think about; this wasn't what he wanted to be doing. She needed to shut up about it. He needed to fuck her quiet.

He covered the hand she had wrapped around his cock and used it to set them both in a stroking motion. His cock instantly came to life. He wanted her on her knees, in front of him, moving her mouth over the shaft. He wanted to experience *la petite mort*—the little death of orgasm—again, so he didn't have to think of the other form of death.

But he didn't want to force her to suck him off. He knew she'd do it if he pushed her to her knees. He knew why she was here now. She was here in case he didn't come back tomorrow. It was a "thing" with these English girls. Young women who never would have done this in other circumstances were giving themselves to the American airmen as some sort of connection to—service to—the war effort. Giving them a night-before fuck in case they didn't come back the next day. Gaining grieving status with their girlfriends if one of their boys didn't make it back. Suddenly given the regard that their girlfriends accorded to Ingrid Bergman on the big screen, which would last until an aviator some other woman was fucking didn't make it home. The longevity of grieving sympathy didn't go much more than a week in this phase of the war.

He hadn't had to force anyone—or seduce them—since he'd arrived here. They buzzed around him and the other American aviators like bees. They always came to him, begging for it. Well, nearly everyone.

"Where is it tomorrow?"

"Where is what?" he asked.

"Where do the planes fly?"

He was on his guard. Was there another motive here. She worked in the scheduling department. She probably knew as well as he did. But there was a "loose lips sink ships" security drive going on now. Was she here to give him a royal sendoff or to check on his discretion?

"I have no idea," he said. "They won't tell us until the mission meeting just before we take off." He wouldn't even tell her when the meeting was or when they were scheduled to lift off. God, he hated this war and its games.

She sighed and switched gears. "I can't face the thought of—"

"Elizabeth! Let's not think of that now. Let's just think of pleasure." With a shock that he'd thrown out a name and that she hadn't rejected it, he grabbed his cigarette out of his mouth and then hers, and dropped them, smoldering to the top of the wooden desk, it's surface already scared by hundreds of cigarettes before it. Then, rising from the desk and kneeing her thighs apart and pushing her skirt up to her waist, he embraced her, set his legs, and thrust inside her again.

She cried out, "Yes, yes, like there's no tomorrow!" and raised her ankles to his shoulders.

He plastered his lips to hers, more to stifle more of what he didn't want to hear from her, or anyone else, and sliced into her again and again and again—deeper and then deeper yet—to the cadence, once he'd gotten her mind off death and released her lips, of her cries of "Yes. Yes. Yes! God you're big!" He *was* big, and he knew it. It's one reason he had to flick them off like flies.

"Fuck me! You're a fucking god!" He *was* a fucking god, and he knew it. It was another reason he was a honey pot to the bees.

He was good and he knew it. He was a star, and he knew it. He might be dead tomorrow at this time—and he knew it.

She was Ingrid Bergman, desperate to give him one last fuck, turning her cow eyes on him, her lower lip trembling, and he gave her several inches of what she wanted to feel that her sacrifice to the war effort was noble and had meaning.

* * * *

Alex sat at the desk in the hangar under the swaying, dim light of a single fluorescent tube. Elizabeth, if that's what her name was, had left more than an hour before, puffed up and all aglow from having made what possibly was his last night on earth memorable. He wondered if she thought he'd be thinking of her as his plane nosedived into the English Channel. Well, she *did* have memorable tits, he thought. Those possibly were as good as anything else to think about when he knew he was going into the drink. But why fool himself? He knew he'd be thinking of someone else.

She wasn't what he'd been waiting for. She wasn't why he was spending the evening here in the hangar rather than at the flight club, chugging with the other aviators—well, the ones not being given farewell presents by the local girls. They weren't supposed to drink the night before a mission. They were supposed to be bright eyed and bushy tailed on mission day. That, at least, was him tonight. He was bright eyed as he hadn't touched a drop and Elizabeth, or whatever her name was, had bushed up his tail.

He stood up from the desk and walked over to his P-47 Thunderbolt, *Lucky Linda*. As he did every night or morning before he went up, he went through the ritual of running his hands over every square inch of his plane's fuselage. If he had a loving relationship with anything, it was this plane, *Lucky Linda*. When he got to the other side, he looked over at the other plane in the hangar. It was Pete's plane. *Make Your Own Luck* was painted on its side. All of the planes in the squadron had some form of "luck" in their title. Any who came into the squadron and refused to rename their plane to the squadron standard had gone down on their first mission out of Duxford, so it wasn't hard to enforce that custom anymore.

They were all captains, except for Major Flint, the squadron commander, but here, as about everywhere else in the world, there was a hierarchy. Peter Porter wasn't the longest-serving pilot in the squadron, but he unquestionably was the leader and, as the name he'd given his Thunderbolt hinted, the most cocky. He also was dominant, self-confident, and so "tall, dark, and handsome" that he was the honeyest of the honey pots.

Alex considered himself blessed to have his plane in the same hangar as Pete's. They were as close in relationship as their planes were. Alex had been naïve and reticent. Pete, in full command, had sensed the vulnerability and need of this new, young flyer in the squadron. These all were factors that had paired the two of them up within the squadron—the dark and sultry, boisterous, flashy, and bossy Peter, scion of a leading textile manufacturing dynasty in Boston, and the blond, all-American Alex, son of a single-mom seamstress in Richmond. Alex had been the wettest of wet behind the ears when he'd reached England. Pete had brought him along and formed him into a gentleman to the point that the locals couldn't tell which was prince and which pauper.

Alex heard them before he saw them as he had finished the "hands-on" ritual with *Lucky Linda* and was strolling back to the desk. The "chug-song" drunken singing drifted in from afar and grew louder until the field ambulance—probably the stolen field ambulance—with young aviators hanging all over it pulled to a stop outside the hanger. The passenger door opened, and a dark hunk, half in and half out his Air Force uniform, his trousers on, but his shirt unbuttoned down to the navel, showing a dark-haired hirsute chest with bulging pecs and a flat belly, stumbled out, holding a champagne bottle.

Pete had arrived at the hangar. He turned and waved the ambulance away and then turned again and walked toward Alex. As he walked, he lost any awkwardness of a stumble. He may have been drunk while he was riding in the ambulance, if only to hold his position as the life of the party, but he was stone-cold sober as he walked toward the desk, his eyes boring into the figure of Alex, who had perched on the edge of the desk where he had been fucking the English woman earlier. Alex gave a little shudder as he watched Pete approach.

Pete turned when he reached Alex and sat, perched on the edge of the desk, beside Alex. They were sitting so close to each other that their thighs and biceps pressed together. Pete held the champagne bottle out to Alex.

"Here, drink," he commanded. His voice was soft, but Alex knew it wasn't a request. This was as much a ritual as the rubdown of *Lucky Linda*. This was Pete asserting dominance and Alex accepting submission. Alex hadn't allowed a drop of spirits pass his lips before he'd joined the squadron and come under the sway of Pete. Pete had made sure that Alex became a drinker as a mark of Alex's submission to him.

Alex took the bottle and drank deeply from it. After two swigs—he would have put the bottle down after the first wallow if Pete hadn't given him a "take another pull of it" look—Alex carefully set the bottle on the desk on the other side from where Pete was sitting. As he'd taken his drinks, Pete had taken out a package of Lucky Strikes and lit up two. He handed one to Alex and placed the other at a precarious angle between his lips.

"Where did you go this evening?" Alex asked. He tried to keep a note of desperation out of his voice, but they both knew that Pete had said that they would meet here hours earlier. It was yet another of Pete's techniques in control to have kept Alex waiting.

"Cambridge. The pubs in Duxford are boring—except for the ones we've been thrown out of." Cambridge was nine miles to the north of the aerodrome.

Pete's hand brushed against the two half-smoked cigarettes from Alex's encounter with the English woman that lay on the surface of the desk. They both would still be worn; one of them had lipstick marks on it. Pete gave Alex a questioning look.

"I think her name was Elizabeth," Alex responded to the unspoken question.

"The redhead in scheduling?" Pete asked.

"Yes, her."

"She's a good lay. Flaming red all the way down. I like a red muff. She stands out from all those fake blondes she runs with."

"Yes. And nice tits too," Alex said.

"We should do her together. Take turns in the cunt and ass. Maybe do them together."

"I think she'd like that. Maybe tomorrow night." This too was a ritual—mentioning something they'd do in the future. Something they'd do after the next mission was over.

"But I guess I can't tomorrow," Pete said. "There's a party on I've been invited to—that American couple's place. Stanford Hall, toward Cambridge. The actor and his writer wife who were stranded here while he was making a film."

"The Taylors, yes," Alex answered. "Curt and Angela. I've been invited too. A garden party, I've heard. In the evening."

"Ah, you've been invited. The fabulous flyboys are we. I suppose we're the entertainment for the party. Have you had either one of them yet?"

"Curt or Angela? No, have you?" Alex answered.

"No, not yet, but there's always tomorrow. I think they're both in heat for it. They made that quite clear at the cricket club last week. They had sexual innuendo to throw your way too. Curt asked if you were a player and I said you were an American aviator, which seemed to settle that."

"Seems they are important enough that they can command that it not rain tomorrow," Alex said.

"Won't rain all day," Pete said. "That means the mission is definitely on."

"Yes," Alex said, but he looked away from Pete so that his friend and squadron buddy couldn't see the concern in his eyes. Alex had a feeling about tomorrow's mission. He didn't like it when he had a feeling like this before a mission. He became aware of the heat of Pete's body—his thigh and biceps—against his own, and he gave a little shudder.

Pete couldn't help but feel the trembling of the other man. He reached up and took the cigarette out of Alex's mouth and flicked it out into the shadows that had deepened between the desk and the fuselage of *Lucky Linda*. The P-47's wing tip almost reached them, giving an illusion of shelter and aloneness even though the hangar door to the summer night air in eastern England was still open. He flicked his own cigarette out in a perfect arc, and it landed on top of Alex's smoke.

The two men watched what was now a shared glow of ash produced by the cigarettes, one laying on top of the other, burning together, the flame brighter together than the two of them would have been separately—one covering the other. Alex felt the fingers of Pete's strong left hand run up into the blond curls at the back of his head, taking control of his head. Peter turned Alex's face toward his, leaned over, and took Alex's mouth in a brutal, fully possessing kiss.

Alex returned the kiss hungrily and placed his right hand on Pete's right bicep, running his hand into the opening of the other aviator's shirt so that he could feel flesh on flesh. He heard his belt buckle being undone and his trousers unbuttoned, and he raised his hips off the desk so that Pete could push his trousers down to the concrete. Alex kicked out of them as he listened to Pete's belt being unbuckled and his fly unbuttoned. Pete teased Alex's thighs open. The blond groaned as Pete entered him with a finger—and then another—spreading them to open Alex up and vibrating them to cause Alex to start moving his pelvis against them with a deep moan. There would be no more foreplay than this. Pete was thick and long, but he wanted to find resistance to his invasion, to sense the slow opening of surrender to him, the groaning whimper of his partner.

Pete pulled around to where he was crouching between Alex's thighs and hovering over his trembling body, one hand on the small of Alex's back and the other positioning his hard cock. Alex hooked his knees on Pete's hips.

The blond jerked away from the kiss and arched his back and cried out as Pete entered him strongly, tightly, thickly, long and immediately started to pump. "Take it!" Pete cried out. "Take it all."

"Give it!" Alex cried back. "Fuck me into tomorrow. Fuckin' drill me!"

Pete did just that, reveling in the feel of power in his cock and of the groaning stretching of the channel walls, giving way to his relentless march deep up inside Alex. And then the stifled sobs as he began to move, drilling his prey ever deeper, mastering him, conquering him, expertly timing their ejaculations to be near simultaneous—but only when Pete allowed it.

Later, on a thick quilted blanket under the fuselage of *Lucky Linda*, after sixty-nining until Pete signaled they could stop, they reversed positions. Pete was on all fours and Alex was mounted on his ass, fucking him like a dog. Even in this Pete remained dominant, commanding Alex to go still when either of them felt close to coming and then taking over the fucking, Alex still holding steady and Pete pushing back at him, fucking himself on Alex's shaft, until Alex couldn't take it anymore and resumed thrusting. Only coming a second time when Pete gave permission and then coming close to each other again.

Sometimes there was more, with Pete on his back, holding Alex on his body, facing up, Pete's shaft buried up Alex's channel and Alex leveraging off the belly of *Lucky Linda* with his feet to rise and fall on the cock. Alex would never tell Pete, but this position gave him an extra charge, as he felt his plane was part of the act, making it an act of love and not just a ritual and release of sex.

Alex had learned some time earlier not to refer to what they did as love. He had whispered the word once and, in anger, Pete had cold cocked him for two days. Alex had gotten the message. It was ritual release. They'd had a good mission after the first time they'd done it, so it had become part of the ritual. Alex didn't have the courage to reveal to Pete again that it was more than a ritual for him.

They fucked like a well-oiled machine, sensing what to do next, how to move further along the program of their pre-mission ritual, always under the guidance of Pete.

They had observed this ritual for the last hundred and seventeen missions. So far they had come back unscathed from every one of them.

Each time Alex lay with Pete he felt overwhelmed by the strength, masterfulness, and dominance of his squadron buddy. When Pete was fucking him, the rest of the world went away. And in the end he felt almost satisfied. Almost. He just couldn't help to wish he'd gotten something more, something more tender and loving when the immediate heat of the animal need had been satisfied. He felt something more for Pete than Pete seemed willing or wanting to feel with Alex. For all his bravado about how the war and the ever-impending threat of death that hung over all of their heads, he couldn't help but wanting more. Whereas Alex was willing to give his all—to love—Pete was holding that level of affection in reserve. Ever hopeful, Alex remained totally open to Pete, giving him everything. Pete took whatever he wanted, as if by right.

Chapter Two: Party Like There's No Tomorrow

Pete had been prescient in his thought that he and Alex were to be the entertainment at the Taylors' garden party. The American aviators were there for the opening and still there for the closing. And it was obvious that they were there to be the young hunk guests. There wasn't much of any virile man flesh to attend to social events in England at the time, most of the young men being in service and "over there"—or having been over there and not coming back. The latter circumstance increased the value of virile young men such as the American aviators.

The two were already there, on display in tennis togs and swinging their rackets, moving gracefully about the court at the side of the country home, next to the pathway guests entered into the back gardens, as the other guests started to arrive. They were playing a foursome with the Taylors. Pete partnered with the tall, willowy, auburn-haired novelist Angela, and Alex with the short, but solid and handsome Jewish actor, Curt. All four were more than adequate at tennis and expert at posing as the guests streamed past them and into the garden, which fell in tiered terraces to a meadow below, with a pond and folly in the distance. The scale of the folly made the pond seem to be a lake, which no doubt was the purpose of having a folly.

The upper terrace was flagstoned and set up with wicker furniture in a semicircle facing the vista around a dance floor. A gramophone was squeaking away at the standards of the day. Billie Holiday was singing "Embraceable You" as the tennis match was winding down and the stream of arriving guests was thickening. The grass-carpeted terrace in the next tier below supported a long buffet table set up for grazing, and the lowest grass-carpeted terrace featured the drinks tables. It was this terrace and the meadow below where most of the guests, a motley collection of academics from nearby Cambridge, an assortment of over-the-hill film people, aging dowagers with titles and plumed hats, and the somewhat squalid literati were accumulating.

The weather was atypically idyllic, which, of course, all the guests credited to Curt's Hollywood connections.

"Thanks for the game," Curt said as the four gathered at the bench by the fence gate. "You brought your uniforms, I hope. We know you did a run today; everyone here will want to hear about that."

More proof that they were here to provide the entertainment.

"Yes, our uniforms are in the car," Pete answered. It wasn't lost to any of the four that he was standing in a close tableau with Curt and Angela and was palming their butts. The two had made quite clear to Pete and Alex with signaling with their eyes and chatting innuendo when the two aviators had been the first to arrive that this was to be a free-sex-expected evening. And, as the guests gathered and it became obvious that the two aviators were the only hunky males present, it was obvious who was to be free with the sex.

"Well, bring them upstairs and we'll change," Curt said. "Angela will take her room and we can take mine." Angela gave Curt a pointed look of pique, but the day was young and she was assured of her innings.

Once up in the luxurious surroundings of the mansion's bedroom area, it became clear to Pete and Alex that they would be taking their time changing. Curt quickly stripped out of his tennis togs and went to the shower first, as Pete and Alex stripped down. When he came out, he went to a window and posed, naked by the drapes. He was in half erection, and he seemed already to have made out how to make maximum advantage of the shadowing of light filtering through the window to enhance his stance. He had kept his body in good condition, as the demands of his film career dictated. He didn't seem embarrassed at all about exposing himself to the aviators.

While he had been showering, Pete and Alex, both naked, had sat beside each other on the foot of the enormous bed and were kissing and fondling each other. They didn't break when Curt came out of the bathroom and he didn't seem to mind in the least. Indeed, it was clear that he expected it and that he also expected the couplings to unfold quickly. They had a party to go to. Pete stood, full frontal to him, magnificent in dark-haired, hirsute body and in full erection.

"Care to join me in a cigarette, old fellow, while your blond friend showers?" Curt said to Pete, his eyes taking in all there was to see. "The fags are over there on the dresser top."

Pete walked over to the dresser and retrieved the packet of cigarettes. "Chesterfields," he said, as if it was some sort of foreign commodity.

"They won't do? I have them smuggled in from the States."

"I'll bring you a carton of Lucky Strikes next time," Pete said. He crossed to the window. The two men stood there, in the light streaming in through the window, facing each other, leaning against opposite sides of the window well, smoking, and smiling. As Alex stood up from the bed to go take his shower, Curt had reached out with a hand, had jutted his pelvis forward, and was coaxing Pete's pelvis forward with a palm on the aviator's buttocks. Pete complied without more comment than a smile. Without hesitation or embarrassment, Curt encased his and Pete's cocks in a fist, bundling the two hard shafts together. Pete's eyes held Curt's in an unwavering look. It was clear that an understanding was being negotiated. What was in balance was which one of the men was going to be dominant. Alex didn't figure into the negotiation; he was recognized as a submissive. Despite Curt making the moves, Alex's money was on Pete to win this one.

When Alex returned from the bathroom, Pete was setting on the foot of the bed, thighs spread, and Curt was kneeling between Pete's legs and giving him a deep-throated, slow blow job. Pete waved Alex over to sit beside him, and when Alex sat, Pete pulled his face in for a kiss and Curt fisted Alex's cock and stroked it while he was sucking on Pete's cock.

Pete pulled Curt up from the floor, and the party host settled on Pete's shaft, crouching in the aviator's lap, facing him, and began to rise and fall on Pete's cock, using the leverage of his feet flat on the mattress on either side of Pete's hips. Both men had lost interest in Alex, who rose from the bed, pulled on his spiffy American flyer uniform, and went out into the bedroom hallway. He found his way through the maze of the corridors in the mansion to the garden, drawn by the strains of Bing Crosby's "I'll Be Seeing You," playing on the gramophone on the upper terrace.

Angela Taylor, sexy and chic in a backless and nearly frontless silver lamé tight gown that fluidly flowed down her slim body, was standing at the terrace, holding two drinks in her hand, as Alex arrived. She handed one of the drinks to him as if she'd been waiting there to bestow it on whoever arrived first. It was as if she knew they wouldn't all come down together—and, from her lack of surprise at seeing Alex, she appeared to know, as well, that it would be her husband and the dark, mysterious aviator who had held back.

"First out?" she asked, with a twinkle in her eye.

"Seems so. I became a third wheel on a bicycle," Alex answered, without rancor. The evening was young.

"Ah. We can both take heart that there's more cycling to be done. Who is in? Curt or your luscious friend, Peter?"

"In?"

"Who is dominating? Who has established rights of penetration?"

"Pete, when I left."

"Ah, lucky Curt," she said. "Come, you must meet our assorted guests. It's time for you to recite today's war story. Use literary license. Buck them up and all that. Do make sure the Germans lose, though. Sorry, this is more or less a payback event, so there's a dab of everyone here—both the dull and the intolerable. Some are dripping in titles, but as you are as American as I am, I'm sure that will just run off your back without leaving you speechless in the company of majesty. Your body—and that of your friend, Peter—is as majestic as I can take. I love the uniform. Very manly, very virile. I can hardly wait to get you out of it. You should know, though, that I can't handle more than thirteen inches." Her laugh tinkled. Her look of amusement was as much in the enjoyment of seeing Alex blush as anything else.

"The others here will love it too—the uniform, not the thirteen inches," she continued. "They don't often get to see young, virile, and vigorous men with all their limbs intact out and about these days." At this last comment, she'd faced him, came in close, and was feeling him up between the legs. "You *are* virile and vigorous, I trust. Yes, I can feel that you have all of your limbs intact. Thirteen inches wasn't that preposterous of a wish." He didn't flinch. He just took a deep drink from his glass and gave her a steely look. he winced, though, when she squeezed his balls through the thin material of his summer dress trousers.

She laughed and turned away, putting her arm through his. "Come, let's get this small talk with the guests over with before getting down to the business of pleasure."

Putting on her hostess smile, she pulled him down the terrace levels, introducing him to playwright this and countess that, as they descended to the drinks tables. Curt and Pete joined them there, Curt giving Angela a look of flushed satisfaction and Angela returning a cool look and a proffered martini. As she turned from the drinks table so did a young man—very young, maybe barely twenty, who was out of place in that he was young and apparently had all of his limbs and therefore raised the question of what he was doing here. What he was doing here was looking almost too beautiful in a pouty, full-lipped face strawberry blond package to be a man.

"Ah, Vis," Angela said, trapping the young man before he could get away and introducing him to her aviator centerpieces. "Peter, Alex, this is Viscount Cinterton. Peter and Alex are American daredevils of the air and the scourge of Hitler over at the Duxford Aerodrome."

"You can call me Nigel," the young man said, flashing a dazzling smile at Alex and then an even more dazzling one at Pete.

"We call him Vis for short," Curt offered.

"Out of uniform for the night?" Pete asked, and the young nobleman looked a bit embarrassed.

"Vis is in the theatre," Curt interjected.

"The theatre?" Pete asked, not following.

"Yes. Ballet to be more precise," Angela said. "He's a dancer, aren't you, dear boy?" She laid a protective hand on the young man's arm. "Can't you tell from his perfect dancer's body?"

"Inadequate eyesight, I'm afraid," Nigel provided an answer to the question Pete had asked, responding with downcast face and fluttering eyelashes.

"And they don't take notorious homosexuals, especially royals who can't be used as frontline fodder," Curt said under his breath as Angela captured the young man's attention for a bit of chit chat about his father, the Earl of Lockthorn. Curt had said it loud enough for both Pete and Alex to hear and followed up. "I imagine he's been fucked by every baron and lord between here and London."

"Time to play hostess," Angela said, brightly. "I assume you men can play by yourselves until you're needed again," she added. Both she and Curt wafted off to greet and stroke other guests, leaving the three men facing each other rather awkwardly. The strains of "Till Then," sung by the Mills Brothers wafted down from upper terrace.

"I say, when I was coming out of the house I spied a nifty burgundy and gray Jaguar with a crest on the door down in the car park. That wasn't, by any chance, yours, was it . . . Nigel?" Pete asked, breaking the silence.

"Why yes it was. Would you like to inspect it?"

"Most assuredly yes," Pete answered. "I see some smashing food on the buffet table, Alex. You should graze there while the viscount here is showing me his machine."

"Sounds like a plan," Alex said somewhat stiffly. He watched the men drift off, Pete's arm around the diminutive young man's shoulder, while Alex fought hard to discard jealously. Pete wasn't his property. At least he kept telling himself that.

Alex's imagination ran ahead of the tableau in the car park, which found Pete pressing Nigel against the fender of his Jaguar salon car in a close embrace and which included Pete's tongue inside Nigel's mouth and his hand on Nigel's crotch as the dancer bent his leg and rubbed his thigh against Pete's. The tableau was exploded, though, by the headlights of a late-arriving car, Pete's muttered "Later," and Nigel's shudder of submission to whenever Pete wanted to pick up where he'd left off.

Later, to the strains of Les Brown's band on "Twilight Time," the five of them—the Taylors, Pete, Alex, and Nigel—were sitting in the dimming light in wicker chairs on the upper terrace, the last of the revelers. Twilight came late to England at this time of year.

"Vis has seen the folly, but I'm sure Peter and Alex would like to see it," Angela said, casting a "don't question that you want to see it" look around the group. "It's getting late, Vis. Do you have to go all the way back to London tonight?"

"I have a flat in Cambridge I can go to," Nigel answered. "But go ahead and show the men the folly. I can wait."

"You can wait? It may take some time," Angela said.

"The viscount has kindly agreed to drive me back to the airfield. I want to hear the Jaguar purr," Pete offered. "Alex can have the staff car to return to Duxford." He turned a benevolent smile to Alex, who fought hard to return a wan version of it.

"And I can wait," Nigel insisted. "Take your time."

There were two Roman-style marble couches set in the folly, at an angle to each other, the rolled up heads of the couches set close together. The aviators, naked, lay on the couches, Alex on his belly on one couch and Pete on his back on the other. Curt was saddled on Alex's slightly raised hips, the host's hands clutching Alex's waist, and Curt's cock plowing Alex's channel in deep, slow strokes. Angela, slinky dress bunched up around her waist, was atop and facing Pete on the other couch, her hands palming his pecs, her torso thrown back, riding his cock hard, an expression of ecstasy on her face. Pete's face was plastered to Alex's. The two men were running their hands through the hair of the other and were kissing passionately.

As promised, Nigel was still sitting on the terrace, listening to Dooley Wilson's "As Time Goes By" when the four sauntered back up from the folly, Angela dangling her slippers from a hand. Both Angela and Curt walked right on by him and into the mansion. Pete and Alex stopped and stood in front of where Nigel was sitting.

"So, now . . ." Pete said, holding out his hand for the viscount to take with his to help him stand, "Perhaps a circuitous route back to the airfield."

"I have a small flat in Cambridge," Nigel said. "It's not far."

Alex tried to smile, but he suddenly felt the loss. There wasn't even any pretense that the young piece was taking Pete straight back to the airmen's barracks. The impression he got of the sparks flying between Pete and Nigel was that Nigel was assuring Pete that they didn't have to pull off into the bushes at the end of the drive and fuck in the backseat of the Jaguar.

When they were gone, Alex sat in the wicker chair that Nigel had vacated, smoked two cigarettes, watched the night descend over the pond, and listened to the gramophone play "As Time Goes By" over and over again. He worked hard to put Pete out of his mind, and did so by thinking of another man who had been in the garden that day, although by no means one of the hosts or the guests.

A gardener had taken breaks from clipping a hedge by the tennis court fence to watch the play. He was a short man, but solid and powerful looking—muscular. He wasn't young. He had looked grizzled, rough, and primitive. For these reasons alone, though, Alex had found him arousing. In the lower-class world Alex had come from he'd been initiated by a man as grizzled, rough, and primitive as this.

The gardener's face was ruggedly handsome under his peasant's hat, his body looking powerful within his loose garden clothing. And he was watching the tennis with interest—the bodies moving on the court more than the play of the ball. His eyes had followed Alex. At the time, Alex had assumed he was watching the tennis play and just liked Alex's style of play. Just now, though, while they and the Taylors had been fucking in the folly, he was there again, standing in the shadows, outside the doorway into the folly. Watching. So, it hadn't been the tennis form he'd been watching.

So that he didn't have to think of Pete on top of the diminutive Nigel, Alex thought of himself writhing under the body of the crude gardener as he had writhed under the body of the neighbor he had done gardening for in Georgia. No more acting like a prince, but reverting to the pauper he himself was underneath it all. Taking a cock—a huge cock as he somehow knew the gardener would have from the assurance with which the man carried himself—and being taken cruelly, totally, the brute only thinking of his own pleasure and satisfaction—but, in that, heightening the pleasure and satisfaction that Alex took from the encounter.

Flicking the spent cigarette out onto the stones, he rose and walked, deliberately, into the house.

It was as if Angela expected him to push open the door to her bedroom, bang it shut, and stride to her. She had been at her table, brushing her hair. She was wearing a diaphanous robe, open and flowing down from each side of her, and nothing else. Her breasts pushed up and out, the nipples taut, of the open robe and also could be seen in the reflection in the mirror. Alex stood close behind her and kneaded her breasts with his hands as she turned her face up to his for a deep kiss. He ran one hand down and over her pulsing belly, down lower, two fingers sliding between her folds, with one curling inside her and the other continuing on to her clit. She shuddered and moaned for him.

She laughed as he laid her on her back at the foot of the bed, and she opened her legs to him and barely winced as he thrust inside her strongly and began to pump. She arched her back, dragged her sharp nails across his bare back and cried out, "Yes. Harder. Deeper. You're a stud," as he furiously fucked her. Deeper and deeper, faster and harder he fucked her—letting it all out, all the tension and resentment he had inside him. All it was to these people—and to Pete—was sexual release. He was just a cock and a bung hole to them all. To them, this was all just a game of fear of the unknown, a frenzied response to the horrors of war and the threat of a force named Hitler.

The more frenzied and more cruel and brutal he got—thick, long cock pumping her hard, punishing her channel walls, making her flop around like a rag doll, conquered, dominated, mastered, the more she cried out for him to do just that—conquer, dominate, master—her. She dug her fingernails into his shoulder blades and bucked against him, laughing and crying at the same time, screeching, "Yes. Oh, god yes! Pound me!"

Curt must have expected this visitation too, as only moments went by after they moved into uncontrollable frenzy before he was saddling up behind Alex, working his way into the blond aviator's ass with his cock, and taking over control of him fucking Alex and Alex fucking Angela. Collapsing on top of Angela with a deep groan, Alex went spongy and soft inside, feeling Curt reach deeper up inside him—thickening and hardening inside him—as Alex went completely submissive, conquered, dominated, and mastered by the actor's pounding shaft. "Oh shit, yes. Punish me. Pound me!" he cried out as Angela held steady now, gripping his shoulders in a death grip, sending her channel walls to clutch at and shimmer over his throbbing cock just as Alex was making his channel walls undulate over and make love to Curt's demanding shaft, and took his seed—spurting once, twice, thrice, subsiding only as Curt's explosion commenced.

* * * *

Pete came out of the washroom, a towel around his waist. The bedroom of Nigel's flat—more a pied-à-terre than a residential flat—was small. There was nothing in it but a single bed, a bureau, a nightstand, and an overstuffed chair. What was there was very good quality, however. This, after all, was a viscount's bedroom in his university town retreat flat. The furniture, oversized for the rooms, probably came from a palatial manor house. The washroom itself had been small, barely accommodating Pete's hulking body and set under the eaves so that a man Pete's height couldn't stand up straight to shower or pee. Nigel was much smaller than he was—delicate, almost effeminate, with the grace of a ballet dancer—so no doubt all of the space looked bigger to him and fit his body more easily.

There were two lamps on the bureau, both with red shades that cast a rosy glow across the room. The color of heat, hot sex. Pete was hard in anticipation. He was looking forward to fucking the shit out of this hot little piece who had avoided going to war. Nigel was a strawberry blond—all the way to the bush, as Pete had found while he was kissing the dancer in a standing clutch of exposing and revealing before he'd broken and growled that he wanted to take a shower to clean the effects of the earlier sex from his body before he started again. Nigel's strawberry-red bush, closely trimmed in tight curls, turned Pete on. He was keeping a separate count of the redheads he'd spiked—more women than men, so Nigel essentially was a bonus for him.

Nigel already was naked, stretched out on his belly on the white sheets of the bed, the red chenille bedspread puddled down to the floor at the lower three sides of the bed, when Pete emerged from the washroom. He was trembling slightly. His head had been turned to the wall when Pete appeared, but now he turned his face toward the other man. Pete dropped the towel to the Oriental carpet. Nigel's eyes went large and his moan was audible.

"God, you're big," he murmured, the sound coming out in a whimper.

"I think it's because your flat is small," Pete said, with a smile.

"No, it's because you're huge."

"And getting bigger," Pete said, wagging his cock at the young man and giving it a couple of stretching and thickening strokes.

"And you're hairy; your chest is pelted with curly, black hair. I'd seen it on your forearms before—"

"Does that put you off? Do you want me to wear a shirt when I fuck you? Do you want to shave my body before we do it?"

The "when I fuck you" might have gone a bit too far at this point, Pete was afraid. Nigel seemed to withdraw into himself, but what he said showed that it had been more his arousal at what Pete said than what Pete had said that had affected him. "No, I have fantasies about hairy men. And are all Americans that big?" What was that in his voice? Was his banter covering something? Fear, reluctance? Less experience with men than had been rumored?

"Yes, we're all monsters. We split our men asunder and leave them unable to feel Englishmen inside them ever again. It's a service we do. It's our present to the young men of England."

"I don't know if I can . . ." Nigel moaned again. "Please, be good to me." Nigel turned his face to the wall again. He was trembling more, and Pete could hear him panting. Pete almost laughed when Nigel raised up on his knees, lifting his tail in a sign of a dreaded "just do it."

Pete's need to dominate and punish drained out of him. This one was young, and not nearly as hardened and experienced as he'd thought he would be. Curt Taylor had exaggerated both his experience and wantonness. But Pete was here and had his needs. He also sensed that it was something Nigel wanted. He'd have to readjust his usual "take 'em fast and hard" technique, though.

He went to the bed and sat down beside Nigel's thighs. He laid the palm of his left hand on Nigel's plump left butt cheek and felt the young man tense up. But Pete did so just to let Nigel know he could go flat, that this wasn't going to be a hard and fast taking. They would get there, but Pete would prepare him for it. The size of him and his reaction to seeing Pete naked told the aviator that Nigel probably couldn't take him without extensive preparation. But Pete was determined that the young man *would* be open for him. He wasn't in the mood just to walk away and call it an unfulfilled night. Nigel was too much of a luscious piece for Pete to deny himself. But he had to move carefully here. Who knows what trouble one of these royals could raise if he was taken by force and didn't like it? This one certainly was sending mixed signals.

The fingers of his other hand went into the red curls of the young man's head, and Pete played there for a while, waiting for Nigel's tension to lessen, which it did. He let the hand come down to the back of the young man's neck and he massaged that and Nigel's shoulders. Nigel turned his face back and gave a sigh.

"That feels good," he murmured.

"I'm going to make you feel a whole lot better," Pete answered. He felt the young man tense up again slightly. He was skittish. Pete wondered just how many times Nigel had done it before—and how expert, big, and virile were the ones he'd done it with? Maybe it had mostly been a façade.

Using his left hand now, Pete stroked softly and slowly down Nigel's spine, stopping when the young man tensed and only starting again when he had relaxed. Pete put his right hand down next to Nigel's face. He stroked Nigel's full lips with his thumb and, almost without realizing it, Nigel sucked the thumb into his mouth. Pete's arousal built and he went harder at the feel of the soft, resilient skin overlying the steel of the well-toned body, alabaster marble white—the body of a Michelangelo's "David," the skin glimmering in contrast to the tanned, curly black hair covered hand of Pete's as it glided across the skin. Pete lowered his face to the crease between Nigel's shoulder blades and breathed in the honeysuckle scent of him. A kiss there caused Nigel to moan and tremble. Pete knew the intoxicating, fresh scent of the young man contrasted with his own, which he was aware, from what conquests had told him earlier, was musky, masculine.

The process of tensing, relaxing, progressing continued as Pete softly stroked and then more deeply massaged Nigel's buttocks with circling strokes following the curves of the mounds, taking care to separate them to expose the bud of his entrance. From time to time Pete leaned down to blow on the hole to watch it pucker for him. The young man was relaxing more, trembling less as Pete took his time with him. The thumb wasn't just in his mouth, Nigel was sucking on it.

Pete turned the young man slightly and ran a hand down his belly and into the strawberry-blond bush. Nigel moaned as Pete let his fingers play in the curls there, occasionally descending as far as the root of the cock and lingering there. Nigel's moans became deeper, and Pete watched the young man engorge and then shudder as Pete ran his fingers down the top of the young's man's cock and then back up the vein on the underside.

Turning Nigel back onto his belly, Pete stood, hovering over the trembling young man. He reached over for a couple of pillows and Nigel answered his nudge and raised up on his knees for Pete to push the pillows under his belly. As he finished doing that, he let a finger run down Nigel's perineum and down the line of the young man's cock again, extending out from below his belly, between his slightly spread thighs. The young man's cock stiffened rock hard to the touch. Nigel moaned and tensed up but when Pete pulled his hand away, he immediately relaxed. Pete was crouched over Nigel. He pulled his thumb from Nigel's mouth and cupped the young man's chin with that hand, moving Nigel's head to the edge of the mattress so that he was facing Pete's hard cock, the bulb resting on the mattress, almost touching Nigel's lips.

The butt cheeks were kneaded some more and rhythmically pulled apart, and Nigel involuntarily spread his thighs more and began to move his pelvis with the rhythm. He didn't notice at first the finger descending to rest on his rim, but his eyes went big and he moaned when he felt the first penetration. Pete moved his pelvis more into the bed, the bulb of his cock now pressing on Nigel's lips. Nigel opened his mouth and took the bulb in. He knew how to suck, Pete was happy to find. He may not have taken many shafts up the ass before, but he'd given blow jobs.

Two fingers were in his ass, spreading him open, vibrating and increasing the sway of his hips. A finger tip found the young man's prostate and rubbed, causing Nigel to tremble and groan with each rub on the hard mound. His stance widened even more, inviting, whether he knew it or not, deeper, thicker penetration, and another of Pete's finger tips pressed on the prostate. Nigel tightened his lips' hold on the base of Pete's bulb, his flicking tongue licking at the precum he found there.

It was Pete's turn to groan. He hadn't realized how arousing slow and sensual long foreplay could be.

Pete seemingly was taking the young dancer slowly, Nigel hardly noticing how quickly they actually were progressing. Pete moved his hips forward and Nigel took three more inches of the cock inside his mouth, closing tightly over it.

But then he seemed to awaken to the seduction and he moaned, pushed the cock out of his mouth, and raised himself on his elbows as if he was contemplating rolling off the bed and away from Pete. Pete didn't allow him to escape, though. He sat down on the side of the bed, twisted Nigel's torso around to where they were chest to chest, embraced the young man strongly with his right arm around Nigel's waist and took his mouth in a deep, passionate kiss. Pete's left hand, slid through the strawberry-blond bush again, grasped Nigel's cock and, holding the young man captive, Nigel gasped as Pete's index finger went to the young man's urethral opening, pressing it and rubbing it, insisting on it opening to the tip of his finger, which, with a moan from Nigel, it did, moistening Pete's finger with precum.

Pete stroked him slowly, rhythmically, determinedly, to an ejaculation. Nigel struggled against him at first but soon settled down and gave up his seed with a sigh. The fingers of Pete's left hand went back to Nigel's ass opening, which Pete worked with one, two, three, and finally four fingers slick from Nigel's own cum, once again paying attention to the prostrate, while Nigel groaned and produced a second, weaker ejaculation, and Pete possessed his mouth in a kiss.

Nigel was spent, but Pete was just beginning. Nigel also was mellow, completely under Pete's control now and, his flexible little body was fully responsive to Pete's manipulation. The young man was purring.

At length Pete rose back off the bed, let Nigel go down onto his belly, all the time with four fingers up the young man's ass, and, when he pressed on Nigel's lips with his cock this time, Nigel took him in almost to the hilt and, although gagging, lay there docile, taking him deep, as Pete face fucked him.

Nigel gave no more than a groan and a "Please be good to me" plea as Pete moved up onto the bed, mounted over him, extracted his fingers from Nigel's ass, and started penetrating him with his hard cock, the soft walls of the young man's passage only reluctantly giving in to the invading shaft despite the effort that had gone into opening him up. He may have been fucked before, Pete thought, but not by a real man.

With a gasp at the first penetration, Nigel reached up and grabbed the brass rungs of headboard and whimpered, as Pete slowly possessed him deep and started a slow pump. Nigel groaned and moaned, the knuckles of his hands white and bruising as the headboard started to rhythmically grate on the wall from the forward and back motion of the fuck.

Pete took him fully but gently that first time and then lowered himself on Nigel's back, kissed him on his neck, and Nigel turned his head for a more passionate, deeper kiss. After they'd come out of that, Nigel whispered, "Fuck me again. I want you to fuck me again. I won't fight you; I know I can take it now. Stay on top of me all night."

"Oh, yes," Pete answered in a low, guttural voice. "All that and more."

Pete went up on his knees and slowly turned Nigel over on his back, repositioning the young man's hips on the pillows. Nigel looked up at him with awe and want in his eyes, risking a tentative smile, his lips forming the whispered words, "Fuck me; make love to me," as he raised his legs up and straight out from his body, grasping his lower calves with his hands. Hovering over him, between his stretched legs, Pete buried his fists on either side of Nigel's shoulders and lowered his lips to the younger man's mouth, which hungrily opened to him, Nigel sucking Pete's tongue inside.

Nigel gave a little jerk when the bulb of the cock breached his sphincter muscle again, but he had been well opened before and the shaft slid right in. He arched his back and set his own passage wall muscles and his pelvis in motion as the deep stroking commenced. Pete, who usually drove it right in to savor his partner's gasp and the total dominance that this represented—and had fully intended doing that with Nigel for the second penetration—moved instead up into Nigel's passage slowly, enjoying the feel of his hard shaft rubbing over shimmering channel walls and the series of small gasps and deep moans and Nigel's whispered, "Yes, yes, deeper. Yes, just like that. Possess me. I am yours. Oh, God, I've never been taken like this before."

Taking it slow and easy and showing some regard for his partner was a totally new experience for Pete. He'd never fucked a man this slowly before, focusing on the progress of the hard cock up through the soft sponginess of the man's channel, opening him up, stretching his walls, exploring into new territory. This was something beyond animal sex. This was affection—maybe something deeper even than that, something that Pete could not, would not, voice. Nigel enhanced the experience by murmuring, whimpering, and sobbing of his own pain-pleasure wonderment of being penetrated, invaded, conquered, fully possessed by a mammoth, throbbing cock deeper, thicker, harder than any man in his limited experience had gone before.

Being with Nigel was something strange and new too—something special. Nigel had expressed it as "making love." Pete had never thought about it like this before, but now he did. Now, with Nigel, that's what he thought he was doing—making love. All this time trying to deaden himself to face his dangerous life as a fighter-bomber aviator in war—going up every other day to the prospect of never coming down in one piece again—and suddenly now he felt totally alive again.

They both gave a little jerk and then a long, harmonious sigh as Pete's ejaculate flowed, bathing Nigel's channel deep. Pete held the smaller man tight and both sighed a second time as Pete released more seed—and then again. "Oh god, oh god," Nigel whimpered.

Oh god indeed, Pete thought. He drew his cock out to the rim, but then took another long, deep slide. "Oh god! Oh shit! Oh FUCK!" Nigel cried out as he let his legs sink to the mattress and collapsed in complete surrender under Pete. Another withdrawal and long slide, the dancer's passage now completely open to and measured to this specific cock. "Oh, fuckin' shit, Peter!" and then a hold deep inside Nigel as his channel walls rippled over the hard shaft, slightly moving still in the lubrication of his cum. Not withdrawing, Nigel turned them both onto their sides, pulled the little dancer's body into his, buried his lips into the hollow of Nigel's throat, and gave a long sigh of satisfaction, continued his deep-probing movement as Nigel whimpered and moaned.

"Don't leave me; don't ever leave me," Nigel murmured.

"I have to return to Duxford tomorrow," Pete responded, with a low laugh.

"Never take your cock out of me again," Nigel whispered.

Pete went to sleep, his mind for the first time, thinking of flying out over the channel to deliver death and destruction on the continent and, for the first time, fear creeping into where he'd only allowed the thrill of the flight to live before. For the first time that he could remember, he had something—someone—to live for.

Light was streaming through the small room's one window, when Pete woke, Nigel's body spooned into his,

Nigel's buttocks nestled into Pete's crotch, Pete inside him, hard, but Nigel's torso twisted around so that he was able to stroke Pete's nipples and run his fingers through the curls of Pete's black chest hair. He had a fascination with the swirling patterns of Pete's hairiness and couldn't get enough of running his fingers through the curls and licking them into a swirl around the man's nipples.

"You're awake," Nigel whispered. "It's late. You'll be needing to get back to the aerodrome."

"Last night you told me never to take my pecker out of you . . . to spike you forever."

"Last night was fantasy. Today is reality. You have an important job to do."

"I prefer the fantasy."

"So, do I, and you smell of musk."

"Do you want me to clean myself?" Pete asked.

"No, I love the scent. It's manly."

"It's sex. Cum. It's the smell of a healthy, cum-filled young man in heat."

"Yes it is, and I wish we had time, but . . . oh shit, oh fuckin' shit."

Pete had nuzzled his lips into the hollow of Nigel's neck and kissed him. His right hand grasped Nigel's right hip to hold him in place, and Pete started moving his cock—out, in further, out, in further yet. Nigel sighed and stretched his right hand back to cup the back of Pete's head and hold it close into the hollow of his neck.

"We need to stop," he murmured. "You'll be late getting back to the airfield." Pete's right hand moved around to encase Nigel's cock and started to work him. Nigel gave him a deep moan and set his pelvis in countermotion to Pete's hardening, thickening, lengthening, throbbing, and relentless expanding up inside him. The action of his pelvis also had its effect on his cock, sheathed in Pete's fist. Pete loosened his grip but left it encasing Nigel's shaft, and as Nigel was moving his channel on Pete's cock, he also was fucking Pete's loose fist with his own. Nigel came with a sigh.

Slowly, gently Pete turned on his back, taking Nigel with him, draped on the front of him. His cock was so deeply embedded that it didn't lose its purchase in the channel. Lacing

97

his arms under Nigel's pits, he put the small dancer into a full Nelson. Whispering, "Yes, yes, yes," Nigel reached over his head to take a grip on the rungs of the brass headboard, as Pete laced his legs through Nigel's and raised and spread them. Holding steady, his own sighs and moans a rich baritone to Nigel's tenor, Pete remained rock hard for Nigel, as the flexible dancer raised and lowered his hips, fucking himself in long strokes on the thick shaft.

"He is mine, all mine—like no man before has ever been" went through Pete's mind over and over again, in waves of wonder and appreciation. The sun rose higher in the sky and the minutes ticked away on the clock on the nightstand. The two men fucked on in an increasingly synchronized ballet of single-mechanism perfection.

* * * *

"He's around here someplace. I'm sure that he's getting his pilot's prep work done."

Alex stood at attention behind the wooden desk in the Duxford Aerodrome hangar while Major Flint gave him the evil eye, turned, and did a walk around *Make Your Own Luck*, Peter Porter's P-47 Thunderbolt. He didn't seem to see anything he didn't like as far as preparation today, although there was more pilot preparation to do before the squadron took off on the next day's mission. Alex knew he wouldn't find anything to complain about, because what he'd told him was at least half true. This was the third day since the Taylors' garden party. Pete had appeared at the aerodrome every day, but he hadn't spent all of his time here. He hadn't spent his nights here. And he hadn't done all of the pilot preparation on his plane himself. Alex had done some of that.

And Alex was exhausted from doing his own work plus some of Pete's while Pete had a fine old time laying the cute little redheaded viscount in Cambridge.

Major Flint finished making the circuit and came back to the desk. "Well, when you next see him, tell him to report to me."

"Yes, Major," Alex answered and then wearily sank into the chair behind the desk when the major had left the hangar.

98

Pete hadn't, in fact, been around much the last two days and when he was here he was dragging around in a stupor and was yawning. And he certainly wasn't laying Alex, so the little redheaded piece must be wearing his pecker out. It wasn't just that Pete was neglecting Alex; he was neglecting protocol on preparing for tomorrow's mission, and there wasn't margin for error in preparing for a mission.

Part of that preparation was their rituals too. Alex should return to the airmen's barracks and get some shuteye himself. He was exhausted from this extra work—and from the worry of where Pete was and, more important, what the status of their own relationship was.

But it was rituals they always went through that he'd always thought were as important to Pete as they were to him. They had to go through their rituals tonight and it was already getting dark.

Alex's eyelids were growing heavy and he . . . just . . . felt . . . like laying his head down on his folded arms on the desk top and getting a nap while he waited for Pete to return. And then that's exactly what he did.

The next thing he knew, Pete was standing over him, shaking him, and telling him they were about to wheel the planes out and takeoff would be within twenty minutes.

"Can't be," Alex complained as he slowly regained consciousness. But then he looked up and saw the sunlight streaming into the hangar through the open door that a truck was towing *Lucky Linda* through. It couldn't be, but it was morning already. Pete was half in his flight suit and Alex wasn't.

"The rituals," Alex mumbled.

"No time for those now," Pete answered. "The lead birds are already on the runway."

"The final prep," Alex said.

"No time to finish those this time either. It's time to just do it, good buddy." The crew was pulling *Make Your Own Luck* out now, and Pete followed his plane out into the sunshine, while Alex dove for his flight suit. When he was adjusting the last of his straps and walking out onto the apron, he saw Pete ahead of him, waving. Instinctively he waved too. This was their last ritual before they took off in missions, Pete's plane taking off close behind Alex's. They waved to each other and gave each other a salute.

Pete was doing that now and Alex was going into his salute. But that's when he noticed the two-tone burgundy and gray Jaguar salon car parked by the gate. Nigel was standing on the hood and waving for all his might. It was Nigel Pete was waving to and saluting, not Alex.

Dejected, Alex climbed into the cockpit of *Lucky Linda*, pulled the plane out onto the runway, and waited for instructions to take off. The whole procedure was closely orchestrated, with very little time separating each flight up into the air, where the squadron would form into their V to cross the channel. Alex's eyes snapped open at a yelled instruction to fly coming over his radio from the tower. It had just been a second or two that he'd blanked out, but the drill didn't allow for extra time.

He revved the engine, started the bird down the runway, picking up speed, and pulled her up into the air. He felt the jolt he shouldn't have felt and then the heat from the explosion behind him, as *Make Your Own Luck* plowed into his tail, going faster than he was—faster than Pete should have been going—and its bombs exploding. The blinding flash caught his attention more than the heat of the blast. He saw the tree tops he was dipping into upon the jarring jolt, but the flash blinded him totally before impact—and then that was that.

Chapter Three: Holding Pattern

They told him they put him in the conservatory on sunny days because the doctors had said he needed the sunshine. Autumn had arrived and it was too cold for him to sit, immobile, on the terrace. Immobile was Alex's only option these days—at least for a while. A broken arm and leg and being blind—it was hoped only temporarily—meant he wasn't going anywhere on his own for a while. He'd been lucky, they said. Inexplicably, they said, he'd been thrown from the plane and landed on strong, leaf-cushioned tree branches. If he'd remained with *Lucky Linda*, he would have been burned to a crisp. They'd said the accident was inexplicable, but Alex knew it was because he'd been sloppy about strapping himself in the plane on takeoff. He'd said nothing about that.

He'd said nothing about the sloppiness and the lack of following ritual, because he knew that had a role in what had happened. They—his aviator compatriots at the aerodrome and even the Taylors here—had, in turn, not responded to his questions about what had happened to Pete. Their nonresponse was all the response he needed.

Angela Taylor was giving him a sponge bath on a wrought-iron chaise in the glassed-in conservatory. He was stripped down and embarrassed at all the areas she was touching in giving him the bath—this in spite of being in her bed every night. It just wasn't the same—what happened in a glass room in the day and what happened in a bedroom in the dark of the night.

He was at their mercy—both Angela's and Curt's—at night too. Just a cock and a bung hole for their pleasure. Not that it didn't give him pleasure too—it's just that he was completely submissive to however they wanted to use him with the constraints of his wounds. And not just his wounds—their hospitality as well. It would have been agony in the base infirmary.

The bright flash when Pete's plane exploded had blinded Alex. It had fried his retinas, they'd said. They also said that should be a temporary issue—that they'd rejuvenate themselves and when his arm and leg were mended, he'd be able to return to the air. They'd said it like Alex wanted to return to the war—to get back to raining death down from the skies over Nazi-held territory on the continent as soon as he could. And he supposed he did. He couldn't think of anything else he had to live for until he fell out of the sky again. Pete was dead. And he hadn't fully realized what Pete meant to him until Pete wasn't there anymore.

He'd had to convalesce somewhere, and the Taylors had stepped up to take over his care. The doctors and the squadron commander, Major Flint, had thought they were bricks for doing that—that they, as displaced Americans, not able to travel over dangerous waters back to the States, were doing what they could for the war effort here in taking a wounded American airman in to care for. Although he was, certainly, grateful for the care, Alex knew the Taylors had really taken him in for the use of his cock and bung hole beyond the public recognition of their contribution to the war effort.

While Angela worked his cock up now, as he lay on his back on the iron couch, under the guise of giving him a thorough sponge bath, he could hear her humming. And then he could feel her climbing up onto the chaise; settling herself on his hips; holding his cock in position; and then impaling herself with a quickness of breath, from both of them, making deep moaning sounds, and rising and falling on the staff, as his breathing became labored and he felt the sap rise, until, increasing her gyrations and urging him to be good to her, he gave her his seed.

She spoke of it, with amusement in her voice, as his exercise time. But in more serious moments she spoke of growing older, coming close to no longer being about to produce, and of how important motherhood was to her. When she was drunk, she spoke of the waste of Pete and of how she'd wanted his child. She was more circumspect when sober, talking of how Curt was sterile but they both wanted to be parents—that they could afford children, that she wanted to have Alex's baby, no strings attached. But there was always the tone there of "If I can't have Pete's baby."

Alex didn't really care if this was true or if she was just trying to rationalize wanting to be fucked regularly. If she wanted to ride his cock nearly daily and take his spunk, that was OK with him. He didn't care much about anything these days. She rode his cock and he took Curt's cock. In exchange, they housed him, fed him, and were nursing him back to health—so he could go back up in the air, bomb more Germans, and fall out of the sky again. Well, OK.

With slight embarrassment on his part, she sponged and jerked him off and rode his cock by day, and by night, he slept between them, him inside Angela and Curt inside him— him blind and in splints entirely at their mercy and manipulation. It was OK with him until he was well enough to take to the skies again. They were arousing enough; he could get it up with them and they all were satisfied with the results.

What he actually looked forward to were the visits by the viscount, Nigel. The young ballet dancer came every other day, it seemed, and read to him—and asked him questions about the Pete Alex knew before those few days that Nigel and Pete had been together. Alex initially was jealous that Nigel obviously had had something with Pete, if only briefly, that Alex and Pete hadn't achieved. But sensing how important this was to the young man, Alex painted for him the Pete Alex thought the young man wanted to know. He didn't come close to telling him of the Pete—the forceful, total master—who Alex had known and only now realized that he had loved. He sensed that Nigel had genuinely—and hopelessly—loved Pete too, and he didn't want to steal the young man's memory of Pete. He sensed that Pete would not have wanted him to. But Nigel's Pete obviously had been a different man than Alex's Pete had been. Alex wanted to have his memories of Pete entirely separate from Nigel's.

Still, this was just a holding pattern. Alex knew it would all come to a head one day—and it did, partially because of Nigel's need and partially because of his own. In bringing a new novel by Somerset Maugham to read to Alex, Nigel brought it all out into the open. It was only while the Taylors were gone on an excursion, leaving Nigel to visit with Alex and as Nigel was reading from *The Razor's Edge* that Alex realized how close Maugham had come to describing him—and his underlying struggle. Despite their generosity, he had been put off underneath it all by the Taylors and their lifestyle ever since their sex-driven garden party earlier in the summer. And that had brought forth something that existed as a barrier between him and Pete too.

The Razor's Edge was about Alex himself, he realized, as Nigel read it. He, Alex, was on the razor's edge and had been ever since he'd arrived in England and came under the sway of the patrician Peter Porter. Alex was anything but patrician. He was living a lie here, stretched out on a fancy iron couch in the glass conservatory of a fancy manor house, with a notable actor and best-selling novelist in his bed—well, their bed.

Larry Darrell, Maugham's protagonist in the book, was a World War I aviator who had been wounded and who fell into high-flying society and traveled the world, taking construction jobs and trying to live an authentic life at his natural level, but always being swept up into society. Pete and

103

the Taylors had done this to Alex under strikingly similar circumstances. As Nigel read, Alex's frustrations grew in seeing himself in Maugham's new book. Maugham could be writing about him, he thought. For a brief moment he wondered if Curt and Angela knew Maugham and that, indeed, Maugham had written about him. But then he realized that the book must have come before he met the Taylors, even if it only recently had been launched.

He didn't realize that tears were streaming down his cheeks from underneath the blindfold he wore to protect his eyes, until Nigel pointed it out. "You're crying," he said. "It's Pete, isn't it, because this Darrell character is a fighter pilot and so was Pete?"

"Yes, I suppose so," Alex said, not wanting to reveal that the connection to the book was closer to him than that— that Nigel seemed incapable of seeing beyond Pete and that his only true regard for Alex was in his past connection with Pete.

"I miss him too," Nigel said. And from the way he said it, Alex realized Nigel was crying too.

Then Alex felt it—Nigel's hand on his crotch, feeling him up, causing Alex to harden. Alex had no more trouble hardening for Nigel than Pete ever had, but he was shocked by what was happening now. Nigel was unbuttoning his fly and pulling his cock out.

"Nigel?"

"I can't stand it anymore—not knowing. You are an aviator too. You were so close to Pete. You are so much like Pete. I've wondered . . . hoped . . ."

"Nigel?" Alex said again, but then he was moaning as Nigel took his cock inside his mouth and gave him deep-throated suck.

"Nigel, Nigel," Alex whispered, as he cupped Nigel's head lovingly with his free hand, held it in position, and began to move his hips. He realized that, for the moment, he was Pete for Nigel, that Nigel was only doing this because of that illusion. But Alex had wanted to fuck Nigel from the very beginning too. If he had to be Pete for the moment to do that, so be it.

When Alex was hard, Nigel was moving up the wounded aviator's body with his tongue, licking up the trail of

104

fine hair leading up Alex's flat belly and on up sternum to expand out to cover his pecs, as his fingers unbuttoned Alex's shirt, flaring it open. Alex realized that Nigel already was naked. Nigel sucked on one of Alex's nipples while thumbing the other one. "Your chest is hairy, like Pete's," he said. "But blond." He ran his fingers through the fine, downy hair and licked the hair around the nipples into a swirling pattern.

"Yes," Alex said. What else could he say? He realized that Nigel was using him as a surrogate for the unattainable Pete. He felt guilty taking advantage of that, but he ached to fuck the young man.

"And you're big, like Pete. Hung." His hand encased Pete's staff, stroking it and thumbing the slit in the glans.

"Yes," Alex answered, flinching as he felt Nigel hold his cock in position and descend on it.

"Pete said all American men are hung."

"Did he? Oh god, oh shit." Nigel was fucking himself on Alex's staff. Alex was hard as a rock for him.

"And so far he has been right."

Alex didn't answer because Nigel had lowered his face to go into a passionate kiss, and Alex was lost for the rest of the fuck, using his more serviceable hand to stroke Nigel off as the small ballet dancer rode him to an ejaculation.

It was nice, but, disappointing and deflating, nothing earth-shattering for Alex. It obviously was the same for Nigel, as the young man came off the cock with a sob. "I'm sorry. It was good, but not the same. You're not Pete."

"No, Nigel, I'm not Pete, nor will I ever be Pete." At this moment Alex realized he didn't want to be Pete. He didn't want to be in Pete's league. And he didn't want to be in the Taylors' league either. He didn't want to run along the razor's edge. He wanted to be Alex.

"Nigel," he said, wanting to give the young man comfort but also wanting to help him to see reality—no, all Americans weren't sexual gods. Nigel had to find his own gods now. But Nigel didn't answer. He wasn't there anymore.

But someone was there. The Taylors couldn't be back yet, surely. But Alex could hear the heavy breathing. He felt the hands on his thighs. Calloused hands; a strong grip. A gag or some sort was wrapped around his head, covering his mouth.

He was being roughly treated. His wrists were being bound, pulled above his head and secured at the top of the iron chaise. His legs were being gripped in those strong, calloused hands and were being raised and split. No quarter was being given for his casted arm and leg—now in just tightly wrap bindings—and the sharp pain when they were jerked caused him to shriek through his gag. It also brought flashes before his eyes, giving him the first hopeful clue that his eyes were on the mend.

A mouth was at his ass, sloppily, but very effectively eating him out, and Alex groaned at the crude pleasure of it, of the slurping noises and grunts, and dirty mutterings of the man, who obviously was taking great pleasure from this.

It was a man, he now knew, because the man had his cock out and was positioning it between Alex's thighs and was slapping it on Alex's stomach and thighs. The man had pulled Alex's buttocks up off the chaise and had run Alex's legs up his chest. Alex could tell he was both heavy and muscular.

Alex arched his back and screamed through the gag again, as the man thrust something hard and thick inside him— not as flexible as a man's cock—twisted it full circle. and then fucked Alex with it. Both he and the man doing this were panting hard.

"You be needin' this to take me," a deep, peasant's voice whispered in his ear, and, indeed as the hard, slickened-up dildo-like object slid in and out of him, Alex felt his passage walls give into it and his muscles undulate across it. The man felt him relax to the rhythm of the penetration and something more flexible than the dildo, a man's cock, was inside him and immediately started to pump. He was huge, thick and long. Curt was large too, so Alex was able to accommodate to him, but not without some initial pain and difficulty. The man was growling in a thick, nearly indecipherable accent and obscene words what he was going to do to Alex with his dick, and then Alex understood what it was, screaming in pain-passion through his gag, as the man did it again and again—and again.

The pumping was suspended but the hard cock was still inside him deep, when the man leaned over and bit Alex on one of his nipples before sucking it hard. Alex cried out again. He now knew the man was bearded, as the thick, kinky hair was brushing on his sternum. The mouth came up for a brutal, possessing kiss on the lips. He smelled of garlic and of the earth. He put his mouth close to Alex's ear and growled, in a heavily accented bass voice, "This be what you want. You be wanting a cocking like I can give you—like I now be giving you. I know this is what you want. You taint a laud-dee-dah pansy like the others. You be wanting a real man between your legs, giving it to you honest and hard. Tell me." He jerked the gag off.

"Yes, this is what I want," Alex screamed. And, in fact, it was exactly what he wanted.

The man went back to grabbing Alex's hips between his hands and pulling Alex's pelvis into the thrusts as he plowed him. Alex very vocally let the man know that this indeed was what he wanted. This is something like Pete gave him, but cruder, crueler, more satisfying. This was so much more of Alex's class and needs. This was a down-to-earth, primeval fuck.

When the man had come, blasting Alex inside with a prodigious wad of cum, which was after Alex had, he quickly whipped the restraints off Alex's wrists and was gone. The aviator was still lying there, moaning in his completed, satiated pain-pleasure when he heard the Taylors' cheery return.

"Oh, dear, you look like you've been wrung out," Angela said, as she came into the conservatory. "Where's Nigel? Have you two been naughty boys?"

There's been a naughty boy in here, that's for sure, Alex thought, but I don't know who in the hell he was. But then it hit him. It wasn't all darkness inside his blindfold. He ripped it off.

"What is it, love?" Angela said, coming over to him.

"I can see color and make out blurry forms," Alex said.

"And it's about time," she said. "I'll go have your doctor fetched. Oh, I see Nigel has left his book. *The Razor's Edge*. I haven't heard of it. Is it good?"

"It's very real," Alex said, busy turning his head here and there, willing himself to make out what objects in the conservatory—indeed, in his life—were. He was searching, if truth be known, but unsuccessfully, for the form of a crude, totally dominant peasant with a magnificent cock, lurking in the shadows where Angela couldn't see him—where Alex couldn't see him today either. But maybe tomorrow or the next day. A blinding charge of realization told Alex where to look for him—when he was able.

* * * *

Alex had to escape the lounge. If he heard Bing Crosby's song, "White Christmas," one more time—even though it was a Boxing Day party at the Taylor mansion, he'd go mad. No one would miss him anyway. He'd overstayed his convalescent time with the Taylors, and they hardly noticed he was around anymore. Well, he'd be gone in the new year. He'd have left earlier if the Duxford Aerodrome hadn't been virtually closed down during the week between Christmas and New Year's.

The usual assortment of writers, theatre people, and titles were wandering around in the mansion's public rooms, grazing on the spread in the formal dining room and gathered around the drinks tables nestled into the corners of other rooms. There was a decorated tree in every room, with the tallest and most majestic one located in the glass-walled conservatory.

That Alex could walk a straight line at all wasn't because he hadn't dipped into the holiday punch—he had remained sober as a defense against the guests such as the bear of a older man thinking he was younger and more attractive than he really was, the London impresario, Felix Nelson, who was specializing in Gilbert and Sullivan this year. Curt had owed the man a favor or two, had told Nelson about the charms of Alex, had told Alex about the needs of Nelson, and then, not too subtly had reminded Alex of how much he and Angela had gone out of their way to bring Alex back to life— this during a period when Alex wasn't sure he wanted to be brought back. He was over that depression and thoughts of guilt now.

And he knew he owed Angela and Curt favors—and that he'd prostituted himself enough to them that a few more times wouldn't make any difference. To them having a good-looking American aviator at their beck and call was a valuable chit they could play to maintain their social standing in England.

Alex had missed an early half hour of the party because Nelson was fucking him in the bedroom the impresario had been assigned upstairs for the holiday week. It had been a straight, hurried fuck, with Alex bent over the side of the bed, his back arched to provide an indentation for Nelson's beer belly while he crouched over Alex's back and fucked him from behind. The impresario had predicted slower, more inventive fucks in the days to come before New Year's, and, before he rejoined the party, Alex said he could hardly wait to experience Nelson again. He didn't know what was more noxious—mingling with Angela and Curt's bovine and pretentious guests or pretending that Nelson's small dick was doing something arousing inside him.

No, Alex was able to move about the party freely because he was cured. His arm had been the first to come out of the cast, and by the time his leg was healed, his vision was coming back strong. He saw everything differently now than he had before he'd lost his sight, but it was a matter of naiveté having been turned to cynicism than one set of colors being turned to another.

He'd probably always have a slight limp, but Angela had declared that to be sexy and to add to his allure. She said he'd always be viewed as a war hero. He didn't disabuse her images about how heroic the circumstances were that had put him into the casts to begin with. To the guests who came to the Taylors' parties, he indeed was both heroic and tragic—a beautiful young-in-age but old-in-life figure worthy of a movie plot all his own. It didn't detract from the image that he was sexy as hell and could enthusiastically be bedded by women and men alike. He was the Taylor's pet whore.

He craved a large room with breathing space, the conservatory being the largest one on this floor, and passed Angela in the wide center hall en route there. She was holding court in the space where everyone had to traverse in moving to any other room on this floor. She was mastering a small group of guests, but she smiled at anyone who passed and placed her hand on the small bulge of her stomach. She wasn't pregnant enough to be making a fuss over, but she *was* pregnant. Alex had asked her outright who the father was and she had coyly replied, "Curt, of course." Alex knew that he could be the father but so could Sam Bolton, a recently arrived American aviator at the Duxford Aerodrome and the Taylors' new bed partner. Alex, more often than not, was made available to warm the beds of their guests, and Alex had become expert in the conversation of offering his services without using crass words.

Alex hadn't been in their bed for nearly six weeks—not since they'd moved on to new man flesh from the aerodrome. He didn't mind a bit. He enjoyed having his own bedroom when there were no seeking guests in the house. It had made him an extra wheel, though, and was smoothing his transition back into the life of an air jockey and into a class that suited him better.

Nigel wasn't at the party. He had returned to London after he had tested Alex as a replacement for Pete's role in his life, and Alex hadn't heard from him again. The American had made the mistake once of asking Angela what Nigel was doing and had received the response, "Oh, you didn't know? He begged the ambulance corps to take him, and the last I heard he was somewhere dangerous in France." This had depressed Alex a bit, and he was sorry he had asked. He couldn't help thinking of it as other than a suicidal decision. It made him feel guilty about having come to terms with Pete's death. It was depressing evidence that he hadn't loved Pete as much as Nigel had.

Bolton was there, in the group holding court with Angela. He put a hand lightly on her arm as Alex passed and gave Alex a slight, smug smile. Don't look to me for competition, Alex tried to silently convey to him as he went past. I'm well out of this, and you'll eventually regret you're in it. Bolton, like Alex, had come from humble beginnings. They would light him up and snuff him out in this rarified aristocratic air.

He almost cut around the corner of the formal dining room en route to the conservatory, but he saw Curt in there. He was conversing with a tall, ascetic-looking man in Arab dress. This was another guest Alex had rather pointedly been asked to accommodate sexually this week. Alex wasn't ready for the first round of whatever that entailed.

Spying Alex out of the corner of his eye, Curt called out to him. "I have Doctor Musadeq here, Alex. He says he'd like to see the stables. Could you—?"

But, pretending he hadn't heard Curt, Alex moved on. I'll bet there's something the Arab wants to see in the stables, Alex thought. He wants to saddle and ride me on a hay bale, and indeed Alex had seen the hopeful and hungry look in the hawk-nosed man's eyes as he passed.

There weren't many people in the conservatory even though it was the largest room in the mansion. It also was the coldest one, considering the late December low temperature outside and the expanse of badly insulated glass that brought the cold seeping inside this room. The Christmas tree there was magnificent, Alex had to allow, but it wasn't what caught his attention. He looked beyond that to the glass wall, and beyond that yet to the man standing on the other side of the wall and looking in. The gardener, Toby, had come to take a look at how the upper crust was faring the day after Christmas. He and Alex locked eyes. Toby gave an almost imperceptible gesture, and Alex made one in return. Toby turned away from the window and disappeared into the shrubbery. Alex turned and walked through to the kitchen area and the mud room beyond, where he retrieved a coat, and quietly exited into the chill of the evening.

If it had not been for Toby, Alex would have declared himself cured a couple of weeks earlier and would have returned to the aerodrome earlier than he should have medically, but freer than he had become here.

* * * *

Rubbing his wrists to lessen the chafing of the leather bonds and to return circulation to them, Alex turned over on his back on the rope bed, looking out into the room, not much larger than his bedroom at Stanford Hall, from whence he could still hear the music from Angela and Grant's Boxing Day party. Bing Crosby was still singing on every other record, but not always "White Christmas." As the war was showing signs of drawing to a conclusion and the German units were being pushed back, Bing Crosby had become the singer of hope and determination. The laughter and rumbling of the guests' conversation was slowly losing out to the sound of the music.

Although small—and apparently the only room in the gardener's cottage—and humble, the furnishings were comfortable and functional, and Alex felt more in an agreeable element here than up at the main house—this even though he'd just had the shit fucked out of him. Even the rope bed had a give to it that made it almost a participant in the bouncing rhythm set in motion by the strength of Toby's thrusts.

The wooden dildo—a ship's belaying pin, all slicked up with grease—that Toby had used to open his ass up with was laying on the nightstand just inches from Alex's face. Behind that was a photograph of a young, blond man in an army uniform. It didn't take much study for Alex to see the striking resemblance of the young man to himself.

Toby, naked, squat but muscular still in his late forties or early fifties, and solid as a rock, veins popping out as there was no fat on his body for them to run through, was standing over a stove top in the line of cupboards that must serve as his kitchen, watching a kettle coming to a boil. Other than the nakedness, he looked domestic. A plate of cookies he would call biscuits lay on the cabinet top beside him. Who would have guessed that he'd had Alex trussed up and gagged on his bed not more than twenty minutes before and had been banging the stuffing out of him?

He'd said the gag was necessary so that they didn't hear Alex up at the big house—a custom Toby had followed for years, Toby said, and hadn't raised investigation yet.

"So you have brought men to your cottage and fucked them silly before?"

"Aye, I gave them a good fucking. I've gotten no complaints for that." With Toby, the sex act, and his domination of men like Alex, was given as natural, which Alex found disarming and needless to argue with.

Alex had protested, though, that a loud party was going on up at the main house, but Toby only answered. "It's how I do it. It's how I've always done it." As he was tying Alex's wrists over his head to the brass headboard and his ankles to the corners of the brass footboard, Alex belly down to the bed, he'd added, "You like it this way."

And Alex had liked it that way, struggling helplessly against the bonds as the old man sat below him and screwed his channel open with the belaying pin. He'd liked that, the total loss of control, the crude, unyieldingly hard wood screwing. Then he'd loved when Toby had eaten his ass out as he writhed and moaned through his gag and then had mounted him and fucked him like a dog in high heat with that impossibly thick cock of his. There was nothing refined about the fuck. It was a crude working man's taking. It's how Alex realized he wanted to have it from another man—totally controlled and totally fucked. He wanted to know he'd been fucked. Pete had approached that; Curt didn't. Most of the Taylors' guests were hopeless.

Now everything was peaceful and quiet in the cottage while Toby made up "something fortifying before we have another go at it." Alex had trembled at the image of having another go at it. He watched Toby set a bottle of whiskey out on the table by the kitchen area, so being fortified for another go wasn't going to be all tea and biscuits. For the first time in years, strangely, Alex felt like he was home, where he belonged. It was weird feeling at peace after he'd been bound and had his ass pounded, but so much had been fucked out of him by the rough gardener that only the peace and contentment remained.

"The photograph. Is it of your son?"

"My son? Oh, my no. That be Daniel—Danny to me. He was handyman here from the time he were in diapers to when they took him for the army."

"He was . . . you had him in your bed?"

"Yes, had him were right. Had him hard, just like I had you—like I want to have you again. And a right good lay he was too. You're good too. See the likeness, do you? It's there in the lying under me and taking the cock too. Loved that lad, I did."

"You fucked him like you just fucked me? You tied him up, opened him with this wooden dick, and fucked him with no mercy?"

113

"We called it makin' love, not fuckin'. We saw a difference. The lad loved it. Couldn't get enough of it. Down here in the garden we tain't as delicate as those up at the main house. When we fuck, we like to feel it. You took it like you can't get enough of it either. He were a screamer, though. I had to stop him from being heard up at the main house."

"And he'll be back?"

There was a pause before he turned toward Alex, a tear in his eye, and said, "Nay, the lad won't be coming back from the war."

After the tea and biscuits and most of the way through the whiskey, a somewhat morose Toby said, "You can be goin' back up to the main house now, if you want. There still be a party goin' on up there of your kind. I can give you another good fuckin' tomorrow."

"They aren't my kind," Alex answered.

"You be right there," Toby said. "'Tis a good thing you be seeing that for yourself too."

"I don't want to go back to the party yet. How is it . . . how did Danny like it best?"

"You want it as Danny liked it best?"

"Yes. That's how I want it."

Toby walked around the small room on bent, sturdy legs, bearing the weight of Alex, facing away from him, on his thighs. He embraced Alex around the waist with one arm and palmed one of Alex's pecs with the other, while he bounced a groaning Alex up and down on his cock. They wound up on a braided rug in front of a fire in the fireplace with Alex on all fours and Toby covering him and fucking him like a dog.

"Danny liked it that way. It were good for you too," Toby said as they stood beside the table, each with a glass of the dregs from the whiskey bottle in his hand. "It be what you needed."

"I think it's what you needed too," Alex said in a low voice.

"Aye, it were. Been some time since I got a good piece of a young looker like you. The way Danny liked it is a way I like it too. Haven't done it that way since until you asked for it."

114

"It was very good for me," Alex admitted. He also agreed it was what he needed. "But I should get back to the party now. The guests will have thinned out enough that I will be missed."

"Just remember now where you belong," Toby said. "And remember where to come to get what you need."

Alex went over to the nightstand and picked up the photo of Danny. "Was the relationship with Danny good?—I mean not just the sex part but the sex part and the other parts as well."

"It were the best." The sadness had returned to the man's voice.

"Did he ever stay the night? Here? In your bed, with you?"

"That were the best part—just sleepin' together, he in my arms, concentrating on our breathing so that we were one. Spent from the hard fuckin'—he did like the hard fuckin'—but not needin' it ere more just then. Not needin' the fuckin' to be breathin' as one. But if more fuckin' came, more tender, more lovin'."

"I wish I could stay the night."

"I dinna think you're ready for that. You still owe the Taylors, don't you? You still be needed and wanted up at the main house. You think on them takin' care of you, but you been takin' care of them too. In many ways, they be lost souls. They need lovin' as much as the next man or woman."

"Maybe not all night quite yet. Could you try it with me—but for a short while? Try to let me become one with you? Work together on our breathing?"

Toby came back to the bed and gently pulled Alex down with him, stretching them both together, cheek to cheek, beating heart to heart, cock resting against cock, thighs touching close, and Alex concentrated on the beating of the two hearts, working at bringing them into synchronization, feeling both the power and hardness of the older man, knowing and appreciating that he could be a cruel and demanding lover, but, at this moment, only knowing of peace and contentment.

He had nearly dozed off in Toby's arms when he sensed that Toby had gone hard again and the man's heart seemed to be racing.

"I want—" he whispered into Alex's ear.

"Please, yes," Alex answered, "the way you would do it with Danny after becoming one in breath and heart beat with him."

Toby gently turned Alex in his arms so that the young aviator was spooned into him. Toby's insistence was hard and thick. Alex felt it rising up the small of his back, until the stronger man reached down and pulled Alex's thigh on top of his. The positioning of the cock head was then at Alex's hole. Toby rubbed the cock head across Alex's rim and on his inner thighs until Alex was panting and begging for the cock. Then Toby pressed in, starting the invasion that came in peace this time rather than his previous battering down the walls into defenseless taking no prisoners. Alex sighed and moaned as the muscles of his passage walls rippled over the shaft, pulling it in. He opened to it and went soft to the core for the invader. If Toby took him hard now, he'd be split asunder.

But Toby took him in peace.

The cock slowly, surely, went into the hilt, and, groaning, Alex moved his pelvis in consort with the wave-like rhythm of Toby's deeper penetration. Gently still, Toby turned Alex onto his stomach, gripped the young man's wrists with his hands, pushing Alex's arms above his head. Alex grabbed hold of the brass rungs of the headboard and Toby, his lips next to Alex's ear, covered Alex close from above and began taking long, slow, deep strokes inside Alex's passage. Alex went even softer at the core; Toby gained girth and depth, riding Alex's ass like waves surging up onto the shore, retreating, surging again, reaching deeper into the soft core each time.

"I'm coming," Alex murmured and then did.

"I be close behind you," Toby whispered, and was, the prodigious flow coming in peace.

Alex felt the beating of Toby's heart on his back and was sure that his was in synch. It was so quiet in the cottage that he could hear the gramophone in the main house again. Bing Crosby was singing "White Christmas" again. But now it didn't irritate Alex. Now he felt totally mellow and at peace.

116

This. This was that finishing of the satisfaction, that journey into the realm of love, that he had craved from Pete but only now was getting from Toby.

Chapter Four: Into the Sky

"What's this then?" Elizabeth greeted Alex at her door with a mixture of surprise, pleasure, and worry. She was dressed in a shift serviceable to go to work in, which is where she had been heading when the knock came at the door. It was almost time for her to leave for her job in the Duxford Aerodrome scheduling office. She looked over her shoulder, toward the kitchen, when she saw that it was Alex, dressed in his everyday khakis, at her door and then turned back to give him a nervous smile.

"I brought these for you. I didn't think I should give them to you at the office."

"Nylons and a carton of Lucky Strikes?" She reached out a hand greedily, although the gesture also indicated that it was involuntary, that she shouldn't touch them. "Harvey," she then said, with a tinge of worry in the saying.

"Harvey is out in the barnyard. I saw him when I came to the door. He didn't see me. Give him some of the cigarettes. Say they were given out at the aerodrome—perks of the job, maybe Christmas gifts belatedly arrived. I couldn't wait to see you. You said he seemed to be at the outdoor work all day."

"And so he is, I suppose," she said, taking the gifts, "other than that he'll come in for the spot of midday meal I prepared for him and put in the frig."

He put his free hands to use, pulling her to him, clutching her pelvis to his with a strong, squeezing grip on one of her butt cheeks. He knew she could feel that he was hard and the heat of him. He took her mouth brutally in a kiss that took her breath away. When he came out of it, her eyes all glassy, he said, in a low, hoarse, voice, "I want to put the stockings on you myself, and then I want you."

"You best come in then. We'll need to do it in the kitchen, at the sink. It has a window where we can see that Harvey is still out there with the livestock."

They both knew what "it" was.

She was backed up against the sink, her arms bent, the heels of her hands pressed into the edge of the counter beside her, leaving it for Alex to watch out for Harvey through the window behind her. He'd pulled her shift over her head and unhooked her bra and tossed both aside on the floor of the kitchen. She had the presence of mind to be glad she'd mopped the floor just the day before.

She moaned and gripped his curly, blond head hair tightly as he pulled her panties down off her legs, kissed her on the belly, and rubbed his cheek there. He took a deep breath, sniffing in the perfume of her cunt and licking at the edge of where her underbelly went into her strawberry blonde thatch. She was grateful that she had bathed that morning and perfumed herself, anticipating seeing him today, the day before his first mission since he'd been back from convalescent leave. She just hadn't anticipated that he would come for her before work. It gave her a thrill and shiver that he had.

She panted lightly as he smoothed each nylon hose up a leg and turned her thighs outward a bit, exposing her more to him, and then teasing her hips forward by pressing her buttocks forward with his palms. She moaned more deeply as he buried his face between her thighs and then more deeply yet as he went to work on her clit and cunt with his tongue.

At length he stood up, unbuttoned his fly, and pressed down on her shoulders, coaxing her to her knees. He leaned over, fists on the counter, and watched Harvey puttering about in the farmyard as Elizabeth took him inside her mouth and made him long and thick and shuddering.

He raised her, turned her to where she was watching Harvey through the window too. Alex's chin was on Elizabeth's shoulder, his hands were cupping and squeezing her pendulous breasts, and his cock was deep up into her cunt, working her. She groaned and moaned as she watched her older husband slopping the hogs.

They both caught sight of Harvey turning around and coming closer, seeing Elizabeth's face in the window. But Alex had already withdrawn his head from her shoulder. Harvey waved at Elizabeth and she weakly waved back, trying to control the sway of her pelvis back against the thrusting cock and lowering her shoulders enough so that the breasts and the hands couldn't be seen from the outside. Harvey turned and walked into a field a good distance from the house and Alex moved his chin back to Elizabeth's shoulder and maintained the rhythm of the fuck.

At the door, in her shift, but not yet in her panties, she said, "You're worried, aren't you? This is because you're worried. Tomorrow is your first bombing mission since you returned to the aerodrome, isn't it?"

"Yes," he said. He didn't acknowledge that it was "yes" to everything she'd said.

"You can't worry. You have to come back. You have to believe that."

"I know I have to believe that." And then, suddenly, the need swept over him again, and he slammed the door, still inside, grabbed her, and turned her back to the wall. He hiked her shift up to her waist, quickly unbuttoned himself, and, hiking her left leg on his hip, thrust up into her again, possessing her lips frantically, and banging her hard and furiously against the wall.

Sobbing, she didn't fight him. She gave him all that he wanted—all that she hungrily wanted too, and when he finally left, reversing direction and nearly running, mostly stumbling on his lame leg, as he saw that Harvey was coming around the corner of the house, she stood there, weeping, and whispering, "You have to come back."

* * * *

He shook his head and looked up from the desk in the hangar at his new plane. He was told it was a new, improved version of the P-47 Thunderbolt. It had only been here for a week and he'd only been up in it twice so far. Tomorrow he'd have to take it on his first bombing mission since . . . since that last one, when he'd lost *Lucky Linda*. Since he'd returned from Stanford Hall he had trained back in on the other planes in the squadron when they were available: *Got Luck*, *Lucky Forever*, *Lucky Louise*. He'd give anything to have his old ride back.

He'd give anything to have his old fly buddy, Pete Porter, back.

119

As he dozed, he'd been thinking of Pete. Not just that last day but all the days they'd spent together. And he thought of the rituals they'd always gone through—until that last day. He'd done, what, one hundred and seventeen over-the-channel missions with Pete before the breakup? He'd heard that the average life of an aviator in this business was ninety missions. They'd been lucky, that was for sure. And "lucky" was part of the ritual. All of the squadron planes that had come back were named some form of "Lucky." Pete and he had known that. Some of the newer flyers, like Major Flint, didn't know about that. It hadn't been spoken of much because no one wanted to jinx anyone else.

Alex looked over at his new ride and at the name that still was painted on her side. *Horus.* He'd been told that Horus was the Egyptian sky god. Appropriate for a fighter-bomber, sure. But all of the squadron planes had some form of "Lucky" painted on them. Major Flint had promised to have a new name put on the airship before Alex took it into battle. But it hadn't been done. The mission was the next day. It already was late afternoon here. Alex had, with hope, picked the name *Still Lucky.* He'd had his fears and worries about this mission—and also thoughts of being tired of it all, with a view to the survival number he'd significantly outdistanced already.

With a sigh, he stood and walked over to the plane. One of the rituals was walking around the plane, whispering encouragement to her, and running his hands over her flanks to bond with her—calling her his lover and that they were in this together.

But his heart wasn't in it. He felt more of endings than beginnings.

Voicing a disgusted "Fuck it," he took his hand away from the fuselage, turned, walked out of the hangar, and signed out one of the staff cars.

If he'd been fifteen minutes later, he would have been there for the arrival of the two maintenance men who had been assigned to paint over the name *Horus* on the new P-47 and paint on *Still Lucky.*

It was close to twilight when he drove up to Stanford Hall. There was much he was supposed to be doing back at the aerodrome today to prepare for the next day's mission, but he didn't really see the point anymore. He had decided—at least that's what he'd told himself when he'd driven away from the airfield—that he should come see the Taylors and thank them again for putting him up and caring for him through his convalescent period. He hadn't had any intention of seeing anyone else. Not really.

Stanford Hall was dark when he arrived, however. He'd lived there, so he walked right in. The door wasn't locked. His "Hello, anyone here?" echoed through the rooms. The furniture in the rooms he looked into while walking down the central hall were all covered with dust sheets.

A housemaid came out of the kitchen.

"The Taylors have gone to Edinburgh, Mr. Alex. Mr. Taylor has a movie to make there. Can I—?"

"No thanks, Chloe. I'm flying tomorrow. I just wanted to drop by to give them my regards. I'll . . . I'll see them when they get back."

He quickly left the house and returned to the car. He already had the driver's door open when he admitted to himself that he hadn't come to see the Taylors at all. He let the door click shut, turned, and walked toward the entrance to the path that led to the gardener's cottage.

* * * *

The conquering pounding fuck was over fairly quickly, with Alex on his back on the bed, his arms pulled over his head, his wrists bound, and tied by a lead to the brass headboard. He was gagged, even though he'd pointed out that there was no need for it. Chloe had said she was the only one at the main house that day and was about to leave when Alex had arrived.

But Toby had his rituals, and he insisted on maintaining them. Alex could understand the importance of rituals.

So, he was fucked naked, his butt on the edge of the foot of the bed, Toby raising and stretching his legs painfully straight to the side, and Toby's cock pounding the living daylights out of him. For an hour nothing entered Alex's mind but the pain-pleasure of Toby cruelly using and abusing his body. It was all good for Alex, and the exhausting sex was satiating and cleansing. With Toby, a man knew he'd been fucked.

In yet another of Toby's rituals, they sat and took tea and biscuits afterward and Toby pulled out a full bottle of whiskey.

"You cried out 'Peter' several times when I was in deep and going deeper," Toby said. "Was that Peter Porter who used to come here with you?"

"Yes."

"Tell me about him. He fucked you?"

"Yes."

"Many times?"

"Yes. And I fucked him too."

"Ah, he was your lover." It wasn't a question.

"I didn't know how much he was until he was gone," Alex answered. "But it was just me who saw it that way."

"Tell me more about him."

"If you'll tell me more about your Danny," Alex said.

So, they sat through a whole bottle of whiskey, each telling the other of their great love to that point, and of the loss they hadn't been able to get past. For Alex, though, it was a purging process. He could only hope that it was the same for Toby.

Darkness had fallen when Toby put a hand on Alex's forearm. "I want to fuck you again and then hadn't you supposed to be going back to Duxford? Don't you fly tomorrow?"

"Yes, I fly tomorrow."

"Isn't there more you have to do to be ready to fly tomorrow?"

"No, I'm prepared for tomorrow," Alex lied. "I can drive back at dawn. I want to stay here with you tonight. I want you inside me, but I want your nighttime attention. I want it to be dark and I want you to think of making love to Danny."

"And you, what do you want?" Toby asked.

"I want to make love to you."

"Not to Peter Porter?"

"No. Pete's not here. You and I are here. I want you to be my lover."

"I'll do that, but I want you to know that I won't be thinking of making love to Danny. I'll be making love to you. I love you, Alex. That don't mean I love Danny any less."

The fear of tomorrow's run hit Alex at that moment. He had a reason to live now. He had a reason to fight to live. He would stay some of the night now, but not all of it. There would be more preparation to do before he flew tomorrow— more than he had intended to do before someone told him he was loved. The tiredness that had bogged him down for weeks lifted. Only now did he realize that the will to live had returned to him.

Toby held Alex into his body, chest to chest, in the dark on his bed until they both could feel their hearts beating as one. Then, before Toby could take the lead, Alex gently rolled the older man on his back. They both were hard. They'd already been stroking each other to erections. Grasping Toby's wrists, Alex pulled the older man's arms over his head. Toby didn't resist, although, as the stronger of the two, he could have taken control and asserted himself. Positioning his buttocks over Toby's hips, Alex slowly impaled himself on the older man's thick cock. He moved into the rhythm of fucking himself on the hard shaft.

Lowering his face to where he could make out Toby's face close below his, he saw that the old man had tears in his eyes.

So did Alex.

~

Long John Silverman

"Come on, let me at least look at it. I have a bet going. I've declared it can't be true."

"No," John said. But he was smiling. He knew the British bomber jockeys were a boisterous and randy lot, and most were too good-natured to raise his dander. And there was a heart-wrenching war on. And, mostly, he was too embarrassed that he was chained to a desk and, this not being his war, at least not yet, locked into a nothing, thinly symbolic liaison job while they were up there laying their lives on the line.

"Come on, then, John. Just a peek. I'll be dead next month. Would you want me to go without knowing?"

Trevor Chelton was being morbid, of course, but they had to be that way, the British war pilots. And they had to grasp at any humor in it that they could—or else none of them could have made it this far. Six months. That was the life expectancy of a British bomber pilot in this second world war. And no one had known anyone who had retired from this. At least not yet.

When John Silverman had just arrived at RAF Mildenhall air base in September 1939 as a nominal American liaison officer to the British war effort, a twenty-one-year-old, fresh-out-of-college U.S. Army Air Corps lieutenant, the best sign of support the Americans could offer to the British at this point in their war against Adolph Hitler, he had "gotten" it the moment he had arrived. His welcome escort had taken him to a barracks building and told him to pick out the billet he wanted.

"But all of the bunks are taken," he had said, after his eyes had scanned the long room and seen the unmistakable sign of primitive, yet determined domestication around each one of the neatly spaced cots.

"No, they are all available," his British counterpart had said quietly. "None of these lads are coming home." It wasn't until much later, at war's end that John would learn that only 10 percent of the British bomber pilots who ever flew off over the channel survived the war. But just the image of that seeming full, but empty barracks that day was all he ever needed to see to believe the horror of that reality. And that was enough to make him vulnerable.

Which was why, in the end, John had given the young and tragically dashing Trevor Chelton the look he wanted— and why he had softened to the young man when his eyes went wide as saucers when he got that look.

And it was why in late November he let Trevor come to his cot in the ghostly empty barracks and had sat on the edge of the cot and let Trevor lower his naked body into his lap, facing him. Why John had sat quietly and docilely and let Trevor rise and fall rhythmically on John's manhood, nipples rubbing nipples, hands encasing John's head so that their lips met and they kissed while Trevor sighed a satisfied sigh of fulfillment and peace—and momentary escape from the reality of the times and expectations.

For three weeks that late fall they were lovers, John progressively being won over to Trevor's desires and needs so that by that last afternoon, Trevor was laying on his back on the cot, buttocks at the edge, and John was holding Trevor's trembling legs spread wide and was actively entering and entering and entering Trevor to the tune of Trevor's cries of passion and pleasure at the depth of the never-ending, mutually engaged taking.

That had been on the 16th of December. The legendary Wilhelshaven Raids over Germany had started two days earlier. No one knew then when they would end. All suspected it would be when the last British bomber pilot was dead.

There was a frenetic, "forget the world," element to John and Trevor's lovemaking. John had never lain with a man before, but he felt so helpless and superfluous to the brave defense these young men were putting up for their homeland, their great sacrifice in the face of sure death and probable futility. He could deny Trevor nothing in these circumstances. And for these days of impending horror, he let himself go. They fucked like there was no tomorrow, for, indeed, there probably wasn't going to be a tomorrow for Trevor and his compatriots. Again and again and again, Trevor in the deepest throes of passion at what John was willingly and completely giving him now, feeding deep inside him. No need for condoms. Skin on skin. Trevor arching his back and his eyes rolling back in his head, his cries of joy lifted to the ceiling of the eerily deserted barracks room as John sank in, in, in. No thought of tomorrow. Only today, and the frenzy of the deep fuck.

And on that day, John believed that it was Trevor who held his love. No other. Trevor was his whole life. And he was no longer even thinking he was doing this because of the unusual circumstances they were in. Trevor needed him in order to get through the days, to motivate him to climb into that Wellington bomber in the twilight and take his next dark-of-the-moon run into the German, flak- and Luftwaffe night fighter-filled skies. But that was passed them now. They were fucking because they were lovers.

The Wellington Raids ended on the 18th of December 1939, the British force exhausted but having made a decisive, staving off impact on the German war-making capability.

In this last sortie across the channel in the Wilhelshaven Raids, Trevor Chelton's Wellington bomber was shot down by a German ME-109E as it had the English channel in its sights after a successful run over Wilhelshaven, with the plane ditching in the North Sea.

Three weeks later, John Silverman was reassigned to Claire Chennault's fledgling Flying Tiger "support" aid force unit that was forming in Kunming, China, to help bolster the Chiang Kai-shek government's resistance to the Japanese invasion in the east. And it wasn't long before John was fully occupied with an entirely different sort of war and without the time or luxury of private mourning for his lost lover. Young men were dying at every turning. There was no time to think on the senseless wasting of them individually any more.

* * * *

It was late in the November of 1963 in a quiet Cleveland, Ohio, suburb, when a distraught and drained John Silverman answered the ringing at his door. If he hadn't been distracted, he might have just let the doorbell ring and ring until whoever was there gave up and went away. But he had been watching the television coverage of the assassination and burial ceremonies for the U.S. president for days, and he was confused and drained and just went to the door without really even thinking about it.

The man was young and sad looking. John immediately started forming in his mind whatever he could say to get rid of a door-to-door salesman as quickly as possible. He was in no mood for anyone else's hard-luck story or personal tragedy at this time. He had all of that he could manage himself now. He was worn out by life.

But he was wrong in thinking there was no more of this to face.

"Did he suffer?" John asked, sitting there in the dimly lit silence of his living room in the long shadows of the late afternoon, the television set turned off for the first time in a week.

"No, not really. He went quickly, once we knew for sure that he was that ill." The young man, Raymond Bock, as he had introduced himself, dragged up a swelling of old, bittersweet memories for John. It probably was his English accent.

"I had no idea that Trevor had even survived the war," John said in a halting voice. The shock that Trevor Chelton had recently died was magnified by John's assumption that he had been dead for twenty-four years already.

"He didn't want you to know," young Raymond said. Bock was a strikingly handsome young man. Lithe and blond. Fine, expressive hands. Probably an artist of some sort. Certainly artistic, sensitive. He had shown as much sensitivity as possible in letting John know that John's old lover—Raymond's most recent lover—had both lived and died in a completely separate dimension from John's postwar life.

"He didn't want me to know?" John was still stunned and a little confused. This wasn't his sharpest week. He was vulnerable.

"No," Raymond answered in a low, throaty voice. It sounded like he was a bit on edge himself, barely holding in his emotions. "By the time he found you after the war, you were married and had children. How many was it?"

"Six. Six boys. In seven years."

"But your wife?"

"Mary died in having that sixth child. I raised the boys on my own. The last of them—Phil—is off at naval training now."

"Six children in seven years. What took her? A difficult childbirth?"

"She was just worn out. I tried to get her to slow down. But she always . . . she just wanted—"

"Can I see it?" Raymond's voice was hoarse. John sensed a thickness in it. A familiar tone. He looked up sharply at the young man. As if seeing him for the first time now.

"Excuse me?"

"Trevor talked of you . . . of it . . . often. In the throes of passion, he would cry out your name. I was jealous for ever so long. Not that he cried out your name. But jealous of what he had to say about it. I wasn't sure I ever believed it. But he was so sincere. He was fixated, and I'm afraid I've become fixated too. I've come all the way from London. Please, can I see it?"

Perhaps if John had not been at such a low point, his life would not have taken this jolting turn to the past. But the last of his boys gone from home. No one to care for. The tragedy of Dallas. The shock of learning that Trevor had survived the war but now, just as suddenly as he had been regained, was gone. Here and gone on the breath of a handsome young, vibrant man, in a silent, lonely room in a quiet Cleveland suburb as the whole world collectively mourned the irretrievable loss of innocence. A man with an English accent just like Trevor's. A need just like Trevor's.

They fucked right there in the living room as the late afternoon progressed into dark night. Raymond straddling John's lap once they both were naked, sinking down, down,

down as he arched his back and lifted his gaze to the darkening ceiling and warbled in ecstasy at the long, long journey down into John's nestling pubic thatch.

Later, as Raymond was bent over the arm of the sofa, John hunched over and behind him, and Raymond felt the renewed throbbing moving ever more impossibly deep into the quick of him, the young man thought of that suitcase he had set down out of sight of the front door on John's front porch and wondered how soon there would be an opportunity to suggest that he bring it inside.

~

Mountain Memory

We both were wearing our fatigues and bundled up against the fall night air at the edge of the woods behind the mess hall. So far there was no reason to adjust our warm clothing beyond my fly being unbuttoned. My cock was out as I leaned back against a tree trunk, but it was being kept warm by Corporal Hart's mouth enveloping it.

Corporal Hart was just one of my willing boys. We'd come a long way together to Berlin and beyond from the landing at Anzio, and many of us had become as close and comforting and interested in and willing for mutual release as men could be who were on the move on their feet for two years and subject to being shot on the spot for finding their relief in women encountered along the trek across Europe. Not that it wasn't equally dangerous to be caught engaging in the release we did.

Hart looked up into my eyes, his with a pleading expression on them, asking, I knew, if I was ready to belly him against the tree, cover his back, and give him the full length and girth of my cock.

I was, and would have done so, if it hadn't been for the commotion coming from the back door of the mess hall, by the trashcans, where Cook was speaking gruffly to someone in the shadows.

"Hey, what yer doin' there? And who are you? You're not from the camp, are you? A local. A Kraut, I think."

With a sigh, I gently pushed Ted Hart back on his haunches, folded my cock back into my pants, and buttoned up as I walked toward the mess hall. Duty called. It already was nearly pitch black here below a cliff of Kehlstein Mountain in the German Alps, in the most remote southeast corner of

Bavaria. Only the light from the mess hall kitchen windows, cast across the shadows of two men, one rather small and struggling and the other tall and heavy and grasping the smaller figure close, provided any context to Cook's gruff voice and answering whimpers in German. My immediate thought as I approached this tableau was that there would be some sentry I'd have to dress down. German nationals weren't allowed in the camp without escort—and not at night at all.

In fact, we had license to shoot them on sight. There were signs, in German, explaining that plastered on the compound fences.

"I found this Kraut rummaging around in the trashcans," Cook said as I walked up. "I told you that I thought there was a wild animal at the cans for the last week. Turns out it's only this little guy."

"Well, let me see what we have here," I said, as I reached them. "He doesn't look so dangerous."

And, indeed, he didn't look dangerous at all. He looked so weak and emaciated that he might be on his last legs. Pity that, I thought. He was quite a good-looking young man. Not young, young, of course. Maybe his late twenties or early thirties, but life obviously was being cruel to him. It hadn't been all that rewarding to any of us as World War II was winding down across Europe. And some of us had had to walk here from the toe of the boot that was Italy.

I had taken my guys all the way to Berlin to help cut off the head of the snake there the previous May, not losing one soldier in the process. For our reward, we were sent up here into the far reaches of Bavaria to sit in a temporary camp between the mountain town of Obersalzberg, up against the lower cliffs of the Kehlstein Mountain and in the shadow of the third highest peak in the German Alps, Watzman Mountain. I don't wish to sneer at the assignment we'd received as we waited to be shipped home—nearly all of us to wives and children no matter what we'd gotten into for solace and relief during the last two years marching from Italy to here. We actually had a plum assignment. Obersalzberg had been the winter retreat for Adolf Hitler himself and his sycophants, built up here on the lower slopes of the Kehlstein as a retreat for the führer during the 1936 Olympics in nearby Garmish-Partenkircher.

Hitler had spent more and more time up here in the waning years of the war, and he'd stashed a lot of the loot up here that he and his cronies had pulled out of art museums all across Europe during the German occupation. My unit's job was to guard and inventory this stash until it could be properly dispersed again. We were not far from the end of accomplishing this, which was a good thing, because the winter of 1945-46 was pressing in on us, and this place would be one snow-covered iceberg come December.

And a look at the obviously starving young man in the tattered clothing and overcoat who Cook was holding by the scruff of the neck told me that it was unlikely he could survive the winter.

His eyes showed a mixture of fear and resignation. My heart turned over. I'd seen far too much of the suffering among civilians in this war. There was nothing about him that spoke soldier. He fit the bill of starving artist more. The complete look of surrender and vulnerability in his eyes moved me—and not just my heart. Cleaned up and fed he would have been almost irresistible to me and my appetites.

"Who are you and how did you get into the camp?" I asked. He looked at me with a complete lack of comprehension. So, a German refugee no doubt. Certainly not American and most certainly not belonging in this camp. I knew all of my men—more than a few of them I knew biblically.

"Are you hungry. Were you looking in the trashcans for food?"

There was a flash of recognition in his eyes, but still he said nothing. He probably knew that rummaging for food here was inviting a death bullet. He had to have been totally desperate to even contemplate risking it. At that point the assistant cook, Private Green came to the kitchen door.

"Kyle," I said to him. "Is anything left over from the night's mess?"

"We have a bit of ham left and there's bread," the private answered.

"Can you make a sandwich with that please—a big one—and give it to this man, and then escort him back to the main gate, please? I'm too tired tonight to write up an incident report. But on your way back, please make a round of the sentries, let them know a civilian got into the camp. Tell them to look at every inch of fencing for a breach and report to me tomorrow. And tell them that, despite the breach, I haven't released any orders permitting target practice."

"Yes, sir," Kyle answered. When he came back with the sandwich, wrapped in a newspaper, and handed it to the young man, Cook let loose of him and I drew both Cook's attention and that of Kyle to me to ask them just not to say anything to anyone about this. We were not supposed to offer any help at all to German civilians. In the moment it took for me to do that, though, the young German had disappeared.

I sighed. I'd have to write up some sort of report after all. "I still want you to go to the sentries, Kyle," I said. "I hope to God one of them doesn't shoot the young man while he's trying to get back out of the camp. But there's a breach in the fencing someplace. The only side not covered is the cliff below the Kehlstein, and that's a sheer rock wall."

A little sad now—at what war does to us all—and slightly irritated that I'd have to write up an incident report, I returned to the edge of the forest where Corporal Hart was waiting for me in the dark. Reverting to an earlier stage of our preparation, we engaged in a bit of lip play and groping before he sucked me off again. It was with weary thoughts of all we'd been through and the toll it had taken on people like that young man at the mess hall, whose hands I'd seen—the hands of a professional or artisan, not of a farmer or soldier—that I embraced Ted Hart from behind as he leaned into the tree and spread his legs, entered him deep to his moans and groans, and worked him hard to give both of us release and something more pleasant to think of than what we'd been through in the last two years.

I was finishing with Ted, holding him close in my embrace, his head turned to me, our lips meeting, and the last short spurts of my cum ejaculating into the quick of his passage when I floated up out of our "transported elsewhere" time separated from the present and slowly became aware of our surroundings again.

As I drifted back into reality, I sensed that the two of us weren't alone—that we were being observed. I slowly rotated my head around, not wanting to spook off whoever it was. But just that slight turn was enough for me to hear the crackle of pine needles underfoot deeper into the forested area. Just the glimpse I saw was of tattered clothes in browns and grays and black, and I instantaneously thought of the young German who had been caught at the trashcans.

I released Ted, who slumped against the tree trunk, and, after an affectionate stroke of his cheek, strode out in the direction in which I sensed we had been watched. But of course when I got to the tree I had marked as the figure's hiding place, no one was there.

* * * *

Cook approached me in the mess hall two evenings later as the dinner hour was drawing down and men were leaving the hall. We were in a state of unaccustomed limbo here at the base of the German Alps. The men had been warily trudging through fields, avoiding roads, where ambushes could be set, and being ever aware of their environment for years before landing here in the small camp near Obersalzberg below the Eagle's Nest, Hitler's famous mountaintop tea house that was carved out of the rock of the Kehlstein. Here, the march was over. The war was over. Presumably the danger was over, although there continued to be whispers of "lost cause" partisan cells that kept the Americans close to their camps and bases. There was little for the men to do in the evening after dinner and before night when they could surreptitiously move about their barracks into each other's beds. They lingered in the mess hall, but it was dark and growing late.

I habitually ate late, walking around to the tables earlier in the meal, coffee in hand, checking on the well-being of the men—and frequently making assignations with one or two of them for meetings in my separate room in the night.

"Excuse me, Captain," Cook said, his voice hesitant.

"Yes? Is there a problem? I saw the supply truck come in today. We were shortchanged in some rations?"

"No, Captain, that is all good. It's the German refugee from the other night."

"The young man who somehow got into and out of the camp without alerting one of the sentries?" I was still chaffing over that happening. I had doubled the sentries. I also was chaffing a bit from having gone soft and given him something to eat. 1 was somewhat surprised that I didn't have half the population of Obersalzberg at the front gate the next morning begging to receive what he had. I had also conveniently "forgotten" to write up an incident report on his intrusion.

"Yes, the same," Cook said. "He returned. I caught him going through the trash again."

"And did he run off when you found him—like the other night? I can call out the men to search the camp for him. We need to know how he's getting in."

"No, sir. I have detained him."

"Detained him?" A chill went up my spine. The regulations were to summarily shoot any German invading a camp to steal anything, especially food. I thought it was barbaric, but I had been assured that it was the only way to keep the starving population from trying to overrun the camps. An example ran through my mind that had been spread around the country and, I had been assured by high command, was true and was repeated as a deterrent. The story went that a young German boy earned scraps of food at a U.S. base near Heidelberg shortly after the fall of Berlin by shining the shoes of the base commander. He was seen running out of the commander's tent with a pair of shoes in his hand and was shot by a sentry who didn't know of the arrangement. Just beyond where he fell was a rock on which the shoe polish and brush were neatly arranged. He had just decided to shine them outside rather than inside the tent that day.

Deterrent perhaps, but it choked me up each time I thought of the cruelty of war. I knew I could have shot the young German scavenger two nights previously—and that perhaps some of the men would have expected me to do so and would think it weakness that I didn't. That was probably why I only told who I had to about the incident and why I didn't write an incident report as I should have. So, part of me was relieved that he had escaped.

But now he was back, and under control, if I understood Cook correctly.

"Yes, sir, I have him locked in the storage room."

"Well, I guess we'd better attend to him, then," I said, with a deep sigh. "Let's not let the whole camp hear about this, though." I had absolutely no resolve to shoot the young man. After trying to discern how he was getting into the camp, I'd send him on his way. I was still struggling in my mind whether to send him away with food or not. If I fed him again, I knew he'd be back. If I didn't feed him, maybe he would realize this was a blind alley for him. What I was really struggling with in my mind, I knew, was whether I wanted him to come back again—and where that might lead. I hadn't been able to get him out of my mind.

When the storage door was open, I was torn between crying and laughing. The young man was sitting on the floor, in the dark, and had found and torn into a sack of raw potatoes. He was munching on one. He looked up at me in the doorway with a panicked look on his face, but he was holding onto half a raw potato as if his life depended on it. I didn't think he was going to give up the rest of the sack without a fight to the death either. And, as he looked even more emaciated than he had two nights previously, it's possible that his life did depend on it.

There was nothing else I could do. I turned to Cook. "Is there still stew in the pot from the evening's meal?"

"Yes, sir."

"Dish up a bowl of it—and a chunk of bread and some coffee. And bring it to our guest in the mess hall. And, Private Green," I said, turning to the assistant cook, "See if you can rustle up some civilian clothes that will fit this young man. Put them in my room."

I went into the storage room and bent down, and pulled the young man up to his feet. He was as light as a feather. "*Kommen Sie mit mir, bitte,*" I said, hoping my tortured German was understandable. "*Sie mussen essen.*" I'd endeavored to tell him to come with me—that he needed to eat something. I meant he needed to eat something more balanced in nutrition than raw potatoes, but I couldn't manage to say that in German. I could only hope that he'd understood what I had tried to tell him in my inadequate German.

He looked at me with glazed eyes, but he allowed me to guide him into the now-empty mess hall. He was still clutching the sack of potatoes under his arm and I made no move to take it away from him.

After he'd polished off the second bowl of stew and I motioned that any more would probably make him sick and he'd lose it all, I attempted to communicate with him again, wanting to ask him how he was managing to get into the camp and to explain to him how dangerous this was for him. "*Konnen Sie sagen mir*—?"

"Perhaps we should speak English," he suddenly said. "I appreciate your attempts at German, but . . ."

I was too shocked to speak in any language for a few seconds. "You speak English. And I mean English English, and your accent is impeccable."

"Thank you. I have lived in both London and Paris."

This just made it all the more tragic for me. He was educated and spoke with a refined accent. And he'd been brought this low.

"What are you doing here then? And are you English?" I was grasping at anything that would justify me breaking so many regulations by feeding him.

"I'm German. I was painting abroad when the war started. But I had to come back . . . for my family."

Ah, I was right. An artist. He was a painter. "And did you find your family?"

"No," he said softly. "I'm Jewish. My family was gone by the time I returned."

"Oh. My name is Trent. Yours is—?"

"You can call me Jake. But I see that you are a captain. So I must call you captain."

"OK, then, Jake. You can call me Captain Carter. I've asked that some cleaner clothes be found for you and you can come back to my room. I have a bath. You can shower there. I take it where you live doesn't have washing facilities?" Of course I wanted him to tell me where he lived and how he was able to get in the camp without being seen by a sentry—and possibly shot.

"I couldn't possibly . . . but thank you for the meal. I should go now."

We both rose from the table. "Are you going to leave that sack of potatoes here?" I asked. And when he looked lovingly at it, I said, "You can have the potatoes, Jake. But you have to stop coming into the camp. We are supposed to shoot anyone who does that."

"Being shot is not the worst thing that can happen here in this time," he said simply, his eyes downcast. But he picked up the sack of potatoes.

"Winter is going to be bad here," I said. "We should only be here for another month or so, but if you promise not to come into camp to go through the trashcans again—and if you don't tell others of it—I will see to it that you can have some food left for you every evening."

He stood there stolidly, with down-cast eyes, although I discerned a slight tremble in his body that might have be caused by emotion. I was struck with how beautiful he was, even in this condition, and my body was stirring.

"The food must be left outside the camp, though. Do you know of the track up the mountain from here, and the religious shrine about a 100 yards beyond the main gate at the side of the road—the one with a closed wooden container at its base?"

He merely nodded.

"You will find food there for as long as we're camped here."

I told myself I wasn't doing this because he moved me to desire—and certainly not because he was German—but because he was Jewish and had been in freedom and had returned despite the danger to find his family. And because he hadn't found them. The war in Europe was over now—justice and humanity needed to be brought back into the world. Even if only in small ways at the beginning.

"But I have a condition for leaving you food periodically."

"What?"

"You must get cleaned up tonight and take a new set of clothes. Those are in tatters."

When he had showered in the bathroom attached to my room—having my own facilities being the privilege of rank and command even if my unit was a small one—he padded out into my room in the nude. His body was perfectly formed and even as thin as he'd become, he retained muscle tone. He was beautifully equipped.

"Are you going to take me to your bed now?" he asked simply, in a low voice, his eyes, with the long, curly dark eyelashes fluttering.

"Excuse me?" I said. I had taken an overcoat I had replaced out of a closet, and I held it between him and me defensively, wondering wildly how he'd know that I'd developed a hard on from the knowledge that he was naked, in my shower.

"I saw you the other night, with the young man, in the forest. I saw that you made sex with men. If you want me clean, it must be because you wish to use me. You may do so. I will lie under you. I am sorry that I am too thin to be desirable now, but you are being kind to me, and—"

"No, please. That's not necessary," I said, embarrassed—embarrassed mostly because all the time he'd been in the shower I'd been fantasizing about fucking him, thoughts that only ran rampant when he came into the room naked. "I assure you that I have no designs on you. Just put on these clothes and go, please. I'll have someone escort you to the main gate. And take the food from the shrine; don't try coming in to go through the trash. You may be shot for trying."

"I am sorry if I have presumed—or if I have displeased you," he said with downcast eyes.

"Not at all," I answered. "I would not dream of taking advantage of you, though."

"It would not be taking advantage," he murmured. "I do lie under men. And I have seen that you cover men."

This was my opening, but I was too shocked and obsessed with my responsibility to answer. And not having responded at once became the answer.

139

"It's not that I don't . . ." I couldn't complete that thought. "You should dress and go."

I stood, quaking, after he'd left. I wanted him even more now than I had before he'd offered himself to me and I had turned him away. It was only after he'd gone that I considered that what I'd told him meant that, under other circumstances, I would want to fuck him.

I hadn't done what I had for him to get my cock inside him. Surely I hadn't. I didn't want to believe that this might have been a motive, even subconsciously. I wasn't that much of a using predator. Thinking on that made me think beyond that. All that time walking from Italy to here. I was in command. I fucked what, five or six of my men regularly. Was that because they wanted it as much as I did? Had I been fooling myself? Taking advantage of my position. Surely the army would see it that way.

It snowed steadily although lightly for the next two days, accumulating maybe three inches of snow, but promising a blizzard in the not-too-far-distant future. I was under the covers—a pile of covers—reaching "warm" for the first time that day in this indifferently constructed group of temporary camp buildings. I was nearly asleep, when I felt the draft of the covers being raised and a body slipping in under the covers.

Earlier, Corporal Hart—Ted—had been with me in my bed. We had writhed against each other on top of the sheets, as we often did, not being able to be satiated enough with the touch, and smell, and taste of each other but generating all of the heat from each other that was needed for that time.

As was also often the case, I had speared him in a side split and moved in and out of him deeply until he was putty in my embrace—relaxed and completely open so that he took me to the root, murmuring his surrender to me. I turned onto my back, pulling him with me so that he was full length on top of me, both of us bending our legs so that we could get leverage off the surface of the bed with the balls or heels of our feet for me to thrust up into him and him to rear back into my pelvis to meet the thrusts.

I embraced his chest with one arm, latched onto the lobe of an ear with my teeth, and fisted and jacked off his cock as I pounded his ass. We came almost simultaneously, Ted first

140

spouting toward the ceiling and splashing on his belly and chest, and me creaming his channel deep.

As we lay there, panting, the cold of the room crept in to push away the heat of our sex, and, reluctantly, he said, he left me.

I hadn't called for Ted to attend me; he had come to me on his own in the night. I had felt so guilty about the possibility that the men I fucked only allowed me to do so because of my rank that I hadn't been with any of them for two days. Concerned when yet another body burrowed under the covers with me several minutes after the corporal had left my bed, I moved my hand toward the nightstand where I had laced my service revolver, but a hand gripped my wrist.

"Please, Captain Carter, you said I'd only be shot for entering the camp again if I was going through the trashcans. I came for you, not the trash. I meant what I said when I said it wouldn't be taking advantage."

"I told you . . . you don't need to—" I didn't finish that sentence as I was overtaken by a moan as the mouth of the young German who had told me to call him Jake found and enveloped my cock.

When he had subdued me into an irrevocable want of him, which didn't take long, he lifted his head and said, "Although I am grateful, I'm not here because of that; I'm here because I want you inside me. I have lusted for you since I watched you fuck that young soldier against the tree—and then again just now, as I watched you two through your window. I want your cock. I want what you gave that young soldier just now." He slid his lips over my cock again and, with a sigh, I gave in to his ministrations.

With me on my back, he rode my cock for what seemed to be hours. We lay and murmured to each other as we rested between fuckings.

"You do this like a pro," I whispered. "I thought you said you had a family here you'd come back for. I had assumed a wife . . . and children."

"One does what one has to to survive in wartime. All I had for the last year that was marketable was what the guards of the führer's winter house craved. I acquired, first an expertise and then a taste, and then a need for it myself. Yes, I

141

had a wife and children," he answered. "I think of you as having a wife and children too back in your country. You do have a family, don't you?"

"Yes," I admitted, "I do."

"It's the war. It's the same for both of us, I think. It's just the war. A man has his needs, no matter the circumstances he finds himself in."

"Yes, it's just the war," I answered, as he brought his face down to mine for a kiss. But it wasn't just the war. Not with this man. It was more than that. I couldn't fool myself about that. "We'll be leaving in four more weeks," I said, not knowing why I'd brought it up. But, in fact, knowing why. And then, many minutes later, when the panting and rhythm of the fuck had abated into a mutual flow and we were lying there, recovering, knowing we weren't done, only taking a rest to recover, I whispered, "I will miss these mountains." I couldn't tell him what I'd now discovered I'd really miss.

"You don't have mountains where you come from?"

"Yes," I answered, with a laugh. "I come from the Rocky Mountains, running down the middle of America."

"I've heard about those. Like our alps, but not as tall."

"Yes. I'll miss the tallness of these mountains."

"And I'll miss the longness and thickness of you—the vigor and musky scent of you," he said, after a hesitation. "But we'll have these four weeks, if you'll let me come again."

"Yes, we'll have these four weeks. But then we'll be gone and it will be the middle of the winter. There'll be no more food to put out for you."

"There wasn't food before you came. Afterward I don't think it will be the food I miss from your going."

We fucked again then, tenderly, me holding him under me on his belly, and languidly mining his ass passage.

He thought I was asleep when he slipped out of the bed, dressed, and left. But I wasn't. I still needed to learn how he was getting into the camp past the fences and guards. I quickly pulled on my fatigues and followed him at a distance, aided by watching for his tracks in the recently fallen snow. I followed his footsteps up to the base of the Kehlstein Mountain towering over the camp to the south, but then lost the track where the rock started. Still, it all looked like a sheer rock wall to me. That's why we hadn't bothered to fence it in.

Three weeks and five visits from him later, I discovered where he went and how he got there. I managed that by staking out the shrine where the food was left for him and following him from there. His trek took him up a rocky incline at the base of the Kehlstein and then descending by a circuitous channel with rock walls on each side into the back of the camp. Another, nearly invisible, crevice in the rock was accessible by moving sideways. This passage opened up and ascended the mountainside to a glade of trees. A shack close to collapse was hidden in the trees.

I stood at the door as he mussed with the food over a small table, turned away from me so that he didn't see me for the longest time. The room contained the table, a rickety straight chair, and a cot. The rest of the room was taken up with painting supplies. An unfinished oil painting sat on an easel.

The painting was of the nearby Zugspitz, the tallest mountain in the German Alps. The mountain commanded the distance. Nearly centered in the foreground was a ravine leading down toward the base of the mountain, with its walls rising on either side of the canvas. Mist enveloped the floor of the ravine. On the left, rising out of a rock outcropping on the side of the ravine, roots clinging to hard-won crevices in the rock, was a lone pine tree. The branches of the tree were nearly barren, although there was a hint that it was still fighting for life even though its only grounding was solid rock.

Although the painting obviously was of the Zugspitz, upon closer inspection, I knew the painting really was about that lone pine, clinging to the last vestiges of life by tenacious and hopeful roots buried in the crevices of hard, unforgiving rock. The mountain of the painting reminded me so much of the mountain rising above my family ranch in Colorado that it choked me up and I briefly entertained the thought that he'd been to the Rockies. That must have made an audible sound, as Jake turned in surprise.

I expected him to be angry. I had ferreted out his lair, which he obviously had wanted to keep as a secret.

He merely smiled a sad smile though, and started to undress and move to the cot, where I fucked him like the end of the world was at hand.

And for us, it was. I had to inform him that it would be too dangerous for him to visit the camp again, and that I'd now be too busy to break away to visit him here. The orders to pack out had arrived and the last week in the camp would be chaos.

He let me go with a tender kiss at the door of his shack. He said nothing about what this departure meant for him—either in the lost sex or the end to his food supply. And I said nothing either. I didn't want to think about it, and there didn't seem to be anything to say about it. But in subsequent years I was haunted by not having found some way to protect him.

The night before the transport convoy arrived to take us away for the flight home, one of my men came to my office.

"This parcel was left for you at the gate, Captain," he said.

"Who—?"

"It was a German guy, but he didn't give a name. But he's the guy who has been coming into camp at your order." The soldier knew what Jake and I had been doing, of course. All of the men probably knew. It was the greatest sign I had that my men had a high regard for me that none of them reported me.

When I unfolded the yellowed, German-language newspaper print away from the parcel, it was revealed to be the painting of the Zugspitz I'd seen on the easel in Jake's shack. It had been finished. In my melancholy at parting from Jake, the lone pine stood out of the painting even more now than it ever had done.

Regardless of what else had to be done, I left my office immediately and, after some fruitless searching, finally found the entrance of the ravine at the back of the camp that led me to the doorstep of Jake's shack. The shack was deserted. I decided that he probably was right—that good-bye was inevitable and prolonging it would only add to the grief.

Since he wasn't there, I told myself that he had gone into the town and would find shelter and sustenance there. I kept telling myself that for some time. I don't think I ever convinced myself that he'd done so, though.

Like many a soldier before me, I returned to the States, to my lucrative cattle ranch, and to my wife and two children. I fell immediately into a normal, straight life. Like so many others—the lucky ones—I was able to compartment off my war years from the home life I had gone to war to preserve. And like so many others, I wasn't quick to respond to my children's innocent questions of "What did you do in the war, Daddy?" because I had gone to war to save them from knowing what one has to do in war and the totally different person it demands you be.

It was only when I was feeling vulnerable or nostalgic that I thought back on what I had done with men during the war—and inevitably my thoughts at these times went to Jake.

I shouldn't have rewrapped the painting in the yellowed German-language newspaper print. In shipping it had clotted with what must have been still-damp paint on a hip of stone on the side of the Zugspitz and took the top layer of paint away, leaving an impression of the printing on the newspaper. For a year or more I searched for an artist who would touch the painting up for me. All of them in the Denver region and even the Los Angeles area said that the work was too fine for them to touch.

They all asked me where I'd gotten it. I, of course, was vague with my answer. After a while, considering the interest the painting evoked from other artists, I began to fear that someone would think that I had raided the art stash in Bavaria that my unit had been assigned to protect and I hid the painting away. I could not forget it, though, and each time I took it out to look at and my eyes went to the lone pine, I remembered—and I felt myself go hard. The painting kept pulling me back to it and, nearly a year later, when I had occasion to go to New York City on business, I decided to make another effort to have the damage to the painting repaired.

A prestigious gallery in New York said they had an artist who could attempt a touchup. "But I doubt that anyone can match the delicacy and tone of the original artist. You'll be able to tell the difference."

"Do the best you can," I said. "It pains me to see it like it is now. It looks wounded, and I don't want to think of it that way."

"By the way, do you have any idea what you have here?" the gallery official asked.

"Yes, it's of the Zugspitz in the German Alps. I served near there at the end of the war. It looks just like the real thing. It was given to me by a refugee, in exchange for food."

"Yes, it would look like the real thing," she said. "You have here a Jacob Gelmen painting. There's his mark down in the corner. This painting is worth a fortune, even with the flaw. Very few Gelmens survived the war, although he was the toast of London galleries when the war started. It was ironic, but the London studio where he worked and where most of his paintings were stored was bombed out by a German rocket during the London blitz."

"A famous artist?"

"Absolutely," she said. "A real tragedy. He was Jewish, you know. He was safely away in London—well, as safe as London was under rocketing conditions. But his family was in Germany. He left London to go find them long after everyone knew that would be suicide—he was Jewish, you know. Yes, I already told you that. Sometime in 1943, I think. Yes, indeed. Should you ever want to sell this, Sothbys would be delighted to handle an auction for you."

"Thank you, but I don't think I could ever bear to part with it," had been my answer. I was so choked up that I barely could get the words out. Besides the fact that if I did try to sell it, the question of how I got it when I was in charge of protecting an art stash would crop up again, there's no way I would ever give it up.

I almost didn't ask, but I couldn't bear not to. "The artist, Gelmen. Did he stop painting?"

"He must have been killed in the war when he returned to Germany," she answered. "Nothing has been reported of him since the war. This looks like the paintings of his later work. It may have been one of the last pieces he painted."

The gallery's artist did a decent job of touching the painting up—at least it was better than the mar of the paint removed by the newsprint—but the real benefit of having it retouched was that the touchup only highlighted how much finer the original artwork was.

And, even more than before, it no longer offered a "marred" focal point to take away from the centrality of that lone pine, clinging to life on its rock.

Before the end of the decade, I found an excuse to fly back to Germany—and to Bavaria—on my own. On the ruse of wanting to hike in the German Alps, I went back to Obersalzberg, being able to stay in the U.S. Army's General Walker Hotel thanks to having maintained reserve status and risen to the rank of major. I found where our camp had been, now, I was happy to see, returned to productive farmland. And I found the opening in the rock wall at the base of the Kehlstein.

I found the shack, but the roof had caved in and there was no sign that anyone had been there for years. The winter of 1945-46 had been a rough one in Germany. It was hard to conceive that Jacob Gelmen could have survived if he had remained here. I almost poked around in the ruins of the shack but decided not to, being very afraid of what I might find.

But if he had survived, there would have been no reason for him not to have resurfaced in the art world and taken his rightful place and enjoyed his international reputation.

I both didn't want to think about it and wanted to cherish the memory of the short time we'd had together—in what now was a world that was closed to me and taboo to mention to anyone.

The painting, though—and the art gallery official had shown me on the back where it had been titled as "Mountain Memory"—was mounted over the fireplace in the living room of the ranch house.

There was a fire in that section of the rambling, log-sided ranch house in 1952. The only object I was able to save in addition to getting the family out before the roof collapsed was "Mountain Memory."

I had saved from that fire all that was precious to me, though.

~

Pacific

Theater

Naval Dilemma

Dutch came first. It was a particularly busy and boisterous night in the Dick Hut, tucked in the back shadows of an alley off the Nuuanu Stream in the heart of Honolulu's red light district. The sign over the door actually said "Richard's," but that's not what everyone called it—or probably what its owner wanted it to be called. Naval ships were in harbor, more than ninety of them, I was told, and all of Oahu was abuzz at the rumblings of war, with the Japs getting more belligerent with each passing day. All the sailors could talk about was how we were on the brink of something big.

As the night wore on and the drinks flowed and sailors overflowed our little bar, it was getting a little dicey for me. Hung Lee, the bar's proprietor and my virtual owner, as well, kept a string of young Hawaiian men like me in the bar for when the sailors wanted something more exotic, smaller, more lithe and compact—and more undressed—than each other when they poured off their docked vessels, randy, needy, and with a month's pay in the back pockets of their regulation tight whites. Our main responsibility was to keep the men in the bar and paying for drinks. Inevitably, though, we left the bar with one or more of the men and took them to our small rooms in the upper floors of surrounding buildings. This was where the real money was, and Hung Lee let us keep a third of whatever we earned.

I had already left the bar once that night—with a blond, pimply young sailor of no more than nineteen, who was shy and embarrassed and didn't know for sure what to do. All he knew was that he was far from home, he was lonely and a bit scared, and he had had a raging hard on for weeks because he was missing poking some sweetie back in Ohio on the mainland.

I took him to my rooms mostly because he was being circled by the older, much more experienced and aggressive sailors, and I knew from experience that he was in danger of having something far different happen to him than what he had hesitatingly come into this bar for.

When we got to my small two-room working and living space, he didn't seem to know what to do, where to start. So I started for him. I untied and dropped my sarong, the only thing I wore at the bar, and directed him to disrobe, which he did almost furtively in the corner of the room and turned from me. Then I laid him on his belly on my single bed, the most sturdy piece of furniture in the room—out of professional necessity— and I rubbed his shoulders and back with fragrant oil, loosening up both his tension and his inhibitions. He was grinding the bed clothes with his pelvis by the time I had finished with his legs and had moved to his well-rounded butt cheeks. He was sighing and moaning like he was in the heights of sex, but then I turned him over and my hands and mouth showed him what real sex felt like. It had been some time since he'd had sex, so he shot off quickly and prodigiously almost as soon as I sank my mouth down on his throbbing cock.

And then he was very embarrassed and was stammering and was quite beside himself with apologies. I felt sorry for him and didn't want him to leave with a bad impression of how he would be with a man, so I shushed him and covered his mouth with kisses until he subsided back on the bed with a sigh. He was young and virile and in need, so he was already hard again. I mounted him and slid my hole down on his cock, straddling his pelvis as he lay back in the bed, and I taught him that all he had heard on shipboard of what a man could give him was true.

I was late in getting back to the bar because I had instilled such confidence in the young sailor that instead of leaving when I thought we were done, he bent me over the back of a straight chair and took control of a vigorous second fuck, covering me closely from behind. I cried out in the taking for him, telling him how good he was and how fully he was using me and how much I wanted him—all to help him get seasoned in this new lifestyle he was trying out.

When he asked me how much I wanted, I asked for far more than my usual fee. And I did so to be kind to him. I didn't want to leave him with a great deal of money to spend. I wanted him to go directly back to his ship from here, not return to the bar where the predators were circling the waters. I told him that if he just kept his eyes open for the possibilities, that he should be able to find a special friend on the ship who would bottom for him with more opportunities for encounters and less of a risk of falling in with those who would want to use him for their bottom until he was more seasoned.

When I returned to the Dick Hut, Hung Lee was beside himself with anger and slapped me hard across the face and pushed me into the thick of the boisterous, rutting crowd of sailors. There were entirely too many ships in Pearl Harbor, too many sailors free in Honolulu. Too much testosterone flying around the red light district. Too much tension in the air. Too much frantic need with an eye on the curfew time.

And there were very few of us bar boys to go around. We were easy to spot in a swirling crowd like this. We wore only gaily colored sarongs knotted at our waists, hanging low on our slim hips. We were barefoot and bare chested and had orchids over our ears. We left the impression that all a sailor had to do was to pull loose that knot and we'd be accessible and ready for action.

The sailors, however, were heavily regulated to remain in their starched white uniforms, with the tight midsections and bell bottoms and the pullover top. The Navy didn't care too much what they did on port leave as long as they remained squared away in their sailor costumes while in public. The only saving grace was that they still had buttoned codpieces for easy access when they needed to piss. It, of course, provided easy access for other things as well. Thus encumbered, the sailors, in their urgency, gravitated more to the half naked, willowy and exotic Hawaiian and Chinese bar boys than to each other.

And there were few even vaguely private places for the sailors to go together. Hung Lee had a back room, but it was quickly filled—at a premium price. As were the surrounding alleys, even if they were free, if you didn't count the danger of

151

being accosted by a roving military police patrol. The sounds of grunts and groans and slurping floated above the whole backstreet and its allies, as white-uniform dressed sailors gravitated to whatever unoccupied shadow could be found to kneel and suck or cover and dog fuck.

It was late enough in the evening, and there were so many sailors in the bar that most of the rest of the bar boys were off in the rooms over the bars, servicing the highest bidders. Hung Lee thought I'd spent entirely too long with the pimply blond, although he was less angry when I showed him how much money I'd gotten out the bumbling sailor. He, of course, took the money for safekeeping, which was just as well, because some sailor would have gotten it away from me otherwise.

I was no sooner back in the center of the barroom before the situation got out of control. I was surrounded by a sea of white and of lust-filled faces. A sailor was close behind me, lacing his arms under my pits, immobilizing my arms, and lifting my feet off the ground. A drunken buddy of his had a fist at my knot, pulling at it, and my sarong drifted down to the floor.

He was leering at me and unbuttoning his codpiece fly and pulling out a hardened cock.

Sailors were surrounding us, coming in close, licking their chops, and a rhythmic chant of "Fuck him, fuck him, fuck him" was swelling.

Hung Lee had gone up on the bar top and, red faced, was bellowing at the top of his lungs, yelling that he needed to be paid first and that this wasn't allowed in the barroom, that the military police would be along at any minute and shut them down.

I wasn't scared of the sailor's cock or even what he intended to do with it. But I was apprehensive about the ten sailors who might follow him and about the mob conditions in general and that I might be gravely hurt in the process.

The sailor in front of me was lifting and parting my legs and was crouching his hips under me and between my legs. My feet already were off the ground. Most of these sailors towered over me, all of them were bulked up and at least twice my size.

I winced and flinched as the cock head found my hole and just pressed inside and pushed higher and higher into me. The mob was crowding in closer and cheering at the initial invasion and picking up the "Fuck him, fuck him" chanting.

My assailant was sweating and smelled of too much beer. His cock wasn't thick, but it was long enough that he was rising up further in me with each thrust. He certainly was longer and more insistent and demanding than the young, inexperienced sailor I'd just serviced had been. He was palming my butt cheeks and leveraging on them to pull me up and down on his cock. His teeth went to one of my nipples, and I screamed out in pain at that. And the crowd cheered.

The crowd noise swelled and then inexplicably tapered off, and my tormentor had pulled his cock out of me and I was being lowered, more gently than I imagined was going to be the case, down to the floor. The grip of the man behind me lessened, and he was trembling. But he didn't drop me.

I looked up to see the gigantic, broken nose of an angry-faced head pushing its way through the crowd. The mouth was open, showing uneven, broken teeth; it was bellowing at a level that demanded attention. A monster of a man in sailor whites was cutting through the mob that had surrounded me, and the men were shrinking away from him. Those who didn't give way fast enough were being swatted into the men behind them, all struggling hard not to go down like bowling pens. The man mountain was virtually bulging with muscle. His torso was thick, but not fat, and the material of his sailor bell bottoms were straining to hold in his massive thigh and calf muscles. He was a good foot taller than any other man in the room. And he was ugly as sin.

But he had saved me and had quieted the crowd into docile and skittish sailors instantaneously. The two men who were my principle assailants melted into the crowd, and the mob somehow largely evaporated from the bar.

The man leaned down and lifted my sarong from the floor and held it out for me.

"Are you OK?" he asked.

"Yes, now," I replied, "Thanks to you, of course." He looked away, almost bashfully, while I reknotted my sarong low on my waist. I was trembling, but I fought to regain control. Just another night at work.

"May I buy you a drink?" he asked, diffidently, almost in a whisper. He still wasn't looking at me.

"Yes, of course. At the bar." This was what I was here for—to push drinks for lonely sailors. I looked over at the bar. Hung Lee was behind it now. I could tell that he was still half in shock, his whole future having passed before his eyes. I'm sure he figured he came close to having the bar closed down by the naval authorities because a riot had occurred here. And there was no question in my mind that he'd blame me. I'd have to walk very carefully until he forgot this incident.

We bellied up to the bar. I ordered a gin and tonic (which, of course, would come with no more than a hint of gin), and the sailor ordered a Coke. Anybody else in here who ordered a nonalcoholic drink would have been jeered out of the place. But I was pretty sure that no one messed with this monster of a man.

I discovered the source of his almost obscene bulk. He was a boilerman on the battleship the USS *West Virginia*, which was docked at Pearl Harbor. His was perhaps the dirtiest and most muscle taxing—and developing—job on the whole ship. His name was Dutch, which he seemed anxious for me to know. He seemed to want me to know more than that he was just in this bar to find some man to fuck—or be fucked by.

"And your name?" he asked quietly as we worked on our drinks. As required, I quickly downed my first one and was already on my second one, all on the sailor's tab, of course. He had saved me, so I felt badly about doing this, but Hung Lee was right there, watching my every step, and the sailor didn't seem to mind.

"'Ano'i," I answered.

"'Ano'i, 'Ano'i," he repeated, almost in a whisper, treating each syllable like velvet. "What a beautiful name. Is it Hawaiian?"

"Yes," I answered. "I'm Hawaiian. Well, mostly. A little Chinese blood, of course, and I'm told there's a Presbyterian missionary or two from the mainland in there too. We're all a mix of something here."

"And it turned out real good, too," He said, giving me a smile that was almost pathetic as ugly as he was. I almost felt like laughing. It seemed like he was courting me. Here in a bar, where I got paid to lie on my back and open my legs, no real pleasantries exchanged.

"Thank you," I said. Then. "And thank you again for what you did over there; I would have been in a lot of trouble if something had happened to get the bar closed down tonight. Now, I guess I should—" I was standing up, ready to mingle with the much smaller crowd in the room in the wake of the excitement.

"No, please. Can't you stay a bit longer?" he asked, his eyes pleading with me. "I have money; I can pay for the drinks. Barkeep, another round over here, please."

I looked at Hung Lee for a sign of what I should do. But he was being inscrutable. I knew he'd want me to jolly up the men around the tables and get them to drink faster to cool down their hard ons as I flirted with them. But it also was obvious that Hung Lee realized that it was only Dutch's presence that was maintaining calm on this unusually crowded night. A night full of tense talk of what was happening, why so many ships were in harbor, what were the Japs up to?

"'Ano'i," Dutch said again, almost in loving tones. "A beautiful name. Does it have a meaning?"

"Yes," I answered. "It means desired. And it can be either a boy's or a girl's name. They often use that name when—"

"I know what it means to me," Dutch said in a low, hoarse voice, cutting me off in midsentence. "It's the right name for you."

I didn't respond. I just let that hang there. He was ugly and maybe three times bigger than I was, and it frightened me a bit to think that he was that proportionally big everywhere. And his hulking strength. He could smother me or break me in two in his excitement and lust. An uneducated sailor, a boilerman working in the bowels of a battleship. He might be cruel and rough and incapable of holding himself back at the height of passion. But he had saved me from possible harm, had saved the bar from maybe being closed down when there was so much profit to be made.

155

"Can we . . . could we . . . would you . . .? I have money; enough money." he was struggling to get the proposition out. But he wasn't looking at me. He was ugly as sin and frightfully big. He didn't need to be told that. He lived that.

I looked at Hung Lee, who nodded slightly. Not really an acquiescence as much as a command.

"Yes, yes. of course," and then an "I would like that." Ever mindful of the role I played in the fantasies that were mine to weave for the money. "I have rooms across the street. We can go there. Now, if you'd like."

* * * *

He perched precariously, straddling one of my straight chairs reversed, his massively muscled arms folded over the back, resting his bulging chest against the slats, as I stood by the bed and unloosened the sarong and let it slide to the floor in swirls around my ankles. I had no idea how much of me he had seen in the gang banging attempt earlier in the bar, but his eyes at first went wide and then slitted when he saw me fully unclothed, and I heard his intake of breath.

He just looked at me for the longest time, and then he stood up from the chair. "I think I'd better go," he said. But I could hear the regret in his voice. I knew what the problem was. I thought I wouldn't be able to take him.

"It's OK, really," I said. "I can do it."

I could see the conflict in him, but I could also see that the lust would win. After several seconds of indecision, he said, "If you're sure."

"Yes, I sure. It's what I want."

He slowly stripped off his navy whites. It was my turn to take breath in when he was done. His muscling was inhumanely bulky, but all in proportion, and his cock, as I had feared, was enough for three men, not too abnormally long as it stood straight out from his thick thatch of reddish pubic hair but as thick as a normal man's wrist. I had never taken anything that thick. And his balls hung low and were the size of lemons. I hadn't the slightest doubt that they could provide semen to flow for hours.

156

He was holding back, unsure still whether I would want to continue after having seen him. But I lifted my arms in a welcoming, gathering gesture, and, with a sob, he moved to me, picked me up, gently and almost lovingly in his arms, and his mouth went to mine.

I closed my eyes, not least to close out the ugliness of his face. I wasn't resentful, but I wanted him to think my body would respond to him, and I was afraid that the ugliness of him would freeze my desires. But I need not have had any fears about that, because his kiss was soft and tender, and sweet tasting. I couldn't get enough of the taste of him, and sensing that, he tentatively darted his tongue into my mouth, and then when I sighed to that, he probed deeper, yet still tenderly. And all the while we were kissing, his gigantic hands were moving on my body, with tenderness and skill belying the clumsiness that would have been expected of him, knowing just what to do to make me melt.

It was obvious that he knew what he was doing. He probably got what he wanted on his ship. There were men who would go after the challenge of him.

When we broke from the kiss, I murmured "Oh god, take me, fuck me." It was a line I instinctively used to get sailors to get on with it so I could get back to the bar. But I wasn't at all sure that was what I meant now, in this instance.

I could feel him shudder at that. He was still holding me in his arms. But I could tell I had broken through the ice. He knew now that I would accept him.

"Yes, yes, in time . . . if we can manage. That's not always possible," he said in a low, hoarse voice. "But first I want to make love to you. You are so lovely. There are no men on my ship as small and as perfectly formed as you are."

I knew that the only thing that was making his hesitate was the size difference, the question of whether I could sheath him without damage.

He laid me gently down on the bed, on my back and sat down on the side of the bed next to my waist. "Do you have . . .?" he started to ask with hesitation.

"Sheaths? Yes, there, in the nightstand drawer."

"No, not that . . . and I've brought my own. I don't think yours would—"

157

No, probably not, I thought. And then a chill went up my spine at the full realization of what was to come. How monstrously thick he was. He had been thinking of my welfare more than I was.

"I meant oil. I would like to give you a massage. I am longing to feel your curves and crevices."

"Oh, that's in the nightstand as well. And . . . well . . . it can be used for—"

"Yes, that's good," he broke in.

He was a divine masseur. He worked all of my muscles so lovingly and deeply and sensually that I was purring and getting close to dozing off when he gently turned me over. And the sensuality of what he was doing was so strong that I was fully engorged when he turned me. He worked my neck and chest and arm muscles and moved down from my chest to my pubic fringe and then up from my legs to under my ball sac.

And while he was working me, I was gliding my hands over any part of him I could reach. When I could reach his cock, he poured oil on my hand and I stroked him. I couldn't get my fist around what he had so that my fingertips would meet. And it was hard as a rock and was throbbing. I knew it wouldn't be long now before I was put to the test. He was sighing and groaning. With my eyes closed, I could completely blot out that he was a ogre of a man, in both bulk and visage.

I must have drifted off to a purring sleep, because I came back to full consciousness with a warm, moist, fully encasing sensation in my cock, which was completely sheathed in Dutch's mouth. Then I realized my channel was being filled as well—as fully as most men could with their cocks. Dutch was working on opening me to him with oil and his huge thumb.

His thumb had found and was stroking my prostate, and, with a flinch and a lurch, I exploded into his encasing throat. I murmured my appreciation and the extreme pleasure he had brought me in his sensitive and prolonged preparation.

But we weren't very far along in the preparation at all yet. Now it was time for Dutch's pleasure.

He turned me in the bed to where my butt was on the edge. He pulled over the straight chair and sat there. Placing two pillow under the small of my back, he took my calves in his big fists and gently pulled my legs apart and folded them up and made me dig my heels in the wooden side piece of the bed.

Then, using large quantities of the oil, he began to open me up. His thumb was replaced with his middle finger, which was as long and as thick as many of my men's cocks. He gently fucked me with this, in and out and around, opening me slowly. This wasn't so bad, and neither was it that difficult when he added his index finger. I began to pant and arch my back, though, when the third finger went it. He fisted my cock with his other hand and stroked me to another ejaculation to take my mind off the opening of my hole to his needs.

Not long before I spouted off, I felt I couldn't wait any longer. "Fuck me!" I cried. "Take me now! Fuck me. And no rubber. I'm clean. I want you to drown my insides! Now!" And it was true. I was doused regularly because some sailors just wouldn't wait. And I'd yet to have a problem. Hung Lee was Chinese. They knew what to do.

"Sorry, Not yet, I can't yet," he croaked, my begging for him affecting him deeply, almost choking him up to where he couldn't speak. The three fingers inside me were quaking with excitement and anticipation. "I don't want to ruin you, and I'm afraid once I've started I won't be able to stop."

As I shot off, the fourth finger went in, the fingers cupped and gently pressing out, stretching me, if ever so slowly. I writhed under the invasion, moving my pelvis back and forth, trying to help stretch my channel. My fingernails clawing at the bed spread.

"And are you sure about the rubber? I don't want—"

"Yes, I'm sure." I spat out between clinched teeth. "Skin on skin. I want to feel that thick pulsing vein under your cock. Directly on your cock. My muscles moving on your cock, making love to your cock. Pulling you into me, being flooded by you. Deep, deep inside. NOW!"

That did it, With a sob, Dutch rose up off the chair and crouched between my legs, and I felt the gigantic bulb of his cock head at my hole, between his cupped fingers inside me. As the fingers withdrew, his cock head tried to push in, slowly and as gently as he could, but I had him worked up to the limit now and his legs were shaking.

I arched up to him and reached down and grabbed at the root of his cock and held it steady and tried to draw his dick into me, willing the cock head to breech the sphincter. We were both panting and groaning. With a plopping sound, the cock head was past the entrance, and he was inside me.

I screamed and flopped back onto the bed, arching my back up then, though, and clawing at the bed spread with my hands, taking up great globs of material in my fists. Panting hard and groaning and grunting at the strain.

"I can stop. Tell me to stop," Dutch cried out.

"Don't you dare," I yelled back. "All the way. Fuck me. Stretch me. Ah, I can feel the vein! Oh, Shitttttt!"

And then I was taking all of him. He had prepared me well. He was sliding up inside me and my muscles were making love to his cock, undulating around his huge cylinder, inviting him in, wanting him to force himself all the way in.

We didn't say anything for a half hour or more. We were concentrating on giving and taking as much as each of us could. When he had bottomed out and was sure that I could handle him, Dutch bent down to me and we kissed. He buried his face in the hollow of my neck and kissed me deeply and gently bit me there. His mouth went to my pits, as I raised my arms, one after the other, and he licked and kissed and nipped me there. Then he worked his mouth down my torso as far as he could go, giving loving attention to my nipples.

He was pumping me. Slowly, but deeply. Alternating rhythms so I was never sure whether he was going shallow or deep, whether he was going straight or corkscrewing me. Holding me on the edge; taking me over the edge again and again. Both giving and taking a full measure of pleasure.

He nipped a nipple, and I ejaculated again, up his hard belly.

He picked me up with hands on my waist and turned and sat on the bed. My torso arched back and he crouched up off the bed and fucked down into me. Then he stood, still a bit crouched, with me suspended below him, my hands leveraging off the floor, my legs wrapped around his upper thighs, his hands holding my thighs, as he fucked down into me deeper and I met his thrusts with thrusts of my own, pushing off from the floor with my quaking hands.

With a cry of ecstatic passion, he fountained off down into me and then filled me and filled me and filled me, great flowings of semen burbling up around his cock and out the sides of my hole. Flowing for more than a minute. Emptying those lemon-sized balls inside me.

We lay on the bed panting, time in suspension while I reveled in hearing his ragged breathing of fulfilled passion, my back enfolded into the bulging muscles of his torso. When he entered me this time, I required no extra preparation and we needed no oil. His strokes were long and deep and slow and melting, and the flow of his semen was enough to lubricate us. I nestled my butt back into his pelvis, and he lifted my leg for greater access and gently fucked me to an exhausted sleep, his massive calloused fingers gently rubbing my nipples. All the time him whispering in my ear how good I was to him, me knowing that, rather, it was he who was giving me the stretched and sustained loving I hadn't had for several years. The thickness of that cock alone something that few had known and been able to take. Me only taking it because of the patience of his preparation.

I didn't wake until morning. He'd left enough money on the table to shut off any complaining Hung Lee might have done because I didn't come back to the bar the previous evening.

Dutch was a regular customer during the next couple of weeks. And I never again needed the preparation to take him that I did that first time. But I always felt stretched to the limit, fully taken.

We had to be careful how we fucked; if Dutch moved to a position on top of me, there was a danger I would be crushed. There was always the fear that he would lose control. Many men were afraid of his bulk and the size of his cock, and when he came to me he was full of need and aching with semen. But he never did fully lose control; he always let me determine when we should stop to allow me time to open to him. It was only while he was in those long moments of miraculously long flows of semen at the height of passion that he would stroke hard and deep and fast. And by that moment, he had worked me so expertly that these were the most pleasurable moments for me as well.

He visited me every three days, and the men in the bar grew to know that when he entered the door, they were to move away from me. He couldn't get enough of me; he worshipped me. I invariably started by oiling his awesome muscles, hard and as beautifully cut as marble. I tried to give him suck, but I could hardly get more than the bulb of his engorged cock in my mouth. The rumbling groans of pleasure from him were well worth the effort, though.

Usually we would start with me sitting in his lap, facing him, my wrists locked behind his neck, my lips on his jutting nipples, while he stretched me open with oiled fingers. I loved the feel of his pulsating cock pressing against my belly. Then, when I felt I was open enough, I'd rise on my straddling knees and either slowly impale my channel on his tool while facing him and kissing that ugly face of his or turn away from him, arched forward with his big mitts on my pecs, and lower my butt cheeks into his pubic bush. One glorious afternoon, he corkscrewed me, revolving me around and around on his lap as he sank farther and farther into me. In an equally melting, but not so advisable, fuck, he leveraged his back against the wall, crouching down to provide a perch for me on his thighs, and he lap fucked me, moving me up and down on his tool with strong hands at my waist—but the whole building shook when we got lost in passion, so we only did that the once. Invariably we ended stretched on the bed, me folded into his belly, and he side splitting me languidly until we both drifted into sleep. He would be sighing, and I would be thrilled that I had given him satisfaction.

I was awed at the thought of how an ugly sailor like that, only a boilerman on a battleship, could have learned to be such a gentle and expert lover. And a lover he was becoming. All of the rest of the men in my life for the previous three years had been quick-fuck marks—or a young sailor I fancied or pitied. But what I had for Dutch was very close to love. It certainly was love for him. And he told me so. And within two weeks of our first lovemaking, he was telling me that he wanted to take me from the Dick Hut and set me up in an apartment in a safer, less seedy neighborhood and have me for his own. That he wanted us to be life partners.

It pulled at my heartstrings. I'd been taught to avoid this. I knew what could and couldn't be. I knew that I would never be destined for that. But now I had received the offer. And within a week, I'd received another. And that was when the naval dilemma set in.

His name was Richard Randolph, and he made a point of never separating those names. They always went together. I gathered that the Randolph was supposed to mean something. Maybe it did, on the mainland, on the East Coast where he made clear his family was from. He was a lieutenant, serving on the light cruiser, the USS *Raleigh*.

He was all spit and polish, well groomed, extremely well turned out, his body obviously his temple. He marched into Dick Hut one Thursday afternoon, when business was light. He gave the distinct impression that he wouldn't come in such a place at night when the enlisted sailors held sway.

He marched right up to Hung Lee, who was at the bar supervising the Barkeep's cleaning of glasses. I and the other bar boys were milking the few afternoon drunks that we could—mostly civilians, because few of the Navy men were given leave from their ships in the middle of the day.

The lieutenant, standing straight and tall and slim, and pristinely white in his officer's uniform, stroked his thigh with some sort of stick, a swagger stick, maybe, but it looked more like a riding crop, as he spoke to Hung Lee in low tones.

I got both interested and a little apprehensive at the same time when both Hung Lee and the lieutenant started gazing in my direction as they talked. I saw Hung Lee's eyes go wide and his mouth begin to quiver. And then his eyes slitted and he said something to the lieutenant, which caused the lieutenant to take a wallet out of his tight white uniform and slap a big wad of bills down on the counter. And then the lieutenant turned and walked over to the entrance door and stood, as if ready to take a freeing, cleansing step out into the street as soon as he could. He was looking out the door, not at anyone in the bar.

Hung Lee shuffled over to me. "This gentleman has bought you for three days, 'Ano'i," he said. "In your rooms. He says he saw you on the street and wants you and followed you back here. Don't keep him waiting."

As soon as we entered my flat, the lieutenant kicked the door shut and pushed me over to the table I ate on and pushed my chest down roughly on the wood. he held my cheek painfully to the table top with a firm hold on the back of my neck, while he unknotted my sarong with his other hand. Once my sarong was falling down my legs, he had the palm of his hand on one of my butt cheeks and then worked it over to the crack and was roughly fingering the rim of my asshole.

"Open," he said with mild surprise. "Wide open for one so small." I could tell he was pleased.

Of course it was open. Dutch had been fucking me for weeks now.

He had knelt down, and I felt his mouth and tongue at my hole. He was licking and nibbling at me. I started to rise off the table and he slapped me on the rump.

"Stay down," he said. I put my cheek and chest back down on the table, and he went back to eating me out. While he was doing that, he slapped me on both sides of the rump until I felt myself chaffing.

"Where's the lube?" he asked. I noted that he didn't ask for a rubber. I assumed this had been covered with Hung Lee when they were talking. I told him it was in the night stand, and he told me not to move until he returned.

While at the nightstand, he stripped off his uniform, neatly folded it, and put it in the center of the bed. That was the clue that we probably wouldn't be using the bed for a while. Before he came back, he glanced around the room, zeroed in on a stool without a back on it, and pushed it over into the center of the room with his foot.

Then he was back at me. Working my hole with lubricated fingers with one hand and arching my back with his fist in my hair with the other.

He pulled me off the table and propelled me over to the center of the room and pushed my belly down on top of the stool. Then he was riding me like a horse and fucking me like a dog and beating on my thighs, arms, and back with his riding crop.

He had a respectable cock, but nothing I couldn't handle. His rough fucking, however, made something other than his cock the center of our sex. Whatever he lacked in cocking, he made up for in invention and maximizing of sensation and risk-edged ecstasy.

He played me alternately like a violin and a set of drums for three days and nights. He was not unlike the sailors I usually served in his intensity and concentration on his own needs and his cruelty in the fuck. But he went way beyond those others; he took me beyond what had become numbing sameness of the act. He would still be fucking when the others would have had their immediate needs met and wanted to get back to the liquor at the bar. And he would take me far out over the edge each time. I would moan for him to slow down or stop and he would quicken his pace and go on forever—and I would find that awakened me.

He made me hard, something that had been slipping away from me in the routineness of my life at the Dick Hut, and he kept me hard. And he brought me off—repeatedly in a session. The cruelty and invasiveness was overbalanced by the height of passion he brought me to—beyond, I must admit, even what Dutch transported me to. The sailor had to be very handsome and well built and hung to make me ejaculate these days—and most had no interest in doing so. They were only there for their own temporary needs.

I was only there for the lieutenant's needs too, but his needs included having me writhing and quivering like jelly and begging for mercy while incongruously also begging for the cruel fuck and crying out in passion and release—and not pretending to do so as I normally did with the other sailors. I had come to need the cruelty and explosion over the edge that he was providing. It was sweeping the numbness of my life away.

He'd leave for meals and then return to floor me wherever I was and fuck me and prod me and slap me and beat on me with his riding crop. I'd meet him at the door and he would push me down on the floor and fuck me roughly from behind as I tried to move across the floor, wanting to escape the onslaught, but equally wanting what the lieutenant was giving me. Once as I tried to escape him, he pulled a plump, curved cucumber off the table and fucked me with that, reminding me of Dutch's cock stretching me to the limit.

I'd wake up in the middle of the night flat on my belly with the lieutenant straddling me and working his cock into my ass. Then I'd find he'd bound me to the bed and he'd roll me over and attack my mouth with his hardened tool, slapping my cheeks and tweaking my nipples.

And, amazingly I found I loved it. The quick, impersonal, missionary- or dog-style fucks I'd been trapped in for years had deadened me to passion and lust, only relieved by Dutch's gentle, filling attentions. Now I had another lover, equally melting, but entirely different. For three days and nights, I found that I myself was perpetually hard and ready to ejaculate at the lieutenant's will. I didn't know what turned me on and fulfilled me the most, the giant but sensitive boilerman or the demanding, controlling, and cruel, but inventive officer.

But it seemed I would have to make a choice. At the end of the three days, the lieutenant informed me, while I was lashed by my wrists to a hook in the ceiling and he was crouched under me and fucking up into me and flicking my belly with his riding crop, that I had pleased him.

He said nothing then, but the following Thursday night, the young, pimply sailor I had striven to save from the predators in the bar brought the situation with the lieutenant to a head.

The sailor appeared in the bar that night, the first time I had seen him since I had guided his floundering lovemaking. He looked around until he saw me. I saw several of the older sailors assessing him, so I walked quickly over to him.

"I thought I'd convinced you you didn't really need to come in here again," I whispered to him, while I latched on to his arm, as if I was flirting—an attempt to hold both Hung Lee and the sharks in the water off.

"I want to be with you again," he said in a little whining voice.

"Didn't I tell you that you could find someone on the ship to satisfy you. You fuck well. When that's known, you'll have all the bottoms you can handle."

"So far all I've found are guys willing to suck me off," he said. "I know I'll find someone, but my rocks are aching. And they're aching for you."

So, I took him to my room and let him fuck me. He took greater control than he had earlier, and I was laying on my back on the bed, my legs spread, his knees under and lifting my butt, and his cock working nicely inside me, when the lieutenant put in an unexpected appearance.

In the space of five minutes, the lieutenant had the sailor clutching his clothes and escaping the room under the flailing of his crop, and the lieutenant had transferred his anger to me in a rough, wild, and totally satisfying fuck.

Immediately after that the lieutenant told me he must own me for his own and that he'd be negotiating with Hung Lee for my contract and wanted to set me up in an apartment away from here where only he could be fucking me.

This set me back on my haunches. I melted to Dutch. I loved what he did to me and the knowledge that I could take a cock that big and that he was so gentle with me, but Richard Randolph drove me wild and made me experience ecstasy to depths that my life of opening my legs for every randy and drunken sailor who sailed by had driven out of me.

Despite what the lieutenant thought, though, he couldn't just buy up my contract from Hung Lee—at least not without my concurrence. My mother had Hung Lee by the balls; he could shove me around like he did at the bar, but he couldn't "sell" me. He didn't own me. No one would own me without my permission. But if I chose to go with Richard Randolph and the condition was that he owned me, than I would let him own me. Certainly when he was fucking me, he owned me. And owning me was part of the thrill of sex with him, the depth of sensation I hadn't felt for years—until he and Dutch entered my life.

Sundays were my off day. When I brought men back to my place on Saturday night, they left on Saturday night. Sunday I slept in and pampered myself. Or at least I did until that first Sunday in December. That Sunday I was awakened before 8:00 in the morning with the most godawful noise I'd ever heard. I tied on my sarong and ran out into the street—only to see the diving of war planes over Pearl Harbor and a cacophony of explosions. The Japs were attacking the fleet anchored in Pearl Harbor—more than ninety ships of the line, the largest part of

America's fleet. The sky was filled with Japanese Zero fighters, Kate carrier attack planes, and Val bombers.

Like everyone else, I headed up the slopes away from Pearl Harbor, my first thought being for myself.

Later, when all was over other than the salvage of the tonnage bombed to the bottom of Pearl Harbor—not sunk far, because the floor of the harbor was not too much lower than the ship's normally drew, but crippled at the minimum—I remembered my beloved Dutch and the lieutenant who touched me at my very depths and went down as close to the carnage as possible. All I could find out was that my lovers' ships, the USS *West Virginia* and the USS *Raleigh*, were among the ships that had sustained damage and that had lost a large number of crewmen in the Japanese attack.

For three days, I agonized. Men were starting to reappear at the Dick Hut, but they were there to bury themselves in drink after what they'd seen in the cleanup operations, not to pursue hookups, and none of them could tell me about either Dutch or the lieutenant. On the second day, the pimply young sailor showed up, shell shocked, and I took him up to my rooms and we made love like he'd never done before. If nothing else, I was able to push the remembrance of that brutal attack out of his mind for a couple of hours.

But he couldn't fill the needs of my life. Only either Dutch or the lieutenant—or both—could do that for me.

On the third day, within three hours of each other, I found out that both Dutch and the lieutenant were alive and recovering from superficial wounds.

That was two days ago. Now I am back to my naval dilemma. Either Dutch or the lieutenant, both of whom are only fleeting pleasures, as they now surely will be transferred away from here quickly. Or neither—the continuing of my life as relief and comfort for needy, now increasingly frightened and endangered sailors, like my young, pimply sailor.

I don't know what to do. My story doesn't end here. All I can say is that both of my lovers survived that terrible attack on Pearl Harbor. And for now, maybe that's enough.

~

Trapped

There was no transition that I could ever make myself remember. One moment I was trapped in my gunner's seat in the burning B-29B bomber just moments after the raid on Osaka, then I wasn't. Air was whistling loudly through the shrapnel holes in the fuselage, spraying me with blood from the nearly decapitated Pete in the EWO's position beside me, and I was frantically searching for the lever on the canopy over my position so that I could be anywhere but here. And the next minute I was on the deck of a yawing Japanese fishing boat, trapped between the sturdy calves of a hulky nut-brown man and looking up into the slitted eyes of the *chujen*—as Goro and Jun, who I later encountered, told me Iwao wanted to be called—the boss. Sometime between those two points I had lost my Superfortress buddies and cashed out on my service with the U.S. Air Corps in its drawn-out attempt to bring Japan to its knees and end a world war that had already concluded in the European Theater.

The man hunched over me was brandishing some sort of wooden-handled fishing spear, and my first thought after coming to in a sputter of water and vomit on the slippery deck of the vessel was that I was about to meet my bomber buddies on the other side.

I knew pretty precisely where I was. The last thing that was ringing through my mind as the Superfortress moaned and groaned in its disintegration was the pilot screaming a Mayday over the intercom and as far into the ether as he could project. We were coming down in Toska Bay on the east coast of the Japanese home island of Shikoku, having been hit by flak right after dropping our load on Osaka port and pulling up over the northeast point of Shikoku. We barely cleared the roofs of the

169

cliff-top village of Aki on Toska Bay before heading into the drink and oblivion. I must have found the lever to my canopy at the very last moment. All I knew was that I was soaking wet and bloodied and bruised and could feel groaning in very muscle and bone of my body.

I saw the Japanese fisherman stiffen and look out across the bay and, pulling together every fiber of my energy, I lifted my torso off the deck on my elbows and was barely able to see over the gunwale, my attention drawn to where the fisherman was staring. I saw the Japanese coastal naval vessel cutting across the waves out from the dock at the foot of the cliff at Aki. This would be it then. The fisherman would turn me over to the Japanese soldiers; he would then be the toast of the village, and I would be cannon fodder.

But that's not what was happening. The fisherman was nudging me with the blunt end of his spear, herding me toward a tangled web of fishing netting. He lifted it and motion for me to roll under it, which I did, and then he lowered it on me, hiding me effectively from view even as he was being hailed from the military craft.

I heard jabbering, which I came close to understanding, as I had been studying Japanese for months, trying to qualify as a radio intercept operator. I did manage to discern that they were asking the fisherman about a *bakugeki-ki*, which I knew meant bomber, and the fisherman was gesturing farther out into the bay.

I heard the naval craft motoring off, out into the bay, where they undoubtedly would find the flotsam they were looking for. My feelings were conflicted over whether I wanted them to find any of my buddies clinging to the wreckage, still alive. In this late winter of 1945, the Japanese were getting desperate, knowing now the inevitable, but through their blind devotion to their emperor, being determined to take the rest of the world down with them. In our mission briefings, we were being constantly told not to expect any quarter or regard for the Geneva Convention if we were to fall into the hands of the Japanese, especially in their home islands.

It was with this thought that I trembled and shrank away from the fisherman when he came back to me, spear still held in strong, sinewy hands. But it was only to do what he could to get across to me that I was to remain under the netting and to be very quiet.

I spent the next couple of hours until night descended cowering under the netting, mentally and physically checking my body to assess the damage there, and wondering why I was getting this reprieve—and what sort of reprieve it was. And just trying to deaden my nerves. I wasn't dead yet. By all accounts I should be dead now, but I wasn't. I was living on precious, borrowed time.

In the darkest hours of the night, the fisherman quietly steered his boat back to the docks of Aki and stealthily motioned me to follow him. Keeping to the deep shadows, he guided me around the edge of the lower village, its inhabitants tucked safely indoors behind heavy blackout curtaining that protected the fisherman and me from their gaze as much as it protected them from the waves of U.S. bombers coming across overhead in ever-shortening intervals in their campaign to pound Japan into acknowledging defeat.

The fisherman who rescued me led me up a steep and winding lichen-slippery stone pathway rising against the side of the cliff, ever upward, until all that was above us was the clear, moonlit sky. At the very edge of the cliff, set apart from the upper village by tumbles of boulders and pine trees seemingly growing out of the rock itself, was a traditional Japanese dwelling of dark wood frame, white rice-paper paneling, and a grass roof. The man led me around the side of the building to a small garden right at the edge of the cliff. Most of this space was taken up with a series of shallow pools of water that let off steam in the cold March night air. Hot springs. As we came to the corner of the building, though, the man pulled me aside into the shadows. I could see into the garden and had a full view of the springs, which were partially hidden by dense foliage, but I could not be seen from the pools.

We were no longer alone. I could hear men's voices and soft laughter. Several men were in the pools. Flagons of wine—sake—rested on the stones bordering the pools of water.

The man put his finger to his lips to signal that I was not to reveal myself, something that I had absolutely no intention of doing for as long as I could, and then, sliding a panel at the edge of the pavilion, he motioned me to slip my boots off and step up onto the tatami matting on the structure's wooden flooring. He led me through a series of chambers set off by yet more rice-paper-lined screening to the opposite side of the building from the hot springs pools. In the last chamber, he walked over to the far wall and slid the paneling away to reveal a small hidden garden, surrounded by mounds of high boulders. In the small space between the building and these boulders was another pool clouded in steam.

He motioned to me what he wanted me to do, and, understanding him, and thinking of the hot, cleansing, soothing waters of the spring, I gladly stripped down, while he stood there smiling broadly at me, and I slipped into the pool. It was deep enough for me to sit in and be covered up to my neck, and I lay back and, feeling my muscles begin to relax almost instantaneously, I drifted off into a consuming sleep.

I don't know how long I slept, but much later in the night, when darkness still fully possessed the world, I heard murmurings coming from across the room fronting on the small garden—from the next chamber beyond a papered sliding screen. I moved gingerly around to the far side of the pool, my muscles relaxed but still screaming of the indignity that had been forced upon them by the escape from the B-29. When I reached the other end of the pool and turned back toward the pavilion, I could see that lanterns had been lit in the chamber beyond, on the other side of the paper screen. In full silhouette, I could clearly discern two figures in full fuck. One figure was prone on its back on some sort of low bedding, legs spread and knees bent, with thighs and calves set in languid motion leveraging off the balls of both feet. The other figure knelt between the spread legs, torso hovering over that of the prone figure, arms propped on the floor on either side of the prone figure, and buttocks moving back and forth, slowly pumping. I could hear muted moans and sighs.

But the sounds were coming in stereo now. I looked over to the side, where the papered screen of another chamber abutted the room at the edge of the pool. Another lantern flared. A second set of figures, one belly down on a stool of some sort, and the other, arms propped stiffly on either side of the chest of the bent figure, a long, lean body at a straight incline between the first kneeling figure's legs, doing deep and slow pushup movements toward and away from the kneeling figure. The two figures were joined only by a thick rod that appeared and then disappeared inside the buttocks of the kneeling figure, which slowly writhed and shuddered as the two figures became one. More moaning and sighing.

I involuntarily took my stiffened cock in my hand and worked myself as I listened to the sounds of the taking and the increasingly frenzied silhouetted couplings in the two chambers. Exhausted, as I added bulk to the cloudy waters of the hot-springs pool, I drifted off to sleep once more. It had not been lost on me that I was being observed as well as I masturbated or that the waters weren't so cloudy that what I was doing with my hand under the water couldn't be seen by the observer. I was so keyed up from the tension of what I had experienced that day and was so sexually charged that I gave way to my own need.

On the next day, when I awoke, there were two young men in the room adjacent to the pool, just sitting there and watching me. Both were handsome and well-formed and were wearing only light cotton robes. Even though it was only late March and the frost could clearly be seen on the mosses hanging down from the boulders bordering the pool, it wasn't really cold at the pavilion level. It dawned on me that the hot springs at both sides of the structure acted as a natural heating system for the pavilion.

When the two young Japanese men saw that I was awake, they started jabbering at me and at each other. I could only make out half of what they said and made them slow down. I soon learned that the smaller and thinner, and younger, of the two was named Goro and the more handsome and robust and heavily muscled one was named Jun. Through repeated attempts at understanding and hand gestures and the Japanese that I was acquiring much faster by necessity here than I had ever been able to do in the classroom, I discerned that they both worked for "the boss"—the chujen—who owned this retreat where the wealthy men of the village and beyond came to take the healing waters, He also went out occasionally to fish in the Toska Bay. This was why he was on the water and in a position to pull me from the tangles of my parachute, which otherwise would have dragged me down into the ocean in the unconscious state I had been in when I went into the drink. I learned that he went by the name of Iwao—the Stone Man, for the setting of his hot springs—by all but Goro and Jun, who served the spa. And now I was to think of him as the chujen, too, I supposed. My life was in his hands and at his whim.

I was provided with a white cotton robe—a *yukata* is what Goro, the more intelligent of the two, called it—and the mere hint of a loin cloth, and then, when they had shown me how to wear the yukata, held together by a thick sash, they brought me food and chattered away at me and with each other as I ate heartily.

The chujen visited me later in the afternoon—I had slept in the pool, with the healing waters swirling around me, well past noon—and got across to me that an army unit had come down from the northern end of the island to investigate the downing of my bomber and that I was to confine myself to this chamber and the hidden garden pool until and unless he told me it was safe to move more freely about. Then he showed me a hidden place in the corner of the garden, etched out of the rock and entered through a narrow passage hidden behind a cascade of Japanese maple boughs that dipped down to the surface of the pool. If I was to hear a gong sound, I was to hide myself there and not emerge until he came for me.

I already had my fears of being here. I had no idea why this Japanese citizen was shielding me. All of my instructions during mission briefings had clearly stressed that the Japanese hated and would resist the Americans to the last Japanese. But I was wholly at his mercy. And my thoughts kept going back to the night before. What kind of party had been going on here? Was this a frequent event? There had been no sign of any women, other than those silhouetted figures in the other chambers the previous night. In fact, I hadn't heard a woman's voice since I had come ashore on this island.

The shadows were long and the pool outside my room was fully dark as I was finishing an evening meal of delicious but completely unidentifiable bits and pieces of food while kneeling at a low table. Late in the afternoon, Goro and Jen had brought in arms full of heavy, thick quilts and made them up into a bed, topped by several pillows, near the center of the chamber. It seemed as if I was destined to stay here for a while—although I had some hope of an early rescue. Three waves of bombers had gone overhead already today, rattling the very timbers of the delicate structure between the hot springs pools and had come across and out to sea again almost immediately. I couldn't hear the bombs they were dropping on the Osaka area, but I could clearly hear the flak guns of the Japanese, which had been so effective with my own last flight. Listen as I could, however, I didn't hear the dreaded sound of a B-29 plummeting into the sea or into the dense foliage of the island.

What I did hear, though, was a clamor of guttural, demanding male voices at the entrance into the retreat and the sounding of the gong. But I was too far away from the entrance into the hidden garden, and two men were already entering one of the chambers next to mine. A sliding screen was ajar between the rooms, and if I moved across the chamber toward the pool garden and its hiding place, I surely would have been seen, I slipped over to the bedding instead and managed to crouch down behind it so that I could not be seen, but so that I could see into the other room through a gap in the pillows on top of the bedding.

The larger figure was in uniform. A Japanese army officer. He was scowling and had a firm grip on the arms of the smaller man—Goro—who was cringing but not resisting. The officer jerked off Goro's sash, grabbed his yukata at the back of the neck and stripped it off the smaller, younger man, and pushed Goro down on his belly on the pile of bedding in the center of the chamber. Then he stripped off his own khaki tunic shirt, revealing a heavily muscled barrel chest tapering down to a small waist. His chest was criss-crossed with slash marks. I had heard about how the more fanatic Japanese militarists trained themselves to pain and to the heights of dedication to the emperor and the Japanese cause. This no doubt was one of those adherents.

The Japanese officer unbuckled his belt and whipped it out of his pants loops. Then, as he unbuttoned his trousers and spread them wide, he began to beat Goro on the back and buttocks with the doubled leather belt. I had the urge to go to

175

Goro's aid then, but I heard the boisterous voices of other men beyond Goro's room and knew that it was useless. I was trapped in nonaction. To have revealed myself would be suicide—and probably would mean death for the chujen and Goro and Jun as well.

Goro was crying out and groaning and writhing under the lashing, but he was holding fast, bent over his bed on his belly. The Japanese officer was laughing, and his cock, now revealed, jutted insistently out of his open pants, tight across his well-muscled thighs and calves as the leggings descended into highly polished, high-top brown leather boots. His cock was lengthening and thickening and growing redder even as red welts were being raised on Goro's writhing body.

Then, so quick that I hardly saw it happening, the Japanese officer had made a loop in his belt and lassoed Goro's head with it and tightened it around the younger man's neck. Jerking on the end of the belt and setting Goro to arching his body up and scrabbling at the choking leather necklace with his hand in search of relief on his wind pipe, the Japanese officer thrust his cock between Goro's buttocks cheeks and began to fuck him hard.

I was about to rise and come to Goro's aid, regardless of the consequences, when the officer let loose of the belt and covered Goro closely from above with his torso and started to bite on Goro's ear as he pounded his ass with long, forceful thrusts while slapping his butt cheeks with the open palms of his hands. Goro was gasping for air, but he was breathing again. And he was taking it like a soldier. That's when it hit me that this was what he was here for. To take it like a soldier when the men of the area came to take in the hot springs water. And Jun as well. It was Goro and Jun I had seen in those silhouettes the previously night, not women. Plying their trade with the men clients.

Later that evening I began to find out why I had not been turned over to the authorities and just how entrapped I was.

After the soldiers had left, Goro and Jun brought in another late evening meal for me, saying that the chujen said I needed to build up my strength but that this would be the last time that they'd check on me that night—that they had duties to perform out at the larger pools on the other side of the pavilion. I tried to get across to Goro that I had seen what had happened to him and that I was ashamed that I had not been able to come to his rescue. He shyly let me know that he appreciated the sentiment, but that it was Jun who had taken the worst of it. When I showed that I didn't understand, he made clear that while he had been servicing the army captain, Jun had been servicing the rest of the unit. I didn't ask how many—or in what way.

As they left, Goro handed me a flagon of sake and said that the chujen suggested that I soak in the pool again that evening to further restore my torn and sore muscles.

I slipped into the water and raised the open flagon to my lips. The sake was heady, but it was delicious. And the water was oh so soothing. The flagon was also quite a large one. I should have stopped when the sake was no more than a quarter gone. But I didn't. I was keyed up from the danger I was in and all that I had seen in just the last day. I raised the flagon to my lips again and again.

I became bleary eyed, but not so far gone that I didn't see the chujen appear at the edge of the pool and untie his sash and let his yukata fall to the stones. He was a large, solid man. He had the hard, bulging, rounded muscles of a man accustomed to fighting the sea for victory over fish-laden nets. Thick of torso and waist, but all sold muscle. A King Neptune, as befitted his relationship to the sea. Thick of cock and heavy of balls too, I could clearly see.

He did ask me if he could join me in the pool; I have no idea what I answered, but it was his pool and I was his virtual prisoner—and I was nearly gone on the sake—so I'm sure I didn't demur. We sat there at opposite ends of the pool, luxuriating in the heat and mists of the pools and sharing the flagon of sake back and forth as it got darker.

And as it got dark, the lanterns were lit in the paper-walled rooms beyond mine, and, in silhouette, Goro and Jun began to service a procession of male clients in various positions and with varied volumes of vocal response. The rougher clients brought out the louder moans and groans of the two young men I'd grown to like; the more sensitive lovers brought out sighs and gasps that went to the very heart of me—that tugged at me and began to build in me, first, doubts of maybe missing something in life. And then the fingers of desire and wanting began to work their way into me.

Iwao, the chujen, was a master lover. His timing and rhythm were impeccable. That said, he took what he wanted from me, leaving no question that he was going to have it. He selected a moment when Goro and Jun were both receiving men of refinement and skill and sensitivity. I found myself, drunk—possibly drugged as well—and barely conscious of what was happening, sitting in Iwao's lap, facing the two chambers with their silhouetted tableaus of Goro and Jun responding fully to a slow and sensuous fuck. They were being treated as equal lovers, to be pleased as well as to please, and not just as open vessels for frenetic seeding.

Iwao was holding my head to the hollow of his neck with a hand under my chin, holding my face steady and facing the silhouetted takings in the other chamber. He was whispering and half-way singing in soothing tones into my ear, occasionally kissing me behind the ear or taking the lobe of my ear between his lips, or slowly slipping his tongue into my ear chamber—while his other hand was roaming over my body. He was stroking and gripping my chest muscles, tweaking my nipples, running his hands along my biceps and down my chest to my belly. And lower.

As the lovers silhouetted behind the screen began their rhythmic, equally undulating coupling, Iwao was possessing my cock with his pressuring fist and slowly pumping me—just as I had done myself the previous night as I watched the dance of the fuck in the other chambers—and as Iwao had watched me do.

I was close, but he held me fast, not letting me ejaculate as Goro and Jun and their partners completed their coupling and the rooms cleared briefly. When the silhouettes were back in place and their mating was beginning with Goro and Jun working on their new client's cocks with their mouths, Iowa had me up out of the pool, my buttocks resting on the edge and me propped on my elbows on the border stones, watching the cock sucking in silhouette and stereo beyond the papered walls, as Iwao, still sitting in the pool crouched over my pelvis, held me there with his elbows and worked my cock with his mouth.

I did come then, in great gobs of ejaculate and cries of release and then of something else, something more primeval and fearful, as, almost incapacitated with inebriation to the point of being helpless against any invasion Iwao fancied, I realized that while Iwao was pumping my throbbing cock with his soft, sensual mouth, he had worked three of his beefy fingers, lubricated with something greasy, deep into my anus.

The current clients of Goro and Jun, both hulking men of substance, were quickly getting down to business beyond the screens. They had already fully skewered their prey, and the two young men were writhing in ecstasy and agony under full, vigorous fuck. No sensitive lovemaking here. Just full and furious rut.

I cried out weakly as the chujen grasped me by the waist with both hands and pulled me back down into the pool, and into his lap, and onto his thick and long cock. Taking only a moment to center his bulb at my puckered and now-stretched—but not nearly wide enough—channel and slowly, relentlessly pulling me down on his invading pole. Having eventually, with great effort and thrashing and moaning on my part, bottomed inside me, he held me firmly to him with one hand on my belly and the other cupping and squeezing my balls until, with a groan of pain subsiding into a moan of possession from me, he moved his hands to my waist and repeatedly, with increasing intensity and rapidity, lifted and settled me on his probing cock as I watched the taking in the other room.

Thus was I undone and on my way to serving as one of the courtesans in Iwao's male brothel. Iwao visited me nightly for two weeks after that. And then came the night when the sliding screen opened and he was not alone. There was another man with him.

Iwao briefly—and almost apologetically—explained that this client had discovered I was here and would only remain silent if I serviced him. The chujen wanted me to know also that the army unit—and its captain who had visited Goro—was still in the area, barely a breathed whisper from taking me into their possession.

What could I do? I was trapped. Nowhere I could go other than here and be even as safe as I was here. The visitor untied his sash and dropped his yukata and joined me in the pool in the hidden garden. He wasn't nearly as expert as Iwao had been, but I was no less fucked—and felt no less the prostitute.

In succeeding weeks, there have been other men. And I have been led out to the larger pool on the cliffside edge of the pavilion, and while there, I have been with more than one man at a time. So many of the village men wanted their taste of the *gaijen*, the foreigner. It was as if, in these last months, when their whole world was collapsing and they could see it happening—and finally believed it would happen—they wanted to experience as much of what to them was the exotic as possible. Fucking a young gaijen became the ultimate in experiences in Aki.

* * * *

I had thought before of being with a man but I had never thought of serving men in a male brothel. But I'm trapped. The daily waves of bombers overhead have stopped. I want to believe that this means that there is nothing else left to bomb in Osaka, that the path is clear for more safely increasing the bombing of Tokyo now. At least that was the plan. My hope is that one day I will awaken and the hot springs pools of Iwao are deserted and I will hear the sounds of steel ramps reaching out to the sands of Aki's lower village and American troops coming to save me from what I have, by necessity, become.

Meanwhile I feel so trapped—trapped between exposure and death and service—which is another kind of death—but at least a fingerhold on life.

~

Tea with the Prince

June 1929, Tokyo, Japan

I was straining for him to start. I ran my hands down his hard-muscled back from the shoulder blades to his buttocks, pushing his trousers down further on his buttocks and clutching at the orbs, willing him to start the stroking. He was inside me deep and I was panting hard for him.

He spoke from the hollow of my throat. "I . . . we need a favor of you."

A favor? What in the hell was this? He had me on the floor of his hotel room, my legs spread and bent, him lying on top of me between them. My trousers and briefs off, my shirt open to the work of his lips and teeth on my nipples. He was inside me, goddamnit. Why wasn't he fucking me? Why was he picking a time like this to speak of a favor?

"Fuck me," I murmured. "Give me your cum."

He continued, as if he didn't hear me. "A prince, a professor at Tokyo University. We need his permission to get into the private art collection in Kyoto."

Private art collection. He was speaking of the homoerotic art he wanted to see during this university study tour to Japan. This whole study tour was probably because he wanted to get into that collection of homoerotic art in Kyoto. That was what Professor Tyndale did on the side himself—sketches of men fucking. And Tyndale was good at it. He had shown me his art that first time, that old "Come up and see my etchings" ploy, and it had aroused me so well that I'd laid down and opened my legs to him then—and whenever he wanted me to since then. And I'd let others of his choosing fuck me too so

181

that he could sketch us. I'd brought this on myself in letting him choose men to fuck me to meet his own needs and wants.

"Fuck me," I whined. The professor was old—maybe in his late forties—and gaunt and ugly. But he had a good cock. I wanted his cock now. Not just inside me. Stroking. To pump me deep. To fuck me. To blast me with his cum. To make me come too.

"He wants me to come to tea with him. To bring a young student with me. A willing young student. He says he likes young blond men."

"Please do it; do me now," I whimpered.

"I want to sketch an Oriental man fucking you."

Tyndale cupped the side of my head, ran his fingers into my blond curls and kissed me on the lips. Coming out of the kiss, he gave me three slow, deep, long strokes. I buried my fingernails in his butt cheeks, arched my back, and, through my pants, cried out, "Yes, yes, fuck me!"

But he held there. "I would be there too. He wants sketches done; I want to do the sketches. Will you do us this favor? The study group needs to see this collection."

"Fuck me and I'll do anything you want."

He began to stroke, establishing a steady, deep beat. Lost to him, I arched my back, as his lips went to my nipples, and ran my hand up and down his back from his shoulder blades to his buttocks, digging my claws in at the down thrust. I panted and set my pelvis in motion in a counterthrust, writhing under him, no thoughts in my mind of anything but that staff working my passage.

He tensed, held, and ejaculated in two bursts, holding for three after spurts, creaming me deep inside as I purred and sighed and ran my fingers up into his hair, pulling his face to mine for a deep kiss.

Tyndale went up on his knees between my thighs and looked down into my eyes.

"We meet him at the Meiji Shrine tomorrow at 3:00 and he'll take us to wherever he wants to perform the tea ceremony," he said, adding, "You haven't come yet. Masturbate yourself for me, please. I want to see you come."

Dutifully, I encased my own hard cock in my hand and began to stroke it. He slipped his hand under my buttocks, and

I felt one, and then two, fingers enter my ass, search for, and finding, the prostate.

My eyes went to his now-slick cock, slick with his own cum. The best feature of him. It had only gone half flaccid and was thickening again as he watched me masturbate and he fingered my ass. I knew he was going to fuck me again. That knowledge drove my arousal, and minutes later I tensed, arched my back, and shot my load. Immediately, he was lowering his body to mine again, entering me, grabbing my knees in his hands, rowing my legs, moving them back and forth—pushing them wide apart as he thrust in, pulling them together as he drew back.

In ecstasy, I arched my back, threw my head back, and in a panting voice of total surrender, whispered to the ceiling, "Yes, yes, fuck me," as the pumping of his cock picked up speed.

Afterward I lay there, exhausted and satiated, as he sketched me in my postcoital position, my legs still spread and bent, open and vulnerable to him and to anyone who would later look at the sketch.

* * * *

The first indication I had that the man we were meeting was anyone of importance, even though Professor Tyndale had said he was a prince, was when our car was let through in front of the shrine when all others were being kept back. There were three black Duisenberg limousines lined up in front of the Torii—the ceremonial gate—of the shrine, and burly Japanese men in black suits cordoning off the area.

At the top of the steps up into the first shrine hall stood a small-stature, mousy-looking Japanese man, graying hair, wearing wire-rim eyeglasses and a black, tailored suit, complete with vest and top hat.

Professor Tyndale leaned over and whispered, "Prince Satsuma," in my ear.

It was obvious to me then that the man was of some import because a crowd had gathered behind the imaginary line the black-suited guards had set and were bowing their heads in the prince's direction. This was a chore for them, because as soon as Tyndale and I stepped out of our car, I became another focus of attention, and those in the crowds were doing what they could to look at me too. I had grown used to the attention in Tokyo, because, with the exception of a contingent of jackbooted Nazi Party Germans roaming the streets of Tokyo during what later proved to be secret pact talks between the Japanese and Germans, blond young men were few and far between in Tokyo in the later years of the 1920s. And it was supposedly good luck to touch blond hair. So, I was getting a lot of furtive attention during this university art class study tour to Japan, the last, we were told that probably would occur in a while, as the flames of war were building in Asia.

So, this little man was going to fuck me in order for Professor Tyndale to have access to a collection of homoerotic art in Kyoto and to scratch his urge to sketch an older Japanese man fucking a young blond American, I thought. Piece of cake; he was such a runt, I thought. He was all mousy diffidence and refinement as he showed the two of us through the shrine, with his guards clearing the spaces so that we had a private tour. During the tour I had to reassess my impression that he was a weak runt. He led me from space to space with a grip of steel on my arm that belied his looks and his weak, tinny-voice precise English that showed him to be a professor type as well as a prince.

As we stood in front of a massive reclining Buddha in polished wood, he stood close behind me. With one hand he pointed my attention to the *fundoshi*—the loin cloth—the statue was wearing and the subtle peeking out at one side of the bulb of a cock. He moved his other hand around my belly and down and was fondling my package. He also was holding me close into his body from behind.

I look sharply to the side to catch Professor Tyndale's attention to what was happening, and he just smiled, shrugged slightly, and gave me a furtive palms-down signal. Obviously, the permission to view the art collection wasn't a done deal. There was a checking out of the goods phase. I stood there, dutifully, in front of the Buddha of the Peeking Penis, while the short and wiry Japanese prince felt up my body from my throat to my knees with strong, searching hands. Tyndale and the bodyguards stood, pretending not to be watching, as if nothing untoward was happening.

Satsuma grunted and turned, and we were making our way back to car park, the prince and Tyndale in front of me. I heard Tyndale lean over and ask, "Satisfactory?" and the prince answer, "Quite satisfactory indeed." He added, "Pity you didn't bring him to me as a virgin, however. I would have savored— and shown appreciation for—deflowering him."

* * * *

We were sitting on eight-inch-deep, silk-covered cushions with a low tea table between us. Professor Tyndale was sitting across from the prince and me, his sketch book and charcoals at his side. The prince was sitting very close beside me.

In addition to two ceramic tea pots and three cups for tea sitting on the table between us, other objects, one of which had me hyperventilating, were set off to the side. There was a bowl of fragrant oil, a six-inch strand of ivory beads with a tiny eyehook at one end—and a clear-glass knobbly dildo, very definitely a dildo, as it was slightly curved up with a vein on the underside running across the knobs and the head on the end undoubtedly was in the form of a penis bulb.

Nothing was said about the added implements. The conversation was quite refined, with the prince providing a step-by-step explanation of the tea ceremony. The surroundings were sparse, but richly appointed, the setting definitely Japanese, with shoji screens and niches with Ikebana—flower—arrangements in them. There were few pieces of art on the walls; what was there was homoerotic and was lit. A Roman-like bronze sculpture was in one corner of the room. It was of two torsos, rather than the usual one, armless and legless, but with genitals included, accentuating the muscularity of the torsos. The torso in front was in erection, hanging low and jutting forward from the bottom of the bonze torso plate. The torso in front was slightly turned so the root of the cock of the one behind could be seen buried in the ass of the one in front.

Nothing was being hidden about the reality that this was the house of a man who fucked other men and that I was going to be fucked.

The house itself was a conundrum and screamed of refinement, wealth, and power in Japan. The estate took up a whole block in a bustling downtown area of the city. The grounds were so covered in manicured and landscaped foliage that the house could not be seen from beyond the grounds and the traffic in the busy city could barely be heard from the house. The house itself was set on a small man-made hill in the center of the property. The surprise was that the house obviously was the design of the American architect Frank Lloyd Wright. The prince explained that Wright had accepted the commission to design it, the original house having burned down, while he was building the Imperial Hotel in Tokyo, which had been completed six years earlier. The prince had not wanted the commission to be known abroad to ward off curiosity seekers, and he'd had the power—even over Frank Lloyd Wright—to have his wishes honored. No doubt a lot of money had exchanged hands for the silence as well.

Once inside, the blending of Japanese tradition and Wright's style was shown to be perfection.

After we entered the house, both Professor Tyndale and I were led off to a room walled with shoji screens, floored in tatami matting, and overlooking a walled pocket garden with a small pond surrounded by rocks and foliage. The pond turned out to be a tub of fragrant, steaming water, where we were bathed (and embraced, kissed, and fondled each other) before being dressed in silk *yukatas*—robes—Tyndale in white, me in a rich red—with only one-material-length fundoshi wrapped and knotted underneath.

The tea ceremony was long and involved, and my tea came from a separate pot than the one the prince served Tyndale and himself from. It didn't take me long to figure out why. Almost immediately upon drinking the tea, I began to feel all tingly, warm, weak, and ultrasensitive to the touch all over my body.

The ceremony over, servants, with well-formed, muscular bodies, and wearing only fundoshis, appeared, heads bowed and not looking at any of us, and turned the tea table so that it was at the opposite side of the prince from me. They took away the tea implements. They left the bowl of fragrant oil, the string of beads, and the glass dildo.

Tyndale rose and I started to do so as well, assuming he'd take the lead in showing me what I should do. But he motioned me to stay in place, and the prince put an arm around me, in which I again was surprised at the strength of him, and held me in place, pulled close into his side. The servants carried the bolster Tyndale had been sitting on to the far side of the room, and Tyndale settled down there with his sketch book and charcoals.

As pedantic as the prince had been about explaining every aspect of the tea ceremony—other than the drug he was using on me—and as long as the ceremony had taken, I expected a longer phase of getting down to sex. But it didn't happen that way.

It started with a kiss on the lips, but while that was happening, the prince was brushing his blue-silk yukata open—exposing his cock and groin. He already was in erection. With a hand cupping the back of my head, he made my eyes lower as we came out of the kiss to ensure that I saw what he had uncovered. I shivered and gave a little moan. He may have been a small man, but there was nothing small about his cock. It wasn't thick, but it was long, long, long. It was upcurved, in angry erection, accentuated as it was stained red; and it had a thick Prince Albert ring in the bulb.

He turned my head toward the wall to my right as lights came on over two paintings of Japanese men—the older man in a blue yukata gaping open off his naked body and a far younger man in a flared red yukata. The panels stood side by side. In the first the older man held the younger in an embrace. The focus of the painting was his cock, in long, upcurved erection, painted an angry red, and crowned with a Prince Albert ring in the bulb. The younger man appeared to be struggling in the older man's embrace. The painting beside it was a continuation in time, with the older man's red cock buried in the ass of the younger man almost to the root, and the younger man laid out in total submission to the taking.

Upon being assured I'd seen the paintings and his cock, which he could have told from my intake of breath, the start of light panting, and my low moans, he grasped my left hand and pulled it around, nudging me to take his cock in my hand, which I did. Directing me only by movement, not by spoken command, he signaled that my fist should be open and loose, so that he could stroke his cock in the fist, which he started to do.

The fingers of the hand he had at the back of my head—his left—were buried in my blond curls, gripped my hair, and pulled my head cruelly back. With his right hand, he brushed my yukata open at my breast, and he possessed my left nipple with his mouth and teeth. His right hand then brushed my yukata open at my crotch and, with one deft pull at the knot of the fundoshi, he stripped that away and took my cock in his hand. His hand was slathered in oil, and I realized that he must have dipped it in the bowl of warm oil on the tea table. After slick-stroking my cock for a minute or more, he dipped his hand in the oil again and slathered it over my balls, letting it drizzle down between my crack, my pelvis rolled-up, and entering my ass with oiled fingers

I lay, trapped in his strong embrace, breathing heavily, all of my senses sexually energized but feeling physically weak from the drug he'd given me, pinging on what his hands, lips, and teeth were doing to my body.

"Fuck me, fuck me please," I softly whimpered.

He made me come with his hand stroking my cock. Across the room, Professor Tyndale was sketching like crazy, tearing one sheet off when he was done, and moving on to the next, capturing each change of position initiated and controlled by the prince.

The prince moved into the next major change, turning me to face him more, with my groin totally exposed down and under to my hole, with my pelvis rolled up, my weight on the small of my back. My left leg was bent, the sole of that foot buried in the tatami matting. My right leg was raised straight up his chest, my ankle hooked on the back of the prince's neck. We were still mostly covered, with only his crotch, his pubic bush hair; a darker black than the grayer hair on his head, and his angry, long, upcurved cock still in hard erection, exposed. My left pec, with its puckered nipple, and my crotch area were exposed.

I watched, mewing softly, past the unavoidable screaming erection on the man, to the tea table, where he was spinning the head of the glass dildo in the bowl of oil. I watched in fear, and arousing anticipation, as he slowly brought the dildo out of the bowl, moved it to my hole, slowly penetrated me with it, and fucked me. At first in a slow stroke seeking out every surface inside me and then hard and vigorously until, straining against an embrace I couldn't escape, I gave him another ejaculation.

I was still trying to bring my pulse under control from that when I was forced to watch him pick up the string of ivory beads, dip them in the oil, and attach them to the ring in the bulb of his cock. With no further preparation and certainly no explanation and no time for me to try to relax to it, the prince turned his pelvis toward mine; dipped his hips; came back up with his beads-enhanced cock head, deftly targeting my entrance; and plunged up inside me. The dildo had opened me up to where I easily took the girth of him, but my eyes popped open from the effect of how deep he could get up into me.

I cried out and tried to writhe out from under him, but he was too strong for me. One hand was arching my head back with a grip in my head hair. The other was gripping my left thigh and holding my leg out. His cock, the beads aswirl, was pumping my passage hard and deep.

Tyndale was busily sketching on his pad. I knew that the resulting sketches would become part of the prince's homoerotic art collection—and maybe find their way eventually into the Kyoto collection that Tyndale was so hot on seeing.

I didn't really care at that point. The little Jap was giving me the fuck of my life.

He moved me to the position of kneeling over the bolster, my elbows on the tatami matting on the other side of the bolster. My yukata was pulled up and gathered around my waist. The prince was naked, except for his glasses, his body wiry and thin, but his muscles hard, and his small size accentuating the angry length of his cock, the beads drooping down to the tatami. Kneeling at an angle behind me to give Tyndale a shot of my buttocks and erection and drooping balls between my spread thighs, the prince leaned over and ate out my ass, distended and squeezed my balls, and milked my cock through my legs. He mounted my ass and finished me off in a good ten minutes of stroking and swirling the ivory beads inside me.

As I stared at the wall opposite from where I was being taken from the rear, another painting lit up on the wall—a painting showing the face of an older Japanese man with a blue yukata floating around the margin of the tableau, peeking out over the shoulder of a young Japanese man in a red yukata, who was bent over a bolster and being doggie fucked by the older man.

After the prince ejaculated, the light went off over the painting, I felt his body rising from mine, and he left. Tyndale finished up his sketches and I lay in a heap, belly over the bolster, moaning and purring, having been finished royally—in more ways than one.

"Pity you weren't a virgin," the prince had murmured to me in flawless, English-accented English, as he swept from the room.

When a servant came to usher the professor out of the room, I started to rise, having difficulty doing so because of how deeply I felt the prince still inside me in the form of my rippling passage walls and his cum seemly in my stomach. But Tyndale signaled me to remain.

"You are staying here until we return from Kyoto," he said. "You are to help the prince in a project of his own."

If his project included more of his cock work inside me, that didn't bother me a bit, I thought. But then I looked up to watch Tyndale being escorted out of the room, I saw, entering the room, one of the jackbooted German Nazi generals who had been roaming around Tokyo. He had a big smile on his face, he was lightly slapping his leg with a riding crop, and he was unbuttoning his brown uniform shirt.

What followed were days and weeks of brutal ravishment by the contingent of German military officers liaising with the Japanese military establishment, reducing me to a submissive and resigned chattel for the cruel desires of the German soldiers. Whatever Tyndale may have thought about what happened to me when I didn't return to him, I'll never know. I never saw Tyndale again after that day. He returned to the room, briefly, to sketch the first of the German generals fucking me, and then was gone forever.

December 9, 1937, Nanking, China

I moved the pillow from underneath the small of my back and placed it under the other pillows behind my head. After reaching for the cigarettes and lighting up, I looked down the line of my naked body, my legs still spread and bent, and watched the German colonel dress in the black uniform of the Nazi Party. This was the first time I'd seen Heinrich Krentz dressed thusly. He'd told me that it was for expediency. The less-dressy khaki uniform of the Chinese Nationalist Army that he had been wearing as a secret German adviser to Chiang Kai-shek's Chinese Nationalist military was folded into a suitcase set on a nearby chair.

"Do you really have to go, Heinrich?" I asked. "Is it really not safe here?"

"The Generalissimo left two days ago. The Japanese 10th Army is closing in on the city on two sides. I haven't been released by Berlin as adjunct to the Chinese yet. I must follow them to Chungking. You should come as well, Wilhelm. I can guarantee your transport."

"Can I leave on the 15th?" I asked "The university is being packed out to go to Chungking. I have students I'm responsible for."

"That might work. But not much longer after that—especially for your Chinese students. The reports say that the Japanese march from Shanghai has been brutal. No prisoners taken; no one left alive along the track."

"Surely that's just propaganda."

"I wouldn't count on that. In fact, I think you should leave with me today."

"I have responsibilities. But I'll miss you until I can catch up with you in Chungking," I said.

And the strange thing was that I *would* miss him. He was my third lover—no, master—in the eight years since I'd been forcibly taken back to Germany from Tokyo after Prince Satsuma had given me to the Nazi generals who had ravished me mercilessly. I had been beaten so much into submission that I raised no objection when I was hustled back to Berlin with them—I had come to accept and then to seek the rough sex. In time, I'd been given more freedom by the general who controlled me and even permitted to go to the university in Heidelberg to complete my art degrees.

When Heinrich brought me out to China with him on his adviser tour, I was given a professor position at the University of Nanking, and we lived together as partners. I'd almost completely forgotten that I was once an American with free reign of my life. I even was more used to my German name, Wilhelm, now than the name I'd been given, William. And the Toliver surname never was used anymore. I was documented as Wilhelm Krentz, Heinrich's son. For social purposes the father and son relationship was established. Only a few of the Chinese servants knew I slept in Heinrich's bedroom, under him, or that sometimes he lashed me to a pillar, flogged me, and then fucked me still tied to the pillar.

We were believable as father and son, I suppose, if you considered that Heinrich had been quite young when I was born. We were both Teutonic blonds, qualified for the master race. And we were qualified in more ways than hair color too. Both of us were blue-eyed and of strong, handsome features. Our body styles were different—his tall, solid, muscular, hung, and mine more lithe and trim and on the shorter side, but we were similar enough for me just to be considered to favor my mother more than my father.

That he was muscular, hung, virile, and vigorous was enough to keep me satisfied with the third German Nazi Party member who had virtually owned me for the last eight years. At twenty-seven, I was lucky to have a god of a man of forty-four, like Heinrich, serving as my protector and master.

His manner changed when I said I'd miss him. In some ways I was more master of him than he of me. I could arouse him quickly, and as I lay there, naked, reaching for my half-hard cock, and giving him a "come hither" look, I could see his resolve on leaving me melt. He had fucked me twice after we had awakened that morning—more times the previous night—as if he couldn't pull away from me and leave me here in Nanking.

"Do you really have to leave right now? You don't have another half hour?" I asked.

When his trousers hit the floor, I saw that he already was in erection. I barely had time to snuff out my cigarette in the ashtray on the nightstand before he was upon me, turning me, coaxing me up on my knees at the end of the bed.

"Yes!" I cried out as he entered me strong and deep from the rear, grabbed the hair on the back of my head, arching my torso up toward his face. He fucked me hard and brutally, as all of the Germans had.

Just like the Japanese marching on Nanking from Shanghai—taking no prisoners.

December 13, 1937, Nanking, China

"Professor Krentz? Wilhelm Krentz?"

"Yes," I answered, standing at the door, maintaining a position between me and the students in the art studio who were packing up art supplies. A Japanese officer stood there, backed up by several soldiers, all with rifles drawn with bayonets attached to them. There had been sounds of gunshots and screaming as the Japanese soldiers had spread out across the university campus, having easily broken through the city defenses, such as they were, that morning. The government and most of the Nationalist army had already drawn off into the interior of the country.

"You are Wilhelm Krentz, German citizen?" the Japanese officer asked again.

"Yes," I answered, not really lying anymore, I suppose, as I had been in German hands for the last eight years and no American had come looking for me. I handed over the papers that Heinrich had made sure I had documenting me as a German with German government and Nazi Party connections.

I'd asked Heinrich before he left why he was so adamant that I have these papers.

"If the Japanese see these before they shoot you, you should be safe—if you don't leave Nanking in time. The Chinese don't know, but Germany—the Nazi Party—has a secret pact with the Japanese. We're allies. Our leaders in Berlin just don't want to be seen backing both horses in this war until we can see who will win."

I obviously hadn't left Nanking in time.

"Yes, these papers are in order. Come with me, please."

"My students. I have a responsibility for my students," I said. But soldiers had already stepped forward, taken me in hand, and were dragging me down the hall. Other soldiers entered the art studio. I was only half way down the stairs when I heard the shots and screaming, the screaming quickly cut off. I nearly collapsed on the stairs, screaming myself in despair, anger, and frustration, but strong hands carried me out of the building and loaded me onto the back of a canvas-covered truck.

I was taken into the foreign quarter, which was nearly deserted, except for the scurrying about of Chinese civilians, most being pursued by Japanese soldiers—and most being run down and dispatched within my sight until I pulled back from the back of the truck and also in my hearing, which I couldn't deaden and was forever after haunted by.

The truck stopped at a stone villa, built in the Western style, and, dejected and my wits dulled, I was taken up the stairs and to a dining room. The table had been pulled to the wall and a low table supporting a Japanese tea set was in its place. Cushions were spread on the other side of the table, and at one side of these sat an elderly Japanese man in a blue, billowy silk yukata. He lifted his head and I sucked in air. It was Prince Satsuma. He was grayer now, in his early sixties, but he still was trim and his back was ramrod straight. He was nearly bald.

"Come, take tea with me, William," he said simply, gesturing to the cushion beside him, as the Japanese soldiers who had brought me here melted out of the room. "Please take off your clothes and put that yukata on before you sit by me," he said.

"How . . . why . . .?" I stammered.

"It doesn't matter. It only matters that I found you in time and that you are safe with me. Come over to me. We'll take some tea and then I will be inside you again. I've often thought of you, the sweetness and yielding nature of you. I have a room back in Tokyo lined with drawings of you being taken by me and other men. Very sweet and invigorating. They

194

have helped keep me young—my *chinko* hard and vigorous. You'll be interested to know I still can fill and seed you."

And he could. Resigned to giving him what he wanted, I sat by him, brushed the folds open at his groin, and found him still capable of an erection and with the Prince Albert ring in the head of his cock. The cock no longer was painted red, though, there being no artwork around to coordinate visual and tactile sensations with. As he rolled over on top of me, I brushed my yukata open, bent and spread my legs, rolled my pelvis up, and took him deep inside me.

We stayed in the villa—in hiding, it seemed—as the city died around us. Satsuma never left the villa in the five weeks we were there. He wore a general's military uniform but I could see no invasion or occupation force that he commanded and later could testify he was at the Rape of Nanking but couldn't attest to him having had any part in it—quite the contrary. He rarely was anywhere but on top of and inside me. I could hardly say at a military inquest that he was that close to me all of the time, though. All I could say was that I ever was beside him and he was not involved in military matters for that time.

After five weeks of looting and raping across the city, the pillage seemed to die down. There really was no one left to rape or rob. Only then did he say, "I think it's safe for us to leave now."

We did, in a staff car, taking us all the way back to Shanghai and then by ship to Japan. In Japan, after enjoying my body for two more weeks in the room he told me about where sketches of me being fucked were hung, he had me driven to the Swiss embassy and repatriated to my home country.

After what I'd seen and heard in Nanking, there was really only one thing I could do from there. I gave a nearly full report to the American authorities, only leaving out the nature of the relationship between me and a German colonel and the prince—although I'm sure the interrogators could figure that out on their own.

September 15, 1945, Tokyo, Japan

I sat, ramrod straight, in the passenger seat of the jeep, while the soldiers jumped out of the canvas-covered truck behind me, pulled open the leaning gates of the park-like block in the middle of the bombed out Japanese capital, and then fanned out over the grounds, avoiding the cavernous holes dug out by Allied bombs.

My driver drove me up the winding road that had once trailed artfully through landscaped gardens, gardens that now were both overgrown and beaten down by bombs. I took in my breath and nearly teared up as we got within view of the palace that had once been a breathtaking Frank Lloyd Wright creation. Only one wing stood now, the central part of the building having taken a direct hit from an Allied bomb.

As I got out of the jeep and motioned a couple of the soldiers to come with me, the irony didn't escape me that I now was doing what had been done to and for me back in Nanking eight years previously. I had come for a prince, to escort him safely through a city in turmoil.

We entered the building and I felt I knew the place. Indeed, I had been held prisoner in this wing for weeks as the German generals were given free rein in ravishing my body to their brutal needs and desires. Halfway down the corridor I brought the escort to a halt and spent a few minutes in the room where, sixteen years earlier, I had repeatedly been hung from an overhead beam and flogged and imprisoned in stocks and fucked. The prince had occasionally taken me as well, but he had me taken to more comfortable quarters to fuck me, and his attentions were almost soothing and love-like in contrast to the German generals he was trying to impress by gifting me to their sexual pleasures. I, of course, had never heard from or about Professor Tyndale again. For all I knew he was still roaming the private collection of homoerotic art he had sold me to access.

My thoughts were conflicted. I could do an ineffectual search and let the prince go uncaptured. He had saved me in Nanking. But would that be doing him any favors? I doubted he would be the focus of military trials. He quite possibly would be examined and then let go free. But perhaps he should be put on trial for having given me to the Germans in the first place. I never revealed how I had gotten from Tokyo to Germany and then back to China.

Prince Satsuma was right where I assumed I would find him. He had described his "William" room to me well enough in Nanking that I could walk directly to it. He was sitting on cushions behind a tea table in the center of the room.

I stopped the accompanying soldiers just outside the door, as a lieutenant announced, "Major William Toliver, of U.S. Army Intelligence"—a position I had risen too based on my facility with German and personal knowledge, which was put to good use, of the hierarchy in the Nazi Party. After that introduction, I told my escort they could go back to the jeep, that we would be out in a few minutes. I didn't want them to look too closely at the sketches lining the walls of this room. I also had spied something that settled my quandary on what to do here.

"You're looking divine, William," Satsuma said in a crackly voice. "The uniform becomes you, although I always preferred you naked."

"I've come to take you back to our headquarters, Prince. I have no idea whether you will be kept or for how long. But you must understand that there will have to be an investigation of your wartime activities."

"I understand," he said. He sounded so tired—and old. And he suddenly, at seventy-two, was, in fact, at-the-end-of-his-rope old. Despite how he had used me, I found I no longer felt any bitterness toward him. He also had saved me in Nanking and, most important, hadn't, as far as I could see, had anything to do with the Japanese carnage there.

"Do you understand, completely?" I asked. "You were in Nanking, as a general. It's a matter of record. If you go with me, I will do what I can to separate you from what happened there, but you were there, so the questioning will be difficult."

"I do understand. But I don't think it will matter. Not unless your justice is swift. Come, can you come sit by me one last time and take tea with me?"

"We don't have much time," I said.

"No, there isn't much time," he said. "But, please, one last time."

I went over and went down, cross-legged on the cushion beside him. There were two tea pots and he poured our tea from separate pots. That there were two tea pots and that he served us separately made all the difference in what I would do here. He was taking the responsibility and decision out of my hands. We drank.

In the silence that followed, I could hear him sniff back a tear. "If only . . . one more time."

I reached into the folds of his yukata. As old as he was, he still could achieve an erection. As he softly moaned and sighed, I stroked him to a dribbling ejaculation that didn't take long to accomplish. As he came, though, he coughed, sighed, slowly collapsed back onto the cushions, and expired.

I knew I'd have to make sure the tea in the two pots was carefully preserved and analyzed—and I would have to ensure that I expressed surprise at what had transpired here.

~

Relocate?

He'd been so sure when his ship pulled into Norfolk and before he'd come to Hagerstown to check out how his father was doing with the family garage business that he wanted to stay in the Navy—to relocate to the West Coast to take up the cushy billet being offered to encourage him to reup. But now . . . now he was torn. Tom was a hunk, a Marine recently mustered out at the end of the war and hired at the garage, with a cock to die for.

He had to be on a train in five hours, but Tom was ever hard, insatiable, demanding, masterful. He was riding Tom's cock in a cowboy position, Tom stretched out on his back and him spiked on Tom's cock and riding it like it was a horse. He'd been riding it forever. Flailing around, revolving every which way on the young Marine's hard shaft . . . being lifted and slammed down on it . . . turned on it . . . fucked hard and deep and fast. Tom growling of how much fun it was going to be when he mustered out of the Navy, came to work in his dad's garage, and rode Tom's cock every night. "I don't want you to go," Tom had said. "If you do, I might come for you." That had given him chills, but he had gotten on the train anyway.

The conductor was striding through the carriage, announcing an arrival in San Diego in fifteen minutes. Ned's sense of where he was swam up from his dream. It seemed he'd been on the train from Maryland forever. The options were driving him crazy. He'd been so sure at first that he wanted to take this Navy job in San Diego—to reup again. Then, there for a while, he'd thought he'd had his fill of the Navy and of war—and of pretending he wasn't who he was. And then the cushy job came along—and the invitation from the lieutenant—no, a lieutenant commander now—and then Tom, the hunky ex-Marine in Maryland with the monster cock was there, talking of the future they could have together. Someone Ned's own age for a change. Someone who wasn't both Ned's superior and dominator. He dominated in sex, of course, just like the Navy officer did—and just as Ned liked it—but beyond the bed, they were equals.

As the train pulled into the station in San Diego, Ned nervously scanned the platform to see if he could see him. It was easier than he thought it would be as Lieutenant—no, he had to remember to call him Lieutenant Commander now— Lewis Harris was wearing his khaki service uniform, which made him stand out in the crowd on the platform. It helped that he was tall and broad shouldered and had the air of authority and being in control. He was still a handsome devil, Ned was glad to see. The war in the Pacific hadn't done him in like it had so many others. Ned rose from his seat and carried his duffle bag out to the open platform between the two passenger cars.

Harris picked him out in those climbing down from the train, also being easy because the young gunner's mate was wearing the dress blue service uniform of a postwar Navy enlisted man. The two men waved at each other and Harris pointed up toward the station area to note he'd wait for Ned near the waiting room. The station, and, indeed, all of San Diego was full of the hustle and bustle of returning to a peacetime industry footing, with merely a year having gone by since the Japanese surrender in World War Two.

Both men had served in the Pacific fleet in the war. They'd been mates—or at least in the same crew—of the battleship *Maryland*—a ship Ned felt special for serving on, as he was from the State of Maryland. They had fought in the battle for Peleliu and then been stationed there as the U.S. invasion force moved on to Okinawa. But Harris had been wounded on Peleliu and sent back to the States, while Ned Carnes had gone on to Okinawa and the Japanese mainland. He was only now returning to the States, with the decision to be made of whether to get out of the Navy and help his father run the family garage in Maryland or stay with the Navy. He'd been offered a billet here at the U.S. Naval Station San Diego that had just been reformed from a destroyer repair facility a month earlier, in September 1946.

It had been Harris who had sent a letter saying he'd heard Ned might be reassigned to San Diego and invited him out to take a look at the job being offered before he decided what he'd do. Ned had been flattered that the lieutenant commander had invited him out but he had mixed feelings about it. With Ned's interests, which the naval officer well knew about, it was difficult to make it in the Navy. Of course, the lieutenant commander was making it in the Navy and there were more like-minded men in the Navy than there were in Hagerstown, Maryland, so there were risks either way. Ned wasn't at all sure how Harris would receive him either. Their parting had been abrupt—and explosive.

"Looking good, gunner's mate," the lieutenant commander said as Ned walked up to him.

"Well, you know the Navy, Sir," Ned answered. "Lots of backbreaking work and the grub is about inedible, so the balance is good for keeping the body fit."

"And yours certainly is fit." Barely here and the man already was at it, Ned thought—moving into his dominating position. Ned was both aroused and felt beleaguered by that.

"Same with you, Lieutenant—umm, Lieutenant Commander. Don't know how you keep shipshape while riding a desk as you told me you do now."

"San Diego is a wide-open town," Lew answered. "A desk is not all a man can ride here." He gave Ned a wink. "And let's make it Lew and Ned between us when the brass aren't looking, shall we?"

"Fine with me . . . Lew." Ned was a bit off center from what Harris had said before that. He hadn't known how it would be between them. And, yes, he'd noticed that the man hadn't told him to dispense with the "sir"—that the lieutenant commander didn't seem to mind the dominator distinction.

They'd parted so abruptly on Peleliu. And Ned knew so little about the naval officer and needed to know more before thinking of relocating to San Diego. A lot was riding on what he found out. Among other things, he wanted to know what, if anything, Harris had in connection to the offer of a cushy billet out here if Ned stayed in the Navy. The Navy seemed anxious to push men out of the force, the war being over and cannon fodder not being needed now, but Ned's jobs officer had gone the extra mile to talk up the San Diego offer.

"Come on through the station," Lew said. "I have a car waiting. I'm putting you up at the Del Coronado, the fanciest waterfront hotel we have here. The Navy hasn't given up all of the rooms it commandeered during the war yet, and I snagged you one." He obviously wanted Ned to understand that it was something he had arranged.

"I won't be staying in the naval barracks? I'm still enlisted, you know." What Ned really wondered was why Lew wasn't going to put him up himself. If he'd done that, it would answer Ned's most pressing question—well, more than one question Ned had. But by rights Ned knew he should be staying in the base barracks, not in some swank seaside resort hotel.

"The hotel business is strange here. Sometimes you can't get a room without selling your body. Sometimes the Navy can't fill its billets and the rooms go to waste. We're just lucky I could get you in. Bet you're thirsty after all those days on a train too and would love to get a shower. Thirsty first, I think. The hotel's got a great open-air bar, right on the water." He didn't wait for Ned to say what he'd like to do after coming off a long train ride.

The waterfront bar was, indeed, quite nifty, but they didn't stay there long. Ned had checked in at the desk, but Lew suggested he treat them to a drink before Ned went up to the room, so Ned lugged his duffle bag through miles of reception rooms to the outdoor, seaside bar. Lew ordered him a beer and Lew had scotch. They talked for almost an hour and polished off another two drinks each, filling in the blanks of how the life of each had gone since that fateful day on Peleliu Island half a world—and, it seemed, half a lifetime—away, even though it had only been a year and a half. There was a lot to talk about—and a lot of talk to avoid—but Ned could tell that Lew was getting antsy. He wanted something. Ned wanted something too. Chances were good that they wanted the separate parts of the same thing.

As the conversation drew down, Lew had the idea of seeing if Ned's room was nice enough—although Ned could have told him that a triple bunk under cannon shells against a steel bulkhead had been about as nice as Ned had had for years. And then Lew had Ned. This didn't come as a surprise to Ned. Lew had had Ned before.

In the room, which obviously wasn't the hotel's best in either size or view but that was a palace to Ned, Lew plopped down on the side of the bed "to test the springs." Then he invited Ned to plop down beside him to test the springs himself. Ned discerned nothing wrong with the springs. He didn't determine anything was wrong either with Lew putting an arm around his shoulder and turning him for a kiss that got deeper and deeper until Ned was putty in Lew's arms, pinned to the bed under the officer's body, and almost breathless. Then they gave the bed springs a real test. As it turned out, the bed springs did creak noisily when bodies bounced up and down on it in vigorous rhythm.

The naval officer had always had his way with the enlisted man, even the very first time, although by then both men knew that the other went with men—and that Lew was a top and Ned was a bottom. And by that first time the two had given each other looks that signaled want, need, and their respective positions in the dominant-submissive spectrum.

Lew came out of the kiss only long enough to pull the gunnery mate's jumper over his head and for Ned, in turn, to unbutton and pull away the officer's jacket, taking each down to nothing more on their chests than their dog tags on silver chains. Both men were well-developed, Ned slimmer than Lew, who, in his mid thirties, was considerably older than the seaman, who had barely turned twenty-one. Lew was in remarkable condition for his age.

Each ran fingers over the chest of the other as they went into another deep kiss, but before that was finished, Lew was fiddling with the traditional thirteen-button flap in the crotch of the seaman's trousers. Ned gave a jerk and a rattling sound deep inside when Lew pulled the waistband of his briefs down, hooked them under the young man's balls, and proceeded to stroke Ned off.

Ned struggled a bit at having his cock stroked while they were in an initial clutch, but he knew Lew liked to do this to establish his dominance. He was much the stronger of the two, having the advantage of size and weight, and he held fast to Ned, with his arm around the young man's shoulders, holding him close in and his lips locking on Ned's and his tongue down Ned's throat. He wouldn't let Ned go and stroked Ned's cock until his ejaculate arced across the room.

This was the way the officer liked it—to bring the other guy, the submissive, off quickly and then to take his time getting what he wanted.

When Ned had come, Lew let the young man's body sink to the surface of the bed beside him and he rolled over on top of Ned. As he rolled, he unzipped himself. He naturally was in erection. He encased their cocks together and resumed stroking. Ned lay under him moaning, their eyes locked. He assumed Lew would fuck him in a missionary position there, but after a few minutes Lew laughed, rolled back off him, and said, "Go take a shower. You smell like you brought the Kansas stockyards with you. Come out ready for me."

When Ned emerged from the bathroom with just a towel fastened around his hips, Lew was naked, sitting on the bed, smoking a cigarette, and stroking his cock with his free hand.

"Come here," he commanded of Ned and crushed his cigarette into an ashtray on the nightstand as Ned approached. "So nice; I remember you like this," he murmured as he pulled the towel off Ned's waist, palmed Ned's buttocks, and brought him in close. Lew nuzzled Ned's belly with his cheek, lowered his mouth over Ned's cock, found the rim of the young man's hole with the index finger of either hand, and began working Ned's ass open as Ned moaned and sighed for him.

"Turn and grab your ankles," he commanded. Ned did so, and Lew spent a few minutes eating his ass out.

"Now sit on it," he commanded. "It's been too long since I've fucked you," and, with Lew's hands grasping his hips and helping to pull Ned down into his lap and onto his shaft, the sailor descended on the cock and, as Lew wrapped his arms around Ned's belly and nuzzled him below the shoulder blades with his cheek, Ned used the leverage of his feet on the carpet to fuck himself on the hard cock. Ned cried out in ecstasy as he felt the familiar—but not experienced for so long—slide of the master's cock inside him, His gates rolled open and the muscles of his channel walls rippled over the hard shaft as slowly,

slowly, with each thrust, it moved deeper into the soft core of him. He'd been fucked since the naval officer had last had him, but never so well or so deeply—unless it was by Tom back in Maryland. Ned was in no frame of mind to do comparisons at the moment, though.

Lew didn't seem to be in a rush to go anywhere. He fucked Ned in a missionary position on the bed, doggie style on the floor, and even in the overstuffed chair in the corner of the room, with Ned slouched in the chair, his legs hooked over the arms, and Lew crouched down over him and taking him in long, vigorous strokes.

Ned objected to nothing that was demanded of him. He never had—not even that first time. Lew took what he wanted, when he wanted it, and as he wanted it.

Eventually, both were tired and they lay, naked, in each other's arms on the bed, their bodies stretched out along the lines of the other, Lew on his back, propped up on the headboard, smoking a cigarette. Ned was on his side, Lew's free arm around his chest, holding him close in. Ned's left leg was laying on top of Lew's legs. He was letting his left hand glide over the older man's body, worshipping it. He stopped at a scar on Lew's side, near the waistline, on Lew's right side. The scar was puckered.

"Does it still hurt you?" he whispered.

"Only when I think that I didn't see you again after that."

"The bullet was meant for me," Ned said. "I've always believed that."

"And I think you've always been wrong. It was meant for me all along. It wasn't your problem."

"How can you say I wasn't the problem?" Ned asked. That obviously wasn't what he should have said—or asked—though. The spell of the afternoon had been lost. With a grunt, Lew reached over and crushed his half-smoked cigarette in the ashtray on the nightstand, disengaged from Ned, and rolled over to the edge of the bed, sitting up for a moment to steady what had to be tired muscles. He lurched up from the bed and headed for the bathroom.

They'd been over this ground before—in letters, as Ned had been shipped out to Okinawa before Lew had even regained consciousness from the surgery. The Navy was quick to clean up its little messes like that. As soon as he could travel, Lew had been shipped back to the States to a desk job. He'd even been promoted. Beyond that the Navy had seen it in their wisdom to ignore all of the circumstances and give Lew a Purple Star for being wounded. But Lew didn't pretend; he kept the medal in a drawer.

Ned continued to be sure that the eye contact had been with him when the bullets had begun to fly.

It had all happened so fast—the whole two months from being on board the *Maryland* and strafing the island of Peleliu and being on Peleliu and being pulled out from underneath the lieutenant's bleeding body had zipped right on by—and it had changed so much in Ned's life.

* * * *

We'd come to know about each other—that the lieutenant gave cock and I took it—as we moved around the Pacific on the *Maryland*, engaging in one cat-and-mouse skirmish with the Japs after another. And he'd given me the eye of interest and I'd returned one of "it's fine with me." But there was Mitch. Mitch, a chief petty officer, was the jealous type and he had his claws into Lieutenant Harris. He warned off anyone he saw Harris show interest in and he was a nasty piece of work about it. I wasn't going to get in Mitch's sights just to get some fine cock from Lew Harris, even though I'd heard he had some mighty fine cock to give.

There was lots of cock to get on a battleship full of young, randy guys who had been at sea for years. And I was judged as prime tail. I had no trouble attracting guys suffering from blue balls.

What it would require to get the two of us together would be fire and brimstone and a sudden urge not to give a shit what Mitch might think. We got that in the fight for Peleliu, an island in the Palau Islands, during Operation Stalemate Two, in September of 1944. Peleliu had an airstrip, built by the Japanese, that high command wanted to use for a final-push invasion of Okinawa.

The island was being held by over ten thousand suicidal Japs determined to defend the island to the last man, which they did. Our role on the *Maryland* was to join in the blasting of the island back into the stone age to soften it up for a Marine invasion. I worked one of the big guns on the *Maryland*. Harris was the officer in charge of all of the guns. It was hot as hell on deck during the bombardment, not just because of the normal heat in the South Pacific in September, but also because the guns, being fired almost around the clock, were boiling hot.

We all were stripped down to practically nothing and glistening with sweat. Handling the big guns on the deck of a battleship also kept a man trimmed down and muscled up. Harris was a hands-on officer and, before our pounding of the island was over and the Marines were going over the sides of the assembled flotilla and storming the beaches of the small island, the lieutenant was as stripped down and sweating as all of the rest of us were.

He also was standing by my gun when the signal to desist came down. We both were standing there, sweating, nearly naked, and panting hard. Our dicks were hard from the sensation of sexual power that firing off the big guns brought with it. Taking breaths in big gulps and eyeing each other, Harris and I reached an understanding, with no word having to be spoken, that our time had come. Mitch was nowhere around to come between us and our heightened arousal and the needs of our rock-hard cocks.

The lieutenant merely reached out, took me by the forearm, told me to come with him—that he was going to fuck the hell out of me. I went willingly and docilely. I'd wanted his dick inside me for months.

He took me to a nearby storeroom for stuff needed to clean and maintain the decks, locked the steel hatch behind us and bent me over a thick and high coil of anchor rope. He covered me from behind and above, grabbed my wrists to trap me under him, thrust up inside me, and fucked the shit out of me. It was a hard, rough, brutal—and glorious—fuck in which we exhausted the bloodlust of pounding the shit out of the Japs on Peleliu with the lieutenant pounding the shit out of me, and me thrusting back into him with my hips to take every inch of him I could.

That was the only time he fucked me on board the *Maryland*, but we both knew he would do it again—in spite of the close watch Mitch usually kept over him.

We took Peleliu, although there was irony there. We no more than took it, wiping out some eleven thousand Japs but losing nearly four thousand of our own men and putting another eight thousand in sick bay, than the high command changed its mind. Peleliu no longer was good enough for staging the invasion of Okinawa. The staging field for that was changed to Ulithi Atoll, in the Caroline Islands.

The powers that be didn't want to lose any Pacific airfield gained, however, and a holding force was to be left on Peleliu. Lieutenant Lew Harris drew a short straw on that and was assigned to stay on Peleliu to help manage the cleanup and holding of the island. Mitch was able, as a chief petty officer, to grab an assignment of Peleliu for himself, as well. I have no idea how I drew one of the short straws to stay. I was a gunnery mate. There were no big guns on Peleliu like there were on the *Maryland*. It sure as hell wasn't Mitch who wrangled the assignment. I've always assumed it was Harris.

That would stand to reason, because he almost immediately showed that he wasn't finished with me yet. It also lends credence to the possibility that Harris was behind the later cushy assignment relocation offer to San Diego after the war.

The lieutenant thought he was clever. He got us all in the same office—him to give commands, Mitch to paper them over, and me as the general gofer to do whatever either one of them needed. Then he developed a reason for Mitch to drive a jeep cross island every other day on a regular-basis errand. While Mitch was away, Harris would lock the office door, pull the blinds down on the windows, lay me on my back or belly on his desk, and lay me, giving it to me hard and furiously. By the time Mitch came back, Harris would be at his desk, smiling and whistling, and I'd be hobbling around the office with a silly grin on my face, doing whatever gofers did.

I don't know if it was the lieutenant's smile and whistle or my grin and hobble, but Mitch added two and two together. And one day he didn't take that jeep trip across the island. The lieutenant also didn't take into account that Mitch had a key to the office door, since it was Mitch who opened up the office in the morning.

I was on top of the lieutenant, doing a crab position, when the door opened. Harris was on his back, his legs hanging down the front of his desk, his hands gripping my waist, as I hovered above him, looking up at the ceiling, my fists propping up my shoulders by burying themselves beside his shoulders, and my legs bent and my feet leveraging off the desk top on either side of his thighs. I was raising and lowering my channel on his buried cock and he was helping by pushing up and pulling down on my waist with his hands.

We were well into the fuck when Mitch opened the door and stood in the doorway. He obviously had expected to see what he did see. He had a gun in his hand.

It was Harris's quick reflexes that had him pushing me off to the side and taking the bullet in the lower abdomen. He later said the bullet was meant for him. I was the one who saw Mitch's eyes when he burst in. I knew the bullet was for me. The first two bullets missed both of us. The third one got the lieutenant. The fourth through the seventh bullets I heard fired got Mitch in the back. It was his short-sightedness, caused by his blind jealously, that made him forget that the office of the Military Police contingent was just next door.

It must have been obvious to higher authority what had been going on in the office and why Mitch had gone crazy and tried to shoot us—although I still think it was only me he was trying to kill—but they cleaned it all up. The lieutenant went directly into sick bay and then back to the States, and I immediately had orders that got me back aboard the *Maryland* and steaming toward the Ulithi Atoll. From there, it was on to the hell that was the invasion of Okinawa and I was given little opportunity to think about Lieutenant Lewis Harris.

* * * *

After tiring of balling Ned in the Del Coronado Hotel room, Lew rolled out of the bed and went into the bathroom. The sailor waited until he heard the shower running and then searched for Harris's trousers and then for the pocket his wallet was in. Ned had to be sure of the Navy officer who seemed so anxious for Ned to be relocated to San Diego, and Ned didn't think Harris would tell him the truth if he asked the lieutenant commander outright. All the time Ned had known Harris, the Navy officer had deflected any attempts to find out what was in his background. And there was the nagging question of why he didn't invite Ned to stay with him if he was so anxious to get Ned here and into bed—and why Harris told Ned that the next time they'd meet was when he picked Ned up the next morning to go to the naval station.

They were there, in his wallet, just as Ned knew, in the base of my mind, that they would be. Ned found a photo of a smiling woman about Lew's age, and of a young girl old enough to have been born before the war and of a baby, obviously not conceived until after the war had ended.

He wasn't going to be any part of that sort of setup. He quickly pulled on his dress blue service uniform, stuffed everything else in the room that was his back into his duffle bag and walked out of the room. He didn't ask for a cab at the concierge desk but walked out onto the street and managed to reach a bus stop as a bus was pulling up. He had no idea which direction it was going. He didn't really care. Three stops later, he got off. He was near the waterfront in a seedy part of town. He was more comfortable here than he'd been at the Del Coronado. He had no trouble finding a fleabag hotel, where he spent the night, changing into civvies to go out to find dinner.

He found more than dinner. In a hole-in-the-wall bar on the waterfront, he found companionship. He was in a funky mood, and the straightforward propositioning from a brute of a sailor in the bar matched his mood. He didn't tell the guy he was a sailor too. He let himself be taken to a hotel even seedier than then one he'd checked into, and he blew the sailor and got blown by the sailor. And he laid on his back and opened his legs, and let the sailor pound his channel, making him forget the lie Lew Harris had been asking him to live and fucking the Navy officer out of his system.

The next morning Ned shouldered his duffle bag and walked to the train station. He walked rather than splurging for a taxi or trying to find a bus going in that direction as penance for what he almost had done—almost had been seduced into doing again. It was a long way back to Maryland. He figured it would be a good thing for him to walk the first two miles back toward the East.

The gods in the heavens smiled on him, though—and thereafter he always thought it was because he had done the penance of the first two miles on foot. When he entered the waiting room at the train station to buy his ticket back East, there was Tom—The ex-Marine Tom from the family garage back in Hagerstown.

After the first surprise for both of them and an explosive meeting of the bodies and lips that, without a doubt, upset and outraged many around them in the station waiting room, Ned managed to ask, "How . . . why?"

"We need you at the garage, Ned. I need you there—with me. I came here to fetch you back."

Ever the submissive, Ned had heard just the right thing to bring him into line and under Tom's control.

"But how would you have found me?"

"I'm a Marine, Ned. Why would you even think to ask that question? There's an ocean here, ain't there? And there are Navy bases. A Navy swabbie would be found where the Navy is, wouldn't he? But the war's over, buddy. Time for you to get the Navy out of you. Time to come home."

Not just the Navy, Ned thought. It was time to get Lieutenant Commander Lewis Harris out of him—and he loved the way that Tom said the word "home." The only relocating he planned on doing now was back in Hagerstown, Maryland, and underneath an ex-Marine, not a naval officer. It had been a hell of a war—not just the fighting, but also the fucking. But the fighting was over now . . . unless, of course, Tom wanted to make him fight for it as a game.

~

About the Author

Habu is one of the pen names of a former supersonic spy jet pilot, intelligence agent, male model, movie actor, and diplomat. A wild youth in Southeast Asia was spent enjoying whatever sexual opportunities came his way, and much of his gay male writing is about recalling incidents from those days and inventing ones he'd perhaps have liked to experience. He now leads a very quiet and ordinary happily married family life.

An American, he is a published mainstream novelist and short story writer under another name and in another dimension of his life. He has written or cowritten (with Sabb) approaching 1,000 published short stories and over 100 published erotica e-books, primarily of gay fiction but also memoir, straight fiction and ménage fiction. His hand and creative writing can be seen in stories and books by habu, sr71plt, Dirk Hessian, Shabbu, and Stephen Kessel—among unrevealed others that might surprise readers. The fictionalized GM memoir *Flying High, Diving Deep* is loosely based on his life experiences. He can be found at the adults only gay male site www.BarbarianSpy.com, which he shares with Sabb and Dirk Hessian.

Our authors always like to receive feedback, and appreciate it when readers post reviews at distributors and other sites.

BarbarianSpy
FOR LITERARY HEAT

BarbarianSpy Books

Not all books listed below may currently be on release.
* indicates the book is available in paperback and e-book.

BOOKS BY CHRIS CROSS
Multisexual Adult Romance

Pulaski Square
Chocolate in Vanilla (MF)2
Christmas with Chris (MMF) (MM) (MF)

BOOKS BY ALEX LOCKHEED
Transgender Romance

Meeting Jenna

Transgender Other

Being Sarah

BOOKS BY DIRK HESSIAN
Xtreme Historical Erotica

Dirk's Ancient Times Collection (Print only Bundle)*
The King's Men
Shores of Tripoli*
Prophecy of Noto
Pretender's Fate

General Historical Erotic Romance

Dirk's America's Founding Collection (Print only Bundle)*
Soldier,Spy
Ridden West
Deliver a Virgin
Clouds and Rain
Confederate Gold
Puttin on the Ritz
To the Hessian Hills
Fire Down the Valley*
Constantinople*
The Beautiful Way*
Blue and Gray
Colonel's Treasure
Beginning of Time
Labyrinth

BOOKS BY HABU
Gay Erotica
Memoir Faction
Flying High, Diving Deep*
Xtreme Erotica
Fist of Gold
Liaisons
Chain Gang Banged (Short Story)
Tramp Steaming*
Escape to Girne
Silas' Choice*
Last Call
Choke Hold
Apyko: The Greek Pimp
Visits of the Schlange
Second Coming: Emile La Cour Unleashed*
Vortex: Sacrificed by Curiosity*
Dark Angel Sounding (in e-book & included in Sounding:Ultimate Control paperback)*
Sounding: Ultimate Control (Print Only)*
Sounding Five (in e-book & included in Sounding:Ultimate Control paperback)*
Romance
Gift from the Sea
Shore Leave
The Aviators
Poison Pen
Need to be Needed
Key Westing (short)
Finding a New Sam
Bangkok Summer Seduction
The Photograph
Inevitable Case
Turn to Love
Rain Check
Built for Pleasure (Sci Fi)
Danny's Choice*
Pull of the Groove
Sugar n Spice Christmas
Friday Nights with Lenny (Christmas Romance)
Snowy, Snowy Nights (Christmas Romance)
Tank n Bull
Sail to the Sun
War Letters
Ravens Roost
Caribbean Cruise Top to Bottom
Arena Stage

Trading Partners (Valentine's Day)
Four Coins
Lower Than the Heart (Valentine's Day)
Brambleton
Finding Amnad
Platres Conclave
Other Novels/Novellas
Also Want to Thank
Ranger Guided
Key Westing
Syrian Ram
Temptation's Clutches*
Descent into Chaos
Escape to Girne
Journey Through Abilene
Harmony and Dissonance
Stallion Station
Racing With the Devil (espionage suspense)
Prepared in Cape Verdi
Gilded Cage
House on Park*
Anything for Ambition
Dance of the Ravishers
Hard Knocks U*
My Neighbor's Spa*
Man's Man: Tales of a High Priced Gay Hooker*
Trip Money
The Indian Doctor
Sailorboy
Home to Fire Island
Murder Mysteries
Retribution (Hardesty)
Snitches (Hardesty
Gotta Keep Trying (Hardesty)
All Fools Day Foolery (Mike Kavanagh)
Inevitable Case (Mike Kavanagh)
Vanishing Laura
Death on a Ping Pong Table
Clint Folsom Mysteries Compendium Volume 1*
Death to Blonds - Stolen Judgment (Clint Folsom Mystery)*
Clint Folsom Mysteries Compendium Volume 2*
Gay Erotica Anthologies
A Hell of a War*
Earth Cry*
Shunga
Habu's Christmas Balls
Eight in D*
215

DevilMENt
Silas' Choices*
Stallion Station (A Novella in Parts)
Eleven to the Dogs*
Fifty Seventy*
Spy Tails 001*
Spy Tails 002*
Doubled*
Doubled Again*
Tails in the Tropics*
Tails in the Med*
Tails in the West*
Rough Riders*
Grab Bag 1*
Grab Bag 2*
Grab Bag 3*
Grab Bag 4*
Grab Bag 5*
Grab Bag 6*
Grab Bag 7*
Grab Bag 8*
Grab Bag 9*
Grab Bag 10*
Grab Bag 11*
Grab Bag 12*
Beyond the Beaded Curtain*
The Sporting Life*
Fetish Galore!*
Literary Gay Erotica
Cairo Surrender*
The Handyman*
Homeward Bound
Journey to Mirage*
Bisexual/Menage/Multisexual Erotica
And Eat it Too
Two Men, One Woman*
Every Which Way
Summer of Denial
Death on a Ping Pong Table
Cruising Gigolo
13 Ways for Halloween
Luther*
The Indian Prince*
BOOKS BY SABB
Spanish Lovers
Driver Reliever
Hiring in Hollywood

The Legend of Holleystone Grange
Surprise Encounters*
She is He
Wrong Man
Loyal to his King
Barbarian Tales - Book One - Traveler's Tales*
Barbarian Tales - Book Two - Journeys Begin*
Barbarian Tales - Book Three - The Inheritance*
Barbarian Tales - Book Four - Road to Persepolis*
BOOKS BY SHABBU
A Season in Galicia*
Blind Dates*
Velvet Interrogation
Finding Jason
Dirty Pool
Operation Black Jade
Cigars!*
Angel in the Barn
Gayly Complicated*
Despoiling David
The Tree of Idleness*
I Met a Man
Rough Road to Happiness
BOOKS BY STEPHEN KESSEL
Gay Romance
The Forever Man
Two Chances
BOOKS BY KIM BLACK
Lesbian Romance
Transfixed on Tammie (F/T lesbian)
~